The
HARDEST MISSION

My Delia waited for me in my island Stromnate of Valka, that beautiful island off the main island of Vallia. I yearned to return to her. Yet I was under an interdiction.

Until I had once more made myself a member of the Order of Krozairs of Zy I would not be allowed to leave this far-off inland sea. Whether or not it was the Star Lords of the Savanti who chained me here, I did not know, although Zena Iztar had indicated it was not the work of the Star Lords.

Well, I would become a Krozair of Zy once more and escape from the inner sea and return to Valka. Before I did that I fancied I would bring this evil king Genod to justice. So having done all these marvelous and wonderful feats and proved just how great a man I was, I would go home, and I would clasp my Delia in my arms again.

And then—and then I would have to tell her the most tragic news she had ever heard.

"Turiloths! Turiloths!" The cries racketed about.

KROZAIR
OF
KREGAN

by
Alan Burt Akers

Illustrated by Josh Kirby

DAW BOOKS, INC.

DONALD A. WOLLHEIM, PUBLISHER

1301 Avenue of the Americas
New York, N. Y.   10019

Published by
THE NEW AMERICAN LIBRARY
OF CANADA LIMITED

The Saga of Dray Prescot

The Delian Cycle

I. TRANSIT TO SCORPIO
II. THE SUNS OF SCORPIO
III. WARRIOR OF SCORPIO
IV. SWORDSHIPS OF SCORPIO
V. PRINCE OF SCORPIO

The Havilfar Cycle

I. MANHOUNDS OF ANTARES
II. ARENA OF ANTARES
III. FLIERS OF ANTARES
IV. BLADESMAN OF ANTARES
V. AVENGER OF ANTARES
VI. ARMADA OF ANTARES

The Krozair Cycle

I. THE TIDES OF KREGEN
II. RENEGADE OF KREGEN
III. KROZAIR OF KREGEN

First Printing, April 1977

1 2 3 4 5 6 7 8 9

TABLE OF CONTENTS

A Note on Dray Prescot 9

1 The chains of Rukker the Kataki and
Fazhan ti Rozilloi 11

2 Oar-slaves in the swifters of Magdag 26

3 Of Duhrra's steel hand 40

4 Nath the Slinger collects pebbles 48

5 Vax 60

6 Renders of the Eye of the World 70

7 We strike a blow for Zairia and for Vallia 77

8 Rukker does not speak of his seamanship 86

9 Blood in the Hyr Jikordur 95

10 Among the ruins of the Sunset People 101

11 The Beast out of Time 107

12 News of the Red and the Green 112

13 "Ram! Ram! Ram!" 122

14 Of a conspiracy and of Queen Miam 133

15 The Siege of Zandikar: I.
A Savapim holds the gate 144

16 The Siege of Zandikar: II.
I am short with a Krozair of Zy 153

17 The Siege of Zandikar: III.
The turiloths attack 163

18 Pur Zeg, Prince of Vallia, Krzy 168

19 "Then die, Dray Prescot, die!" 180

20 The Siege of Zandikar: IV.
Of partings and of meetings 190

21 Krozair of Zy 206

Glossary 213

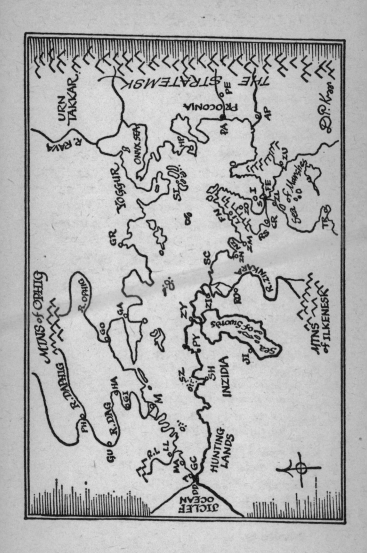

PRESCOT'S MAP OF THE INNER SEA OF TURISMOND, called THE EYE OF THE WORLD

Key

S	Sanurkazz	M	Magdag	A	Akhram
FE	Felterazz	MA	Malig	GC	Grand Canal
ZY	Zy	LL	Laggig-	DD	Dam of
ZI	Zimuzz		Laggu		Days
ZM	Zamu	PH	Phan-	PA	Pattelonia
LI	Lizz		gursh	PE	Perithia
JI	Jikmarz	GU	Guamelga	AP	Appar
ZU	Zulfiria	HA	Hagon	HP	Happapat
ZN	Zandikar	GI	Giddur	SI	Sorzart
SH	Shazmoz	GO	Goforeng		Islands
PY	Pynzalo	GA	Gansk		
RO	Rozilloi	GR	Garles		
CR	Crazmoz	RL	R. Laggu		
ZL	Zullia				
TR	Tremso				
ZO	Zond				
NZ	Nose of Zogo				
FN	Fenzerdrin				
SC	Shadow Coast				
I	Isteria				
SZ	Seeds of Zantristar				
RS	R. of Golden Smiles				

LIST OF ILLUSTRATIONS

"Turiloths! Turiloths!" The cries racketed about.

ii

Map of the Inner Sea of Turismond.

vi

"I swung the sword at the glass and smashed the case open."

62

"The gates flew open."

155

"The struggle carried them to the coaming of the voller."

193

"Like a clump of thistledown, an enormous skyship landed before the gate."

201

A NOTE ON DRAY PRESCOT

Dray Prescot is a man above medium height with brown hair, and brown eyes that are level and dominating. His shoulders are immensely wide and he carries himself with an abrasive honesty and a fearless courage. He moves like a great hunting cat, quiet and deadly. Born in 1775 and educated in the inhumanly harsh conditions of the late eighteenth-century English Navy, he presents a picture of himself that, the more we learn of him, grows no less enigmatic.

Through the machinations of the Savanti nal Aphrasöe—mortal but superhuman men dedicated to the aid of humanity—and of the Star Lords, the Everoinye, he has been taken to Kregen many times. On that savage and exotic, marvelous and terrible world he rose to become Zorcander of the Clansmen of Segesthes, and Lord of Strombor in Zenicce, and a member of the mystic and martial Order of Krozairs of Zy of the Eye of the World.

Against all odds, Prescot won his highest desire and in that immortal battle at The Dragon's Bones claimed his Delia, Delia of Delphond, Delia of the Blue Mountains. And Delia claimed him in defiance of her father, the dread emperor of Vallia. Amid the rolling thunder of the acclamations of *Hai Jikai!* Prescot became Prince Majister of Vallia and wed his Delia, the Princess Majestrix. One of their favorite homes is Esser Rarioch in Valkanium, capital of the island of Valka of which Prescot is Strom.

In the continent of Havilfar, Prescot fought as a hyrkaidur in the arena of the Jikhorkdun in Huringa. He became King of Djanduin, idolized by his ferocious four-armed warrior Djangs. In the Battle of Jholaix the megalomaniacal ambitions of the empress Thyllis of Hamal were thwarted, leading to an uneasy peace between the empires of Hamal and Vallia. Then Prescot was banished by the Star Lords to Earth for twenty-one miserable years. He caught up with his education and learned a great deal during this time.

His joyful return to Kregen was marred by his ejection

from the Order of Krozairs of Zy. On Earth he had been
unable to answer their Call to Arms, when the fanatics of
Green Grodno swept all the Red of Zair before them in ir-
resistible conquest. Determined to forget the Krozairs of the
inner sea and return home to Delia and their children, he
is told by Zena Iztar, who saves him from being banished
back to Earth, that he must again become a Krzy before
he can return home to Valka.

The genius king Genod of Magdag, using a. new army
modeled on one created years ago by Prescot, is sweeping
victoriously across the inner sea. Gafard, the king's right-
hand man, was—unknown to the king and to Prescot—married to Prescot's second daughter, Velia. Now, in order to
escape on a wounded saddle-bird, King Genod has callously
hurled Velia to her death. Prescot, using the name Gadak, is
left holding the dead body of his daughter in his arms as the
overlords of Magdag ride up to take him.

This is where the last volume, *Renegade of Kregen*, finished. Still known as Gadak the Renegade, Prescot picks
up the story as he is dispatched to the horrific fate of an
oar-slave in the swifters of Magdag.

This volume, *Krozair of Kregen*, brings to an end the
"Krozair Cycle" and with the next volume, *Savage Scorpio*,
Prescot is confronted with a monstrous challenge on the
planet of Kregen under the Suns of Scorpio. Because most,
but not all, of the action takes place in Vallia, I have
called the next cycle of Prescot's headlong adventures on
Kregen the "Vallian Cycle."

—*Alan Burt Akers*

Chapter One

The chains of Rukker the Kataki and Fazhan ti Rozilloi

The lash curved high in the air, hard, etched black. I, Gadak the Renegade, grasped the harsh iron chains that bound me so savagely to this coffle of slaves, and which made of us one miserable body. We stumbled down the dusty streets under the lash toward the harbor.

The people of this evil city of Magdag barely noticed us, did not even bother to spit at us or revile us, for we were but one small coffle among many. The iron ring about my neck chafed the skin raw and driblets of blood ran down onto my chest and back.

"By Zair!" the man on my left, for we were chained two and two, gasped, his face a scarlet mask of effort. "I swear the cramph won't be happy until he's had my head off."

"He will not do that. We are needed to pull at the oars."

The overseer, careless in his authority, slashed his thonged whip and my companion yelped and stumbled. I let go of my own chain to help him up. The fellow in front, a giant of a man with the black body-bristle of a Brokelsh, surged forward. The length of chain between us straightened and, by Krun, it felt as though my own head were the one being wrenched off.

"Thank you, dom," the Zairian I had assisted was saying.

Ignoring him, I lurched forward and made a grab at the chain so as to ease the ring about my neck. A voice at my back bellowed in vicious temper.

"Rast! Keep steady, you zigging cramph!"

There was no point in turning about and chastising the fellow. We were all slaves together and I might have yelled as he had done if my own pains had not been caused by myself. The uneven lurching carried back like a wave along the coffle. The air was rent with blasphemies. Listening, I used this occurrence to learn about my fellow slaves, for we had merely been hauled out willy-nilly and chained up together for the walk from the bagnio to the harbor and the galleys.

The stones of Magdag under our feet and rising in wall and terrace and archway all about us held no more pity for our plight than the hearts of the Magdaggians. From the curses and prayers that went up, I knew we were a mixed bunch: Zairian prisoners, Grodnim criminals. And, in truth, I the renegade—who had once been of Zair and who said he was now of Grodno—hardly knew to which of these gods to cleave for the injuries that had been done me.

We were being whipped down to be taken aboard a galley and there enter upon hell on earth.

I knew.

The glorious mingled suns-light poured down in radiance about us, the streaming mingled lights of Zim and Genodras, the red and green suns of Antares. We stumbled along with our twin shadows mocking us, forever chained to us as we would be chained to our rowing benches.

"If I get my hands on that rast . . ." The Zairian at my left side, with his red face and perfectly bald head, showed a spirit to be expected of a Zairian. I wondered if he would be broken by the torments ahead of him, of all of us. All our heads had been shaved as smooth as loloo's eggs. We wore the gray slave breechclouts, which would be taken from us once we were shackled to our benches. All this I had endured before. This time, I vowed, I would make a positive effort very early on and escape.

The enormity of the death of my daughter Velia still had a stinging power to wring my heart. I had known she was my daughter for so pitifully short a time. I had known her as my Lady of the Stars for a short space before that, and we had talked. But I had found her and then, it seemed in the same heartbeat, she had been taken from me.

This mad king, this genius, this king Genod, who ruled in vile Magdag, had thrown her from the back of his fluttrell as the saddle-bird, winged, had fluttered to the ground. Genod had been in fear of his life then, and had thrown a girl for whom he had planned an abduction out to her death. If there was one thing I intended to do upon Kregen under the Suns of Scorpio, forgetting anything else, that thing would be to bring King Genod Gannius to justice.

We passed beneath the high archway leading through the wall of the inner harbor, that harbor called the King's Haven. The cothon, the artificially scooped-out inner harbor, presented a grand and, indeed, in any other city, a noble aspect.

Like all building in Magdag of the Megaliths, the architecture was on the grandest scale. Enormous blocks of stone had been manhandled down to raise these walls and fortifications, to erect the warehouses and ship sheds. Every surface blazed with brilliantly colored ceramics. The tiles depicted stories and legends from the fabled past of Kregen. They exalted the power of Grodno and of Magdag. And, of course, the predominant color was green.

Nowhere was a speck of red visible.

The overseer with the lash bellowed at us, using the hateful word I so detest. "Grak!" he shouted, snapping his whip, laying into the backs of the slaves. "Grak, you Zairian cramphs!"

The lash was of the tailed variety, designed not to injure us but to sting and make us jump. The Kregans have their equivalents of the knout and the sjambok, as I have said, made from chunkrah hide. With these they can pain, maim, or kill. We dragged along in our chains in the bright light of the twin suns, the smells and the sounds of the harbor in our nostrils and ears, the sight of the galleys motionless by the yellow stone walls. I looked at everything. For I had once been a Krozair, and this place was the arch-enemy of all Krozairs, all the Red Brethren, and knowledge conferred power. Mind you, I might possess a vast amount of knowledge right now; I was still chained up in a coffle of shuffling, whipped slaves.

The particular slave overseer entrusted with the task of bringing us down to the galleys was a Chulik. A Chulik has a yellow skin and a face that, although piglike, is recognizably Homo sapiens in general outline, save for the two fierce, upward-thrusting three-inch tusks. A Chulik will normally shave his head and leave a long rearward-descending pigtail, braided with the colors of whomever happens to be hiring his mercenary services at the moment. I will say here, at once, that my comrade Duhrra, an apim like myself, wore his hair shaved and in a short tail at the rear; I had never thought to compare his shaved skull with a Chulik's. A Chulik may possess two arms and legs and look vaguely human; that is all he knows of humanity. I eyed this specimen as he strode past slashing with his whip and I guessed he was taking what he could from the hides of the slaves before he reported back to the bagnio.

"I'd like to—" began the Zairian to my left.

"Shut your mouth, onker!" came that fearsome bellow from my rear. I had not seen who had been chained up aft of me and I'd been too careful of my neck in that damned ring to care to turn to look.

The Zairian bristled. We passed into the shadow of a warehouse wall, past slaves hauling bundles and bales for the swifters moored alongside the stone wharves. I fancied the swifter for which we made lay past the galley ahead of us. She looked large. If I was shoved down in the lower tier, to slave in almost nighted gloom in that airless confined space, I'd really go berserk. I had been holding myself in admirably, looking for a chance. Not a single chance had been given me. Chuliks and the overlords of Magdag form a formidable combination in manhandling. Like Katakis, who are ferocious slave-masters, they leave no easy chances for escape.

The hoarse rumbling voice at my back sounded again.

"Onker! You make it worse by your prattling."

The Zairian's red face turned even more scarlet, if that were possible. He started to speak, and I said, smoothly and swiftly, "Lean a little this way, dom—quickly!"

He was struck by my tone of voice. He leaned in, bringing the chains with him. We remained in the shadow of the warehouse wall, marching beside the edge of the wharf where the galleys waited. We were almost on the low-slung ram of this swifter, just passing the forward varter platform on her larboard bow. Beyond the ram stretched a space of open water, before the upflung stern of the swifter I fancied we were destined for closed that open space. I stumbled.

The Chulik was there. He had been waiting to get a few good lashings in with his right arm before he signed us over to the oar-master of the swifter.

His arm lifted and as I sagged against the chains the

Zairian at my side sucked in his breath. The Chulik lashed. I took the first blow and then the bight of chain looped his ankle. I straightened and heaved, and the cramph sailed up and over. I had hoped he might bash his head against the stones. As I flicked the chains and so released his ankle, he toppled, screeching. The lash sailed up. He went on, staggering backward, his arms windmilling, his legs making stupid little backward steps. He wore mail. He went over the edge of the wharf and the last I saw of the rast was his flaunting pigtail, streaming up into the air in the wind of his fall, and the damned green ribbons flying.

We all heard the splash.

We had remained absolutely silent.

We all heard the beautiful sound of the splash, and then helter-skelter, willy-nilly, dragged by the frantic ones up front, we were pelting for the far side of the warehouse.

"Haul up!" I bellowed.

"Stop, you rasts!" boomed that vast voice at my back.

"Halt! Halt!" cracked from the Zairian, in a voice of habitual command.

But nothing we could do just yet was going to stop that panic.

The Brokelsh in front of me was screaming and running.

We rounded the corner of the warehouse in full cry, a crazy fugitive mob of men chained together. This was no way to escape. Anyway, the high wall surrounded the dockyard and harbor, enclosing the arsenal and the ship sheds, and there was no way over that, and certainly no way through the guarded gateways. I wondered if the Magdaggians would feather us, for sport, or if their war-machine was so desperate for oar-slaves that we had, grotesquely, become valuable.

The bellowing voice at my rear smashed out again.

"You! Dom! Throw yourself down!"

The Zairian and I immediately dropped down. I held on to the chain in front with both hands. The Brokelsh went on running. The jolt was severe. I felt the chain haul out and I tugged back, the Zairian doing likewise.

Then—I swear all thoughts of my being a slave for that moment were whiffed from my mind and I was once again a fighting-man confronted with a hated enemy—the tip of a long and sinuous tail curled under my arm. The tail looped the chain that was held by my hands, so the three gripping members formed a lock on the metal. I felt at once the physical power in that tail. The strain sensibly slackened. We skidded over the stones in our slave breechclouts, and then more men at the rear must have stumbled over the Kataki at my back, or thrown themselves down, either because they saw the sense of that or because they expected the arrows to come shafting in.

In a tangled, cursing pile we came to a skidding halt.

The guards surrounding us appeared with mechanical swiftness. They were not gentle sorting us out. I did not see the Chulik among them.

In a welter of blows and curses we were thrashed along to the swifter and pitched aboard. I tried to see all there was to see, for, even though I am cynical about power and resigned about knowledge, still, as I have indicated, knowledge is power, even to a chained slave, even in his abject condition. It might not do me much good right now; but, although still in a partial state of shock after the death of my daughter, I held tenaciously to this idea of an early escape. Then knowledge would be vital.

If I do not for the moment mention the swifter it is because her arrangements became important later on. The chains were quickly struck off, to be returned to us in the form of chains binding us to the rowing benches allotted. As we filed from the entranceway forward I counted. We were conducted below, whereat I cursed, for this swifter was three-banked, and I had no desire to heave my guts out among the thalamites.

The thranites already sat at their apportioned places on the upper benches, eight to a bench. We passed below them down narrow ladders where the chains clanged dolorously. This was like descending a massive cleft, the sky-showing slot between the larboard and starboard banks, with the grated deck aloft.

I blinked and peered along the second tier. I cursed this time, cursed aloud and cursed hotly.

"By the stinking infamous intestines of Makki-Grodno! Every zygite is in place." I shook a fist upward, the chains clashing. "The bottom for us! The bilge-rats! The thalamites!"

The Zairian said, stoutly, "We will survive, dom."

The Kataki, above him, his tail looped about a stanchion, leaned over. "This is a strange and doomed place—you know, do you, apim, whereof you speak?"

"Aye," I said, descending into the bottom tier. "Aye, I know."

I did not wish to address him, and I wouldn't call him *dom*, which is a comradely greeting. I did not like Katakis. The whip-Deldars were there to welcome us.

They cracked their whips and herded us along and I saw one poor devil, a big fellow, tough, a Brokelsh, strike out at them. They surrounded him like vultures. They carried him away. I knew what would happen. Later on he would be used as an example to us all. He was, and I shall not speak of it.

The whip-Deldars were backed by marines with short-swords naked in their fists, their mail dully glimmering in the half-light. We were sorted into fours. The Zairian, the Kataki, and I shuffled up and were clouted into a bench. The fourth who would row on our loom fell half on top of the Zairian. He was a Xaffer, one of that strange and remote race of diffs of whom I have spoken who seem born for slavery. He looked shriveled. As the smallest, he was shoved past us to the outside position. The Zairian sat next. Then came myself—to my surprise, really—and, outside me, the Kataki. The locks closed with meaty *thwunks*. The chains and links were tested. We were looked at and then, the final indignity, our gray slave breechclouts were whipped off and taken away.

Bald, naked, chained, we sat awaiting the next orders.

For the moment I could think. The oars had not been affixed as yet. That would be the next operation and was being done with us in position so as to show us what was what, how the evolution was carried out. I felt a surprise I should not have felt. Normally, oar-slaves would serve a period of training aboard a dockyard Liburnian with her two shallow banks of oars. Now that the Grodnims of the Green northern shore of the inner sea were carrying forward so victoriously their war against the Zairians of the Red southern shore they needed every craft they could put into commission. There was just no time to go through the protracted period of training when oar-slaves were weeded out. The vicious weeding-out process would take place in this three-banked swifter, and the dead bodies would be flung overboard. Already, after us, the batches of spare slaves were being herded down and stuffed into the holds and crannies where they would wait and suffer until required.

This swifter was a good-sized vessel. There were a great number of slaves forced into her, and we were packed tightly.

The chanks, those killer sharks of the inner sea, would feed well in the wake of this swifter, whose name was *Green Magodont*.

The noise from the slaves echoed and rebounded from the wooden hull. For the moment the whip-Deldars were leaving us to our own devices. Once the oars started to come aboard they'd show us the discipline Magdag required of her oar-slaves.

The Zairian said, "My name is Fazhan ti Rozilloi, dom."

I nodded. The *ti* meant he was someone of some importance in Rozilloi. And that city was known to me, although not particularly well. . . . I knew Mayfwy of Felteraz must have sad thoughts of me, still, for I had used her ill. Her daughter Fwymay had married Zarga na Rozilloi— and the *na* in his name meant he was, if not the most important person of Rozilloi, then damned well high in rank.

"And your name, dom?"

Well, I'd been called Gadak for some time now and had been thinking like Gadak the Renegade. But this Fazhan ti Rozilloi was a crimson-faril, beloved of the Red, and so I deemed it expedient to revert in my allegiance to Zair. Truth to tell, I'd never seriously contemplated abandoning the cause of Zair and the Red; but recent events had been so traumatic—to use a word of later times—that I had been so near to total shock as to be indifferent to anything. Tipping that damned Chulik into the water had been not only a gesture of defiance, it signaled some return of the lump of suffering humanity that was me to the old, tearaway, evil, vicious, and intemperate Dray Prescot I knew myself at heart still to be.

"I am Dak," I said. I did not embroider. I did not wish to involve myself in dreaming up fresh names, and I had taken the name Dak in honor from a great and loyal fighting-man upon the southern shore. And, too, I was growing sick of names, sick of titles. This is, of course, a stupid frame of mind. Names are vital, names are essential, particularly upon Kregen, where so much is different and yet so much is the same as on this Earth four hundred light-years through interstellar space. . . .

This is true of names. As to titles, I had collected a hat-

ful already in my life upon Kregen and was to gather many
more, as you shall hear. Of them all I had valued being a
Krozair of Zy the most. And the Krozairs of Zy had ejected
me, thrown me out, branded me Apushniad. No, I would not
tell this Fazhan I had once been Pur Dray, the Lord of
Strombor, the most feared Krozair upon the Eye of the
World. Anyway, he wouldn't believe me. Since I had taken a
dip in the Sacred Pool of Baptism with my Delia I was assured of a thousand years of life and a remarkable ability
to recuperate rapidly from wounds. This Fazhan betrayed
the usual ageless look of Kregans who have arrived at
maturity; he could be anywhere from twenty to a hundred
and fifty or so.

"Dak?" He looked at me, and then away. Then, seeing
that we were to be oar-comrades, he said, "I salute you,
Dak, for dumping that Zair-forsaken Chulik in the water."

He made no mention of jikai in the matter, which pleased
me. Too many people are too damned quick to talk of some
trifle as a jikai. A jikai is a great and resounding feat of
arms, or some marvelous deed—the word should not be
cheapened.

"And I am Rukker na—" boomed the Kataki, and stopped,
and looked at us, with his evil lowering face dark with
suppressed passion. "Well, since you are Tailless Dak, I am
Rukker." He lifted one massive hand. "But I shall not like it
if you call me Tailless Rukker."

The recovery had been swift. But he'd said *na*, and then
checked. Whatever place he came from, he was its lord.

Carrying on his recovery, the Kataki swung his low-
browed, furrowed face toward the Xaffer, looking past
Fazhan and me. Katakis usually grease and oil and curl
their black hair so that it hangs beside their faces. Their
flaring nostrils curl above gape-jawed mouths. Their eyes
are wide-spaced and yet narrow, brilliant and cold. They are
not apim, like me; they are diffs. Perhaps their greatest
physical peculiarity and strength is the tail each one can
sinuously twirl into vicious speedy action, and with a
curved razor-sharp blade strapped to its tip bring slicing and
slashing and darting in against his opponent. No, I did not
like Katakis, for they were aragorn, slave-managers, slavers,
slave-masters.

"Xaffer!" roared this blow-hard Kataki, his dark-browed
face fierce. "And what is your accursed name?"

The Xaffer surprised me.

"You are a Kataki," he said in that whispering, hushed, timid voice of a Xaffer. "Your devil's race has brought great misery and anguish to my people. I hate Katakis. My name is Xelnon and I shall not speak to you again."

The Zairian shifted his eyes from the Xaffer to look at me, shocked. I looked at the Kataki, this ferocious Rukker. The blood pulsed in his face, veins stood out on his low forehead, his eyes looked murderous. "Cramph! Were we not chained you would not speak thus! Mark me well, Xelnon the onker! Your day will come and I shall—"

"What, Rukker," I said loudly. "You will beat and lash and enslave him, as you are undoubtedly a Kataki and that is what Katakis are so good at doing."

His shocked gaze shifted to me. We sat next to each other, with the steps of the bench lifting him a little higher than me so as to reach the loom. He glared at me. His chains rattled.

"You—apim—" He swallowed down and his thin lips showed spittle.

"Do not fret, Rukker the Kataki. Your tail is safe from me. If you do not cause me trouble."

He bellowed then, raving. I kept a sharp eye on him, for I knew a little of chain fighting by slaves, and I had no desire to be strangled or have an eye flicked out. He reached down to grab me with his right hand, for we sat on the larboard side. This confrontation was no sudden thing; it was long overdue. He tried to seize me about the neck, for the iron rings had been removed after our walk here and tame-slaves were going about with pots of salve made into paste to ease us. The blood on my neck and back and chest was congealing. If he did as he intended he'd not only open up the sore places, he'd squeeze my throat into my neckbones, and if he did not choke me, he'd give me a damned sore throat and head. So I took his right hand with my left. His face convulsed. Struggling silently, for a space we held, he pressing on and I resisting him.

He glared with a mad ferocity upon me. Vicious and feral and violent are Katakis. This one thought to overpower me and subdue me and punish me for my words. Yes, Katakis are all those terrible things. Confident in his power Rukker bore down. It was his misfortune that the man upon whom he happened to choose to release his own frustrations

labored under torments he knew nothing of. It was his hard
luck, as a vicious, feral, and violent man, to meet a man
who was more vicious, more feral, and more violent. I do
not say these things in any foolish state of inverse pride. I
know my sins. But, here, violence met violence and recoiled.

His eyes widened. I bore back harder, twisted, and so
brought my right hand up to block the savage blow of his
left. As for his killing tail—I stomped it flat against the
planking of the deck, whereat he yelled.

"Desist, Rukker, or I shall break your arm off."

"You—apim—I'll—I'll—"

"Do not think I would not do it, Rukker. You are a
Kataki. Do not forget what that means."

"I do not forget, you rast—"

I twisted a little more, and as his left fist still looped
around at me, I took his wrist in my right hand and jerked
most savagely.

He let a gasp of air puff past those thin twisted lips.

"You cramph! You'll pay—"

A lash struck down across his broad naked back and he
snapped upright. A whip-Deldar, sweating in his green, his
dark face sullen, lifted for another blow. "What's this?" he
shouted. "I'll discipline you—you—"

"Whip-Deldar," I said, speaking quickly and loudly enough
to make my words penetrate. "There is no trouble here.
We were testing the height and the stretch of the loom."

The odd thing was that our motions might have been taken
for a practice evolution. The whip-Deldar lowered his lash.
He looked tired, tired and spiteful.

"You dare talk to me, you rast!"

"Only to save your trouble, whip-Deldar. The oar-master
would not welcome damaged oar-slaves now."

The whip-Deldar glowered, flicking the lash. He might be
a poor specimen of humanity anywhere, let alone in evil
Magdag, but the sense of what I said penetrated his sluggish
brain. He gave me a cut with the lash, stingingly, just to
show me who was in charge here, and went off, cursing
roundly.

I do not laugh, as you know, nor smile readily. I kept my
ugly old face as hard as a bower anchor as Rukker, the
Kataki, said, "He was flogging me, not you, apim."

"If you wish him to continue I will call him back for you."

"By the Triple Tails of Targ the Untouchable! Were you a Kataki I would understand!"

Fazhan leaned forward and looked up past me. "But for this apim Dak, you would have been beaten, Rukker."

"I know it. But it would be best if you did not mention it again."

"Ah," said Fazhan ti Rozilloi, "but it is worth the telling, by Zantristar the Merciful!"

The swifter shook and a shudder passed through her fabric. In the next instant, to the accompaniment of distant hailing above decks, we all understood we had pushed off from the wharf. A long, slow gentle rocking made us all aware that we had been cast off into our new life. Until the oars were in, the swifter would possess this gentle rocking motion, for she was of large enough build to remain steady in the water without her wings.

Rukker the Kataki and Fazhan ti Rozilloi glared for a space longer at each other, then I stuck my old carved beak head between them and said, "If we are to pull together it will be easier if we do not try to fight one another all the time."

Rukker nodded. He was a man accustomed to instant decision.

"You say you understand these infernal things. Tell me."

"You have never sailed in a swifter?"

"Aye, a few times. But I sat in the captain's cabin and drank wine and the way of the vessel did not concern me."

"It concerns you now," said Fazhan.

"Aye, that is why I would learn of it."

"All you need to know," I said, and I spoke heavily, "is that you will pull the oar, and go on pulling the oar, until you are dead. All else will mean nothing."

"Where are these oars, then?"

"We are being towed out from the cothon through the narrow channel. It is too narrow otherwise. Once in the outer harbor we will receive our oars from the oar-hulk. They will arrive soon enough, bringing misery and torment, and for some, a happy release in death."

Rukker mused on this. His dark Kataki face scowled.

"You appear to me to be a man, Dak—of sorts. I will allow you to assist me in my escape."

Fazhan gurgled a little cynical laugh; but it was not a

laugh a refined lady would recognize. Oar-slaves do not often have either the opportunity or the reason for laughing.

We bumped and the swifter rocked, and then we bumped again and remained still. We had been moored up to the oar-hulk. Noises began from forward, spurting through the confined space, hollow, echoing. Bangings and scrapings, and at least two shrill yells. It was common for a slave to be crushed or injured when the oars came inboard. We waited for our turn and we did not have long to wait, for we pulled six oars from the bows. A sudden shaft of suns-light speared through the oar port as the sliding cover went back. Sailors busied themselves—hard, adventurous, callous men—hauling the oars in, adjusting the set and balance, cursing the slaves who brought down the round lead counterweights. The oar shoved past Xelnon the Xaffer, past Fazhan ti Rozilloi, past me, Dak, and so past Rukker the Kataki. The loom end was inserted into the rowing frame, which was hinged up to receive it, and locked, and the counterweight was hung on and locked in its turn. The four of us sat, looking at that immense bar of wood before us. The carpenters followed to affix the manette, which we would grasp, for the loom itself was of too great a girth.

I had noticed immediately on boarding the swifter that she smelled clean. She smelled of vinegar and pungent ibroi and soap.

She was not a new vessel, this *Green Magodont;* but she had been in for a refit and was now as sweetly clean as she would ever be. All that was about to change.

Amid the usual barrage of curses and yells, slaves came running along the grated decks and hurled sacks of straw and ponsho fleeces at us. Men scrabbled for well-filled sacks, for fleeces that did not appear too mangy. Rukker hauled in half a dozen and the slave yelped; Rukker knocked him back and examined sack after sack. He took a fine-filled one and as he discarded the others, I snatched up the best and threw them along to Xelnon and Fazhan. The fleeces were likewise gone through, and the slave, jittering with fear, reviled by the other oar-slaves opposite us, squealed at Rukker to let him have back those he did not want.

"Quiet, kleesh," said Rukker, and the slave shook.

A marine, his shortsword out, walked up along the grated deck and I looked forward, not without interest, to a little action; but Rukker hurled the last sack back and cursed.

The marine chivied the slave along and he went off to throw the fleeces down to the next set of oar-slaves. We were all busy spreading the fleeces over the sacks, arranging them. Already I had nipped three nits under my thumbnail. *Green Magodont* was no longer a clean swifter. I glanced up at Rukker.

"You were allowed the pick of the sacks, Rukker, because you have a tail. I understand that. But do not think to take the best of everything the four of us are issued with."

He might have bellowed his head off then; but a whip-Deldar ran along, not hitting us but cracking his lash in the air with a sound most doleful and menacing, violent and frightening. He impressed us poor naked slaves, he impressed us mightily.

"Silence!" shouted the whip-Deldar. "The first man to speak will get ol' snake—I promise you."

I did not speak.

No one else spoke.

We had learned one elementary lesson we would not forget.

A deal of confused shouting bellowed down from aloft. I, who had been a swifter captain of the inner sea, could understand what was going on—but only to some extent. I knew these oar-slaves with me on the lowest tier, the thalamite bank, were raw, untrained, useless. I could not understand why the oar-master had ordered our oars fixed and threaded—that is, placed in the rowing frames. Presently, amid a deal of noise and confusion, fresh sailors and slaves poured below and took the oars from the rowing frames, slid the oar-port covers back, and we all had our first lesson in pushing the oar looms forward so that the looms lay as close to the hull as they would go, which brought the outer portions and the blades close to the outside hull. The thalamites were not trusted to pull yet, and *Green Magodont* would begin her journey with only the two upper banks pulling.

We heard the orders, the whistles, the sudden deathly silence in the ship. Then the preparatory whistle, and then the twin beat from the drum-Deldar, the bass and tenor, thumping out. We heard the creak of the upper oars, the splash of water as they dug in. We all felt the swifter surge forward, slowly at first, but gathering momentum. All rocking ceased and the swifter struck a straight, sure path out through the harbor, out past the Pharos, out from vile Magdag into the Eye of the World.

Wherever we were going, we were on our way.

Chapter Two

Oar-slaves in the swifters of Magdag

We rowed.

We oar-slaves pulled at the massively heavy looms of the oars, up and back and down and forward and up and back and down and . . .

A week. Give a galley slave a week, more or less, and he will be either dead or toughened enough to last another week, and then another, and then perhaps, if his stamina lasts, to live. If the existence of a galley slave can be called living.

The Xaffer, Xelnon, lasted five days.

He would have died sooner, but *Green Magodont* caught a wind swinging out of Magdag and so we slaves were spared much of the continuous hauling that is the killer. But he died.

He did not tell us what he had done to be condemned to the galleys. Usually Xaffers are given the lighter tasks of slaves, household chores, secretarial work, record-keeping. Most often they, along with Relts, are employed as stylors. But he was here, with us, slaving, and then he was a mere cold corpse, blood-marked by the lash, a bundle to be thrown overboard to the chanks.

A Rapa took his place, brought up from the slave-hold. His gray vulturine face with that brooding, aggressive hooked beak and the bright feathers rising around his crest fitted in with the stark horror of our situation.

We spoke rarely. We learned the Rapa's name was Lorgad,

that he had got himself stinking drunk on dopa and had
run amok in the mercenaries' billets. Exactly what he had
then done he did not say, presumably because he could no
longer remember. He pulled on the loom with us and we
labored and sweated in the stink and dank darkness of our
floating prison.

On the day after Xelnon died we beached up on a small
island, one of the many small islands that smother the larger
maps of the Eye of the World with measle spots. The swifter
was hauled up sternfirst onto a beach of silver sand. I have
said that the old devil the teredo worm is nowhere as fierce
on Kregen as upon Earth and often the swifters are not
sheathed in copper or lead. Often, especially in the cases of
the larger types, they are. *Green Magodont* was not sheathed,
and so despite her size her captain had her hauled up out
of the water as often as he could. The task was formidable;
but we slaves, still chained, were flogged up and over the side
and so set to work hauling the drag ropes.

The island glimmered under the distant golden fire of two
of the moons of Kregen; the Twins, eternally revolving one
about the other, smiled down upon our agony.

We were herded back into the swifter and chained up, for
in the ship lay the best prison for us.

In the normal course of events the gangs on a loom remained together in duties of this kind; but the captain of
Green Magodont, although undeniably a cruel and vicious
overlord of Magdag, was of the school that liked to rotate
his oar-slaves between tiers. Once the agonies of learning
how to pull correctly to the rhythm of the whistles and
drums and to conduct the necessary evolutions smartly and
promptly had been hammered into our skulls and muscles,
we thalamites of the lower tier were rotated to the center
tier, where the zygites pulled.

Green Magodont carried on the short-keel system eight
men to her upper bank, six to her middle, and four
to her lower. We did not aspire to the center tier until some
time; but, at last, we were deemed sufficiently proficient to
be rotated.

We had left that island where we had gone ashore to
work, and since then, although the swifter had touched land
each night, we had not gone ashore again. As to our journey
and its direction, apart from my guess that we were headed

southwest, I knew nothing. Oar-slaves are not consulted on
the conning of the ship.

"Will they really let us onto the middle deck, Dak?"

"Once we can be trusted to pull correctly, Fazhan. Aye."

Rukker the Kataki grunted and turned to find a more
comfortable position, his tail curled up and looped over his
shoulder. We rested this night, as we rested any time,
chained to our bench. "Do we ever get up onto the upper
deck?"

"Only when we are considered fully proficient." I did not
want to talk. More and more I had been thinking about my
daughter Velia, of the tragically short time I had known her
and known she was my daughter, of the manner of her
death. "I can tell you that if I captained this damned swifter
this loom would remain in the thalamites forever."

"You!" scoffed Rukker. "Captain a swifter!"

"I said *if*."

"And yet you know about Magdaggian swifters, Dak." Fazhan had lost much of the scarlet in his face; he had thinned
and fined down on the food we ate, on the daily exercise.
"I was a swifter ship-Hikdar before we were taken. But I
know little about Grodnim swifters."

"I have been oar-slave before," I said, and left it at that.

Fazhan grunted and turned his head on his arms, spread
on the loom. But Rukker showed instant interest. "So you
escaped?"

"Aye."

"Then you will certainly assist me when we escape."

"I escaped," I said, "when we were taken by a swifter
from Sanurkazz. A swifter captained by a Krozair of Zy." I
said this deliberately. I wanted to probe Fazhan—and Rukker, too. For the martial and mystic Order of Krozairs of
Zy is remote from ordinary men on the Eye of the World,
strange, and dedicated to Disciplines almost too demanding
for frail human flesh.

Fazhan turned his head back quickly.

"The Krozairs!" he said. He breathed the word as a man
might in talking about demigods.

The Rapa, Lorgad, snuffled and hissed. "Krozairs! We
fought them—aye, and we thrashed them."

"Thrashed?" I said.

The Rapa passed a hand over his feathers, smoothing

them. "Well—it was a hard fight. But King Genod's new army won—as it always wins."

"But one day it will be smashed utterly!" said Fazhan. His voice blazed in the night, and surly voices answered from the other rowing benches in the gloom, bidding the onker be quiet so tired men might sleep.

I had learned what little Rukker would tell me of his story, and I knew Fazhan's, that he had been a ship-Hikdar in a swifter from Zamu. Yet he was not a Krozair Brother, not even of the Krozairs of Zamu. As for Rukker, as he said himself, he was essentially a land soldier, and knew nothing of ships and the sea. As a mercenary he had hired out his— And then he had paused, and corrected himself, and said he had been hired out as a paktun to Magdag. I knew, if I was right and he was a gernu, a noble, that he had taken a force of his own country to fight for Magdag for pay. Now this was, to me, passing strange, for my previous experience with Katakis had been of them as slave-masters, slavers who bartered human flesh. There were a number of races of diffs living up in the northeastern seaboard of the Eye of the World, notably around the Sea of Onyx. Rukker had said he came from an inland country there, a place he had once referred to as Urntakkar, that is, North Takkar. He did not refer to it again.

I said, "Have you heard of Morcray?"

"No."

So I let that lie, also.

But if the Katakis were moving out from their traditional business and becoming mercenaries, then the future looked either darker and more horrible, or scarlet and more interesting, depending on the hardness of your muscles and the keenness of your sword.

We sailed in company with other swifters; just how many we thalamites in our stinks and gloom could not know. We anchored for the night and then took a wind and so rested the next day, and on the following day, the wind fell and we pulled. That was a hard day. Another ten slaves were hurled overboard, either dead or flogged near to death. Those who remained hardened, and the replacements from the slave-hold were those who failed.

That night we once again hauled *Green Magodont* out of the water. I saw six other swifters being hauled up, and also there were signs of a wooden stockade being constructed on the shore into which the slaves might be herded. I knew that Magdag, no less than every other Green city of the northern shore, was utilizing every possible sinew of war. Slaves were now becoming valuable, even though many a poor devil had been captured by the new army of King Genod, the genius at war.

In the stockade only a few fights broke out. Most of us wanted to stretch out—and what a luxury that was!—and sleep. I did not stay awake long. The four of us—for the Rapa, Lorgad, was accepted by us as an oar-comrade—slept together. The morning came all too soon, and with many groans and stretchings of stiff joints, we rose and were doused down with a vile concoction of seawater and pungent ibroi, and then we gobbled the food thrown to us. This was a mash of cereal, a torn hunk of stale bread, and a handful of palines. For the palines everyone gave thanks to whatever gods they revered.

The whip-Deldars stalked among us, the lashes licking hungrily, sorting us out amid a great clanking of chains.

"I believe," said Fazhan, staring about, "that we are to go up to be zygites this day."

It certainly looked like it. The dust from the stockade compound rose thickly as hundreds of pairs of naked feet stamped. The blue of mountains rose inland, and the sky showed that hint of fair weather that heartens the hard-bitten soul of a sailorman. I wanted no trouble. We had been working on our chains. I had experience to go on. The Kataki had the experience of the master slaver, the man to whom the guiles of slaves seeking escape were known as a part of his business. And Fazhan and Lorgad worked at our directions. So I wanted us to stay together, and not to create problems.

We waited in long rows, our chains clanking as men shifted position. The Suns of Scorpio rose over the hills and flooded down their mingled streaming light. I stretched and felt my muscles pull. I was in superb physical shape; but I could have done with more food, as could all of us. A commotion broke out among the slaves to our right.

I heard a bull voice bellowing, and abruptly a whip-Deldar catapulted into the air, turning over and over, his whip thonged to his wrist whirling. He landed flat on his back amid a splash of dust. The slaves cheered. The smashing voice shouted:

"By Zogo the Hyrwhip! You zigging cramph! I'll break your back! Duh, I'll rip your guts out and—"

Dragging the other three, I was running.

The bellow smashed out again, louder, roaring with fury.

"Duh—by Zair! You'll not walk again, rast!"

"Hold, Dak—what is it?" And, "You rast, haul back!" And, "By Rhapaporgolam the Reaver of Souls, you are mad!"

The three of them, I hauled along. The dust, the yells, the confusion, the stink . . . I bundled headlong into the thick of the confusion.

A second whip-Deldar screamed with gap-toothed mouth, glaring unbelievingly at his left arm, which dangled with broken bones protruding pinkish white. Slaves stumbled out of my way. I bashed on to the center and there—standing like a mountain, like a mammoth beset by wolves, a boloth beset by werstings—stood Duhrra.

His bald head already grew a bristly fuzz like all of us. His dangling scalplock had gone. His naked body showed all the splendid musculature of the wrestler. His idiot-seeming face was contorted into a hideous scowl, and I sighed, for Duhrra was normally the most peaceable of men unless someone upset him. Once riled he was like to tear your head off. On the ground at his feet and chained to him lay a young man. A youth; barely come to his full growth, his body showed the promise of a superb physique. He was not unconscious, but a thread of blood ran from one nostril.

I threw a Rapa away, chopped a couple of apims, kicked a Brokelsh, and so grabbed Duhrra by the arm. He whirled, ready to smash my face in, and I said, low and hard, "Duhrra! Calm down, bring the boy, come with me. *Jump!*"

He picked up the boy in a single fluid motion of that massive body, and we turned and plunged back into the throng of shouting, excited, dust-stirring slaves. I had to break the neck of the whip-Deldar who reared up, flailing his whip with his right hand, his broken left arm dangling. He had seen us. I knew what would happen if we were detected. As for the other whip-Deldar—I saw a Brokelsh jump full on him and guessed his backbone would not stand the strain.

With Rukker, Fazhan, and Lorgad trailing on the chain, with Duhrra carrying the youth at my side, we bashed our way through the mob until we reached the line as yet undisturbed. I watched for guards, whip-Deldars, and anyone who showed too much interest.

"Put the boy down, Duhrra."

I bent and scooped up dust, spit on it, wadded it.

"Stand up, lad! Hold yourself straight!"

I shoved the chunk of spittle-wadded dust up his bleeding nostril and then wiped away the blood, licking my fingers. When he looked presentable, and we had knocked the dust from one another—all of us—I said to them all: "Stand and look stupid. By Zair! That should not be difficult! We know nothing of the disturbance."

"Duh—Dak—" said Duhrra.

"Quiet, you fambly. Tell me later."

Rukker, the Kataki, said, "You think fast, Dak, for an apim."

"Shut your black-fanged wine-spout, Rukker. Here come the guards."

We all stood there, in our chains, and looked suitably stupid. There was a considerable quantity of confusion lower down, and shouting, and the sound of the whips lashing. Some of the slaves were too stupid in all reality to run off. When order was restored and we were sorted out, the six of us were herded back into *Green Magodont* and chained down in the middle tier. We were to be zygites, six to a loom, and if the oar-master of the swifter discovered he had two slaves too many, he would give thanks to Green Grodno and smile. As for the swifter from which Duhrra and the lad had come, her oar-master would curse and rave—and I felt damned sure that the oar-master of *Green Magodont* would continue to say nothing and smile even more broadly. As the quondam first lieutenant of a seventy-four I knew only too well the avariciousness of shellbacked sailormen in the matter of ship supplies—and in the Eye of the World of Kregen, ship supplies included slaves.

Green Magodont, as I had previously observed, was broad enough to accept six oarsmen abreast on a loom. Above our heads on the thranites bank the men were arranged to push and pull, the eight men forming a convenient pattern. This tended to cramp them a little more than us lower tiersmen; but the shipwrights of Magdag had done their sums well so that the leverage and power required on the differently sized oars evened out. So we sat at the loom of the zygite oar. The six of us, from the apostis seat, the outer seat, were: Lorgad the Rapa, Fazhan ti Rozilloi, Vax, Dak, Duhrra of the Days, and Rukker the Kataki.

"Duh—master," Duhrra had said to me as we sorted ourselves out, "I should take the rowing frame."

He was fractionally bigger than Rukker.

I said, "Fambly! With that newfangled claw of yours! Next to the gangway! Where you will get lashed more easily!"

"Yes, master."

"And, for the sweet sake of Mother Zinzu the Blessed! I am not your master!"

"No, master."

As always when arguing with Duhrra on this point—for he had attached himself to me on the southern shore, when he had lost his right hand, and since then we had had a few skirmishes together and were good comrades—I gave up the argument in a kind of helpless mirth. Even an oar-slave may feel that at times, in the ludicrousness of his position; for, to all the names of the gods in two worlds, it is not a position a sane man can regard without recourse to the black humor of absurdity.

Some bustle attended our departure, and we were forced to throw our backs into the work. The captain was evidently in the devil of a hurry. The stockades and the cooking fires were left on the shore so we guessed we'd be back tonight. We pulled. We heaved up on the oar, those on the gangway sides of the long rows of men shoving up, standing up, and then with all the weight of the body and bunched muscles, hurling themselves frenziedly backward onto the bench. The hard wood had to be covered by the straw-stuffed sacks and the ponsho fleeces. Had they not been we would have been red raw in no time, and unfit for rowing. This is not a luxury the overlords of Magdag extend to their oar-slaves, in the matter of ponsho fleeces and sacks; it is a matter of economics and slave-management.

The swifter squadron pulled about, it seemed to me, quartering in different directions. I guessed the courses were not set at random. We either searched for another ship, or we wasted a deal of energy. Nothing—apart from the eternal damned pulling—occurred, and we eventually and to our surprise heard the terminal whistles and the final double drumbeat. The oars lifted and were looped and held, locked in the rowing frames, and we slaves slumped, exhausted.

Before lethargy could drug us into stupefaction, we
were flogged out and herded up into the job of hauling
the swifters out of the water. The wood from which swifters
are built must have been placed on Kregen either by a god
or a devil. This flibre, as I have said, possesses remarkable
strength for a remarkable lightness. We would scarcely have
shifted the ships had they been built of lenk. But flibre
gives a large vessel the shrewd feather-lightness of a much
flimsier vessel. As I say, flibre was put on Kregen either by a
god or a devil—a god, in order to lighten the drudgery of
slaves, or a devil so that the damned ships could be manhandled out of the water at all.

At last, fed, exhausted, we flopped down on the hard
ground of the stockade and slept.

If anyone had wished to tell the story of his life to me
at that time, and paid me handsomely to listen, I'd have
consigned him to the Ice Floes of Sicce, and turned over
and slept.

The next day the swifters remained high on the beach
and we oar-slaves sprawled in the stockade, still chained,
but able to stretch out and rest our abused bodies.

Parties of hunters went inland toward the mountains and
later as the suns began their curve toward the horizon we
slaves were issued with steaming chunks of vosk. How we
grabbed and stuffed and ate! Provisioning swifters is invari-
ably a complicated process, and the large numbers of men
involved demand ready access to vast quantities of food.
Usually we subsisted on the mash—there are several varieties
—the base of which consists of mergem, that rich plant
stuffed with protein and vitamins and iron that has the
blessed quality of fortifying a man against his daily toil. But
for mergem, which provides so much nourishment in so small
a bulk, we would have been a gaunt and hungry crew and
quite unfitted to haul on our looms. Onions were provided—
how Zorg and I had debated the dissection of a pair of
onions!—and some cheese and crusts and palines.* The
palines helped keep the insanity levels within toleration.

We devoured the boiled vosk with the voraciousness of
leems. Then we lay back with bloated bellies, burping con-
tentedly, to sleep the night away.

---

*See *The Suns of Scorpio,* Dray Prescot #2.

Duhrra at last found time to tell me what had happened since we had stirred up the camp of King Genod's army and stolen his airboat. He had had to be overpowered by the Zairians from Zandikar when I did not return in time, for he would have gone to find me. He spoke of this with some spirit of contempt for himself that he had been thwunked on the back of the head when he should have been alert not only against the cramphs of Green Grodnims but also, apparently, against the Red Zandikarese.

"When I woke up, Dak—duh! We were flying in the air!"

"You cannot blame the Hikdar—Ornol ti Zab, I believe his name was—he had a duty very plain to him."

"Maybe so. But we flew away and left you."

He and the lad Vax had shipped back from Zandikar and their vessel had been taken. It was becoming more and more dangerous for any vessel of the Red to venture into the western parts of the inner sea these days. The Grodnims had placed swifter squadrons at sea, which carried all before them. Only a very slim coincidence had brought us together again, and to Duhrra it was absolutely inevitable that we should meet up once more. As for Vax, he told me the youth was a fine lad, and potentially a good companion; although he would swear so dreadfully about his father, and Duhrra was strongly of the opinion that if Vax hadn't run away from home to escape the continual beatings, he'd have killed the old devil. Or, so Duhrra believed.

I gave him a brief—a very brief—résumé of what had happened to me after we'd parted. He expressed a desire to twist Gafard's neck a little. We had both been employed by Gafard, the King's Striker, the Sea Zhantil, who was the hateful King Genod's right-hand man, when we'd been renegades, as Gafard himself was a renegade. When I told Duhrra that the Lady of the Stars had, at last, been kidnapped by King Genod's men, he thumped his left fist against the dirt and swore. When I told him that the Lady of the Stars was dead, callously hurled from the back of a fluttrell by the king when the saddle-bird had been injured, and Genod thought himself about to die, Duhrra simply sat on the ground. He ran a little dust through his fingers onto the dust of the ground. His head was bowed.

At last, he said, "I shall not forget."

I did not tell Duhrra of the Days that this great and wonderful lady, who had been called his Heart, his Pearl, by

Gafard, and who had loved him in return, was my own daughter Velia, princess of Vallia.

My Delia, my Delia of Delphond, my Delia of the Blue Mountains, waited for me in my island Stromnate of Valka, that beautiful island off the main island of Vallia. I yearned to return to her. Yet I was under an interdiction. Until I had once more made myself a member of the Order of Krozairs of Zy I would not be allowed to leave the Eye of the World. Whether or not it was the Star Lords or the Savanti who chained me here, I did not know, although Zena Iztar had indicated it was not the work of the Star Lords. Well, I would become a Krozair of Zy once more and escape from the inner sea and return to Valka. Before I did that I fancied I would bring this evil king Genod to justice. So, having done all these marvelous and wonderful feats and proved just how great a man I was, I would go home. I would go home and race up the long flight of stairs in the rock from the Kyro of the Tridents, leap triumphantly onto the high terrace of my palace of Esser Rarioch overlooking the bay and Valkanium and I would clasp my Delia in my arms again. Oh, yes, I would do all this. And then—and then I would have to tell her that her daughter Velia was dead.

It is no wonder that on this dreadful occasion I found less thrusting desire to go back to Valka and Delia than I'd ever experienced before. I must return. I must tell my Delia and then comfort her as she would comfort me. It was not just a duty, it was what love prompted. But it was hard, abominably hard.

Duhrra was telling me about his new hand and I roused myself. I had to plan and think. My thoughts had run ahead. Here we were, still chained oar-slaves in a swifter of Magdag.

". . . locks with a twist so cunning you'd never know. Look."

I looked. Duhrra's right stump had been covered with a flesh-colored extension that looked just like a wrist and the hard mechanical hand looked not unlike a real hand. He could press the fingers into different positions with his left hand. He kept it hooked so that he could haul on the manette of the oar loom. I felt it and the hardness was unmistakable.

"That's a steel hand, Duhrra—or iron."

The doctors of the inner sea are not, in general, quiet as skilled as those of the lands of the Outer Oceans. They are good at relieving pain and can amputate with dexterity. But I did not think they were capable of producing prosthetics of this quality. Duhrra had seen Molyz the Hook Maker and this kind of work would have been quite beyond him. Duhrra had been attended to by the doctors attached to the Todalpheme of the Akhram, the mathematical astronomers who predicted the tides of Kregen, and they had fitted his stump with a socket and an assortment of hooks and blades to be slotted in. But this work here was beyond them, also. Duhrra waxed eloquent for him.

"In Zandikar, it was, Dak. Right out of the blue. This lady says she can fix me up properly. Wonderful woman—wonderful. Gentle and charming and—well, you can see what she did."

"You saw her do it?"

"No. Somehow—duh, master—I do not know! She looked into my eyes and then she laughed and told me I might leave and I looked down—and it was all done."

"And her name, this wonderful woman?"

"She said she was the lady Iztar."

I did not answer. What was Zena Iztar—whose role so far had been enigmatic in my life although I felt I owed her a very great deal—doing in thus helping Duhrra? Her machinations, I suspected, might not jibe with those of the Star Lords or those of the Savanti. She it was who had told me I might never leave the Eye of the World until I was once more a Krzy. I believed her implicitly, had not thought to question her. She, I felt, I hoped, wished me well. That would make a remarkable change here on Kregen, where I had been knocked about cruelly by Savanti and Star Lords moving behind the scenes and exerting superhuman forces. So I admired Duhrra's new hand and thought on.

Then the selfishness of my thoughts mocked me. It was all "I"—Zena Iztar could have helped Duhrra because he was Duhrra.

Tame-slaves threw in malsidges and we ate them, for they are a quality anti-scorbutic. We settled down to sleep and I had a deal to think about; but, all the same, I slept.

Sleep became a rare and precious commodity during the next couple of sennights, for we were employed pulling at night as well as day. The swifters called at islands for short periods and then weighed again, and once again we threw our tortured bodies against the looms of the oars. Food was short and we hungered. Men began to die. I fancied Duhrra would last this kind of punishment well, and the Kataki had reserves of strength on which to call. For Fazhan ti Rozilloi the work became harder and harder; but with all the gallantry of a true crimson-faril he struggled on, refusing to be beaten. The young man Vax stuck to his work with stoical fury, sullen, with a smoldering anger in him hurtful to me. We were not flogged more than any other set on any other loom. But we lost Lorgad the Rapa. One day he could not pull any more, and the flogging lash merely made his dead body jump. He was unchained and heaved overboard, and a fresh man took his place.

He was short, and he took the apostis seat, chunky, and with a black bar look about the eyebrows, and a pug nose that was of the Mountains of Ilkenesk south of the inner sea. Yet he was a Zairian, an apim, and he contrived to give Rukker the Kataki a cunning slash with his chains as the whip-Deldars bundled him across.

Rukker bellowed and shook his chains.

I saw the chain between him and Duhrra pull taut. The chain between Duhrra and me began to pull. The link on which we had been working bent. It began to open. I cursed foully, loudly, unable to get at Rukker past Duhrra.

"Sit back you stinking Kataki cramph! You tailed abomination! Sit down or I'll cave your onkerish head in!"

He swung back to glare with murderous fury at me. The whip-Deldars bashed away at the new man's chains. Duhrra tried to sit back as well, to release the pressure on the chains. It was a moment when all hell might have broken loose.

One whip-Deldar flicked his lash—almost idly—at me and I endured it. I bellowed again, something about Katakis and rasts and tails, and whispered to Duhrra, "Tell him, Duhrra! Get the gerblish onker to sit down!"

Duhrra leaned across and his rumble would have told the whole bank if I had not started yelling with the pain of the lash. It was not altogether a fake. Vax looked at me in surprise. I yelled some more. And then Duhrra must have got the message across, for Rukker slapped himself back on the bench, whipping his tail up out of the way, and the strain came off the chain.

When the whip-Deldars had gone, he started to rumble at

me, "You called me many things, Dak, and I shall not forget them—"

"You would have ruined all, Rukker. You must think and plan if you wish to escape the overlords of Magdag and their slave-masters. Onker! I did what I did to make you sit down."

Duhrra said, "Had you ruined our chances, Rukker, I would not have been pleased—duh—I would have been angry."

Rukker glared at me again. Duhrra lifted the chain between us. Rukker looked.

Duhrra's metal hand had worked hard and well. The bent link was on the point of parting. Rukker whistled.

"Well, you onker! Now do you see your foolishness?"

He did not like my tone. But he was a Kataki.

Rukker said, "I understand. I will not speak of it again."

That was Rukker the Kataki. He had this knack of putting his own mistakes and unpleasant experiences into a limbo where he chose not to speak of them. The idea of apology never entered his ferocious Kataki head.

Chapter Three

———◆———

Of Duhrra's steel hand

"Well, Dak, apim, when is it to be?"

Rukker's words whispered in his growly voice in the darkness. *Green Magodont* lay anchored somewhere or other—we oar-slaves had no idea where we were after all the comings and goings of the past days. We knew only that if we searched for a ship we had not found her.

I said, "There is the question of this Nath the Slinger."

"I shall break his neck the moment I am free," said Rukker, in a comfortable way, perfectly confident.

Nath the Slinger turned his pug-nosed face our way, looking up from the apostis seat, and scowled. He looked an independent sort of fellow, who would as soon knock your teeth out as pass the time of day. Rukker had not liked the slash from his chains.

"We can free the link tomorrow. But we shall not let you go, Rukker, if you—"

He bellowed at that, raising a chorus of curses from the oar-slaves about us in the darkness, weary men trying to sleep.

"You are a nurdling onker, Rukker—why not shout out and tell the captain? I am sure he will be happy to know."

In the starlight and the golden glow of She of the Veils the zygite bank showed enough light for me to catch the look of venomous evil on Rukker's face. But it was dark and shadowy and I could have been mistaken; I did not think I was.

"I do not wish to discuss that, Dak. If it is tomorrow night, then—"

"We will release you only if you swear to fight with us. Your quarrel with Nath the Slinger must wait."

"I'll rip his tail out and choke him with it!" said Nath the Slinger, in his snarly voice.

I sighed.

Anger and enmity—well, they are common enough on Kregen, to be sure. But when they interfere with my own plans I am prepared to be more angry and be a better enemy than most.

"When we have taken the swifter, you two may kill each other," I said, pretty sharply. "And curse you for a pair of idiots."

A voice from the bench in front whispered back.

"If you all shout a little louder—"

"We already said that," said Fazhan nastily.

"Then we will join you. The oar-master has the keys."

Duhrra rolled his eyes at me.

"They must think we don't know what we're about."

"They are slaves like us. Now the word will be all over the slave benches. If there are white mice among the slaves we may be prevented before we strike."

"White mice" is an expression from my own eighteenth-century Terrestrial Navy, meaning men among the hands who will inform to the ship's corporals and the master-at-arms. On Kregen these men are called *maktikos* and may sometimes be discovered among slaves who appear and disappear without apparent reason on a tier of oars, moving from bench to bench. I had wondered if Nath the Slinger might be an informer. There were plans to insure his silence once we had begun the escape. The only way to insure our safety before that was to note if he spoke to the overseers or the whip-Deldars. I fancied an apostis-seat man would experience difficulty in that.

"Why not tonight?" rumbled Rukker. "Now?"

"The link must be further bent."

"I would snap it with one wrench."

"You may try—but for the sake of Zair, do it quietly."

Rukker leaned over Duhrra. He took the chain in his right hand and tail and heaved. The link strained open, as it had when he'd surged up before; it did not break.

The veins stood out on that low forehead, his face grew black, his eyes glaring. He slackened his effort and panted. "Onker, Duhrra! Help me! You too, Dak!"

So we all pulled.

The link would not part.

"Tomorrow," I said.

Duhrra said, "You were told, Rukker. Now do you believe?"

Rukker said, "I will not speak of that."

I did not laugh. We were going to escape, I was certain; but I could not laugh—not yet. There would be time, later. . . .

The next day during those periods in which we were not called on to fling every ounce of weight against the looms, Duhrra used that marvelous hand given to him by Zena Iztar. The steel fingers prised against the link like a vise. Even a steel hand that gave the hard pressure necessary would not have accomplished the bending without the superb muscles that Duhrra could bring to the task. I helped as best I could, taking the strain. We had to work surreptitiously. The bent link was camouflaged by a mixture of odoriferous compounds I will not detail and it passed the daily inspection, for a strong pull on it resulted merely in the usual melancholy clang. The whip-Deldars suspected nothing. They were always on the watch, for slavery makes a man either dully stupid or viciously frenzied.

I said to Rukker "Once we are free, everything must be done at top speed. The slaves will yell and cry out and demand to be freed. You will not be able to silence them. They have no idea at all, in moments like that, beyond the hunger to strike off their chains. So we must be quick."

"I'll silence—"

"You will not. You will take the whip-Deldars. We need weapons. I will see to the oar-master."

"I give the orders, Dak. This is my escape."

"I don't give a damn whose escape it is. But if you foul it up I'll pull your tail off myself."

I had warned him, earlier, not to be too free with his tail. He could have upended a whip-Deldar easily enough. They did not carry the keys, as the onker of a slave in front of us had said. If a Kataki used his tail too much in a swifter the overlords would simply chop it off. I had told Rukker this. He had heeded my advice.

So we planned out our moves exactly, each man assigned his part. I listened as Nath the Slinger spoke, in short harsh sentences. I came to the conclusion that he was not a maktiko, that he might be trusted.

The day seemed endless. *Green Magodont* pulled frenziedly in one direction for a bur; then we rested on our oars for another. Then we set off at slow cruise in a different direction and suddenly we were called on for every effort, and as suddenly relieved and sent back to slow cruise. I fancied we were dodging about among islands and shooting out past a headland in a surprise attack that resulted always in nothing. If the Grodnims sought a ship, as I suspected, her captain played them well in this game of hide-and-seek. Duhrra told me he had come from the swifter *Vengeance Mortil,* where he and Vax had been the two slaves chained together to push against the loom. I did wonder if Gafard's *Volgodont's Fang* led this squadron, for our swifter was not the flagship.

One item I should mention here, for it would affect our manner of escape, showed how either development was taking place in the swifters of the inner sea, or the overlords of Magdag were running short of iron; or, very likely, were conscious of the need to lighten their galleys. There was no great chain that connected all the chains of the inboard slaves. We would have to release the locks of each set separately. This would take time. There would be no release of the locks of the great chain thus freeing all the slaves the moment the great chain had been passed through their chains. It was a factor to be figured into my calculations.

"By Zinter the Afflicted!" rasped Nath. "Is the work finished?" We lay on our oars as the gloom deepened about us and *Green Magodont* rocked gently with the evening sounds from an island nearby reaching us mutedly—the cries of birds, mostly, with occasionally the coughing roar of a beast of prey, and then, sometimes, the shrill scream of its quarry, telling us we were anchored well into the island up a river mouth. The chinks of light that streamed their opaz radiance into our prison waned as the suns sank.

"We will escape," said Vax. He spoke seldom and he was, as we all could see, obsessed by some consuming inner torment.

"Then praise Zair," said Fazhan. "I do not think I could last another day." He coughed, too weakly for my liking. "My old father would weep to see me now."

Vax let rip with a rude sound, and a coarse observation

about fathers in general and his devil cramph of a father in particular. The venom in his voice gave me hope that he would fling some of that diabolic energy into the coming fight.

"I do not care to hear you talk thus of your father—" began Fazhan. It was clear to me than Fazhan had been brought up in the best circles of Rozilloi and was, in the terminology of Earth, a gentleman, although the peoples of the inner sea have a trifle different set of gentlemen from the horters of Havilfar and the koters of Vallia.

"You did not know my rast of a sire," said Vax, most evilly. "And neither did I, for he died just before I was born."

This did not accord with what Duhrra believed; but it was of no moment then as the whip-Deldars ran screeching among us, lashing with their whips, and the whistles blew and the drum-Deldar crashed out his double-beat. In the gathering gloom the swifter made a last try to trap the elusive vessel that caused the Grodnims so much trouble and us oarslaves so much agony.

Green Magodont did not catch the quarry.

"I do not know," Vax had said as we bent to our loom, "if I wish my foul father was here with me now. I would not know if I should slay him at once and thus purge his evil crimes, or if I should allow him to live so that he might suffer as I suffer."

"Let the rast suffer, dom," said Nath the Slinger and then we flung ourselves into the task.

The Suns of Scorpio set in a last blaze that penetrated our prison in a mingled veil of colors and gradually died to an opaline glow. Presently the chinks of light through the gratings took on a pinkish golden tinge as the Maiden with the Many Smiles lifted above the horizon and shone down upon us.

Duhrra kept up the work on the link. I helped.

At last I said, "You must sleep, Duhrra. We will have much to tire ourselves on the morrow."

"I am sure it will give—"

"Then all the more reason for sleeping."

We composed ourselves. Rukker's hoarse whisper, cruel and sharp in the night, pierced the darkness.

"What are you onkers doing? There is no time for sleep. Keep working, rasts, or I will—"

A whip-Deldar on watch walked along the gangway between the rowing frames and Rukker had the sense to shut up and drop his head on the loom. Although the swifter's slaves were washed out twice daily with seawater, we still stank. Our hair was growing back in bristles, giving us an outlandish appearance. The Deldar passed on, humming to himself—the stupid "Obdwa Song," it was—and Rukker lifted his head. I caught the gleam of his eyes in the slatted chinks of light from the gratings.

"Shut up, Rukker, and get some sleep. I shall see how you fight on the morrow—or before, if I decide."

"You—"

A ship is never silent. There are always the same familiar sounds, at sea or at anchor. Through that quiet threnody of water splash and creak of wood, the murmur of distant voices, I whispered, "You are becoming tiresome, Kataki. I know you are a fighting-man. Just do not keep on trying to prove it all the time. And remember who it is you fight— the overlords, and not the slaves. Dernun?"*

A marine bellowed some order or other high on the quarterdeck, and Rukker made a visible effort. His moon-shadowed face scowled with the effort as he controlled himself. "After, Dak the High-Handed," he said. "After we have the swifter—"

"Yes, yes, go to sleep."

I heard a low gurgle—hardly a laugh—from Vax, at my right. Dahrra was already fast asleep.

"If my evil rast of a father had been tamed by someone like you, Dak, I might have let him die under my hand, instead of letting him suffer."

A most vicious and intemperate young man, this Vax.

Toward morning, with the innate sense of rhythm of an old sailorman that even the oddities of Kregen and the stresses of being an oar-slave could not break, I awoke. Soon Duhrra was hard at work on the link. Vax yawned when I nudged him, and bid me clear off. "Schtump!" he said, most malignantly.

"Wake up Fazhan and Nath. Jump!"

He gave me a look, all shadowed and dark, that was unmistakable. But he leaned down and gave Fazhan a crack in the ribs. When Fazhan was awake he woke Nath. We

---

*Dernun: "Savvy; capish; do you understand?" Not a particularly polite way of making the inquiry.   A.B.A.

yawned, still tired; but I knew they were keyed up to the work ahead. If I have glossed over this period of my servitude as an oar-slave it is because I do not care to remember in too vivid a detail a time of great agony and fatigue upon Kregen. Suffice it to say I may appear to be callous about serving as a slave and lax in escaping; the truth was I wanted out of that hellhole as fervently as a man dying of thirst needs water.

Duhrra let a low whispering sigh pass his lips. His powerful body eased back. The snap of metal echoed in the night.

We all sat perfectly silent.

Presently, when I was satisfied no other ears had picked up that sharp snip of sound, I eased the chain off. Duhrra clawed himself up and I put a hand on his shoulder and pulled him down.

Without a word, not moving the chain that lay limply on the deck at our feet, I stood up. The gratings above let down a patterned splotching of pink and gold. The long rows of naked feet and legs of the thranites glistered in the light. Here and there the coil of a chain shone dully. A whip-Deldar approached.

Silently—silently—I eased up. The Deldar passed. In one leap, touching Rukker's bench with foot and springing on from there, I reached the central gangway. A hand clapped about the Deldar's mouth. He went limp and I eased him to the gangway.

He had a knife.

This I passed down to Rukker.

I saw the Kataki's face.

"No noise, Rukker," I whispered. "Until we are all free." By all I meant the six of us on the oar. "This end is up to you, now. I'm for the oar-master and the keys."

He would have spit some surly remark; but I padded off along the gangway. The slaves slept and I did not fear discovery from them. Only one more whip-Deldar fell before I had reached the after end of the gangway. I looked up. Up there past the thranites the little tabernacle in which the oar-master sat and blew his whistle and controlled the drum-Deldars and made sure the motive power of the swifter functioned perfectly lay in darkness. I went up like a rock grundal. The oar-master would be asleep in his cabin. The keys were neatly racked on their hooks ready to be issued to the whip-Deldars when the slaves must be taken out of the ship. I scooped them up, reading the labels, made from leather, going back down again to the zygites. From then on the process would be one of progression.

Fazhan met me on the gangway. He shook. He looked elated and yet filled with a dread fury he might not be able to control. There was no sign of Rukker or Duhrra. Vax and Nath took the keys I handed them and began to awaken the slaves.

Fazhan said, "I will go aft, Dak."

I gave him the thalamite keys. I pointed down.

"When you come up again, Fazhan, bring men who will fight with you."

"Aye, Dak."

I shooed him off. Nath was working forward. A noise and a stir began to whisper in the hollow hull of the swifter. In a few short murs all hell would break out. The time for silence was almost gone.

I started off aft again, and Vax threw his keys to a slave three benches forward. He hit the poor devil over the head and awoke him and whispered fiercely in his ear and then clapped a hand over his mouth. I warmed to the young man. He might be intemperate and malignant in his ways, but he knew what he was doing. He looked at me. I was aware that the light was growing and that I could see him quite well.

"I will come with you, Dak. I need a sword."

He merely echoed my own thoughts.

Together, we stole silently aft, aiming for the quarterdeck, aiming for swords, aiming to wrench this swifter from the grip of the hated overlords of Magdag.

Chapter Four

Nath the Slinger collects pebbles

The sweet fresh night air greeted us as we climbed up onto the quarterdeck. The false dawn lingered with fading radiance upon the deck and the bulwarks, the ship-fittings, the ropes and gilding. The men of the watch were sleepy; they'd been hard at work the previous day as had we. There could be no thought of mercy. Truth to tell, for all the grand talk of mercy here on this Earth, in some situations mercy would be cruel. We were going to take this swifter. I had no doubts. What would happen to any overlords, any ship Daldars, any marines, when they were caught by the released slaves would make their swift, painless deaths now merciful to them.

There was time for me to observe this young tearaway Vax in action. I liked his style. The men on watch were dealt with on the quarterdeck. As the last sailor slumped, a shout ripped from the forepart of the swifter. The long narrow length of her lay dim in the tricky light. Shadows moved. Men were stirring. Catching the crew just before dawn might have been good planning, even in a ship. It was doubly clever in that the slaves themselves would be sluggish and slow to understand their own liberty. I had known this before. The slaves would not suddenly snatch up chains and wooden beams and go raving into action. It would take time for them to understand. But as the first shrill yells broke out and the sounds of fighting, I knew some, at least, understood.

Vax and I burst into the quarterdeck cabins.

An overlord completely naked with sleep still on his

48

face tried to stop us and I knocked him down and kicked him as I went past.

"In here, Dak!"

Vax was pointing to the first cabin.

"You go—if you wish. I'm for the captain's quarters."

Vax cursed and followed me. We ran down the corridor leading from the double doors that gave ingress from the quarterdeck. These cabins lay under the poop. I went straight into the aft cabin, seeing the light hazy and unreal through the sweep of stern windows where the gallery overhung the curved stern. Up above, the high upflung stern post, curved and decorated—with a magodont, of course—would hover over the poop. I wondered where Rukker and Duhrra had got to and if they were up there. The cabin was empty, as I had expected it to be. The sleeping cabin's door ripped open under my blow and I leaped in.

The captain tumbled out of his cot—this was a fashion to be followed more and more in the larger swifters—roaring. He snatched up his shortsword. He stood lithe and limber, instantly awake, a true captain. I jumped for him.

The shortsword blurred forward.

"Die, you rast!" bellowed the captain.

He should have saved his breath and concentrated on his swordsmanship.

I slid the blow, not allowing the blade to touch me, and drove a fist into his mouth. I kicked him and as he went back I twisted his right hand with such force the wrist-bones broke. Then the Genodder was in my own grip. It felt fine.

The captain staggered back, blood from his mangled mouth dripping down his chin. His eyes were wild.

Vax said, "Why do you not finish him?"

"He may be useful. Deal with him—but do not slay him."

I barged out of the cabin and almost at once was fighting for my life. Marines ran down the corridor, yelling first for the captain, and when they saw me, yelling blue bloody murder.

I accommodated them.

The Genodder was a fine example of a shortsword in the fashion of the inner sea, invented by King Genod and named after him. I swished it up and thrust, cut and jumped, and, in short, had a fine old time. Normally I do not enjoy fighting unless—well, you must be the judge of that.

Suffice it to say that on this occasion my pent-up fury broke out. That red haze did not fall before my eyes, for I kept a cool head and my wits about me—at least, I think I did—but there are few memories until I was at the double doors again with a trail of dead men in my rear.

The clean tip of a longsword appeared at my side, from the back, and I whirled and the Genodder hovered inches from Vax's throat.

"You onker," I said, speaking reasonably. "That's the way to get yourself killed." I had not heard him over the noise from the swifter. "You move silently. That is good."

"I—" he said. He looked more than a little taken aback. "I did not expect—"

"Expect everyone to attack you all the time. That way you may stay alive." I looked at the longsword. He had selected a good specimen, although it was not a Ghittawrer blade. "Can you use that?"

"Aye."

"Then let us see what we can find."

"Right gladly. I need—"

I shut him up and we ran out. I knew what he needed.

That fight contained a number of interesting incidents. But then, each fight is different in details, even if they all may seem to be merely a blind scarlet confusion of hacking and thrusting. For instance, Duhrra, who appeared laying about him with a longsword, used it in his right hand, the steel fingers closed and clamped about the hilt. Rukker had spared the time to strap a dagger to his tail. With that bladed tail he could cut a man up in a twinkling. And Vax fought superbly. He did know how to use a longsword. As I barged my way through the knot of marines who came tumbling up from their deck above the rowers, I saw Vax elegantly dealing with his men in a way that made me think he might be a Krozair. He was very young, it was true; but given that the blade he used was a common longsword with a short hilt, he contrived quite a few Krozair tricks. I stuck with the Genodder, for I allow that a shortsword can, in the right circumstances, nip inside a longsword in unskillful hands. I fancied a shortswordsman would be at a disadvantage against this young ruffian Vax.

Duhrra was thoroughly enjoying himself. His great voice boomed out, "Zair! Zair!" and other men took up the call. Rukker fought silently, as did I and Vax. Fazhan and

Nath appeared, bearing swords, and threw themselves into the fray. The upper decks covered with struggling men. There were naked men with weapons against men roused from sleep with weapons. We must do this thing quickly, even though there were perhaps seven hundred and fifty slaves against a couple of hundred sailors and marines. I had no desire to swamp the Grodnims by sheer numbers, for that would be mere brutalized force. I wanted the thing done quickly and in style.

Rukker had cleared his area and was about to lead a hunting party to roust out those still below. I bellowed in his ear, for the released slaves were creating one hell of a racket.

"Rukker! Try not to slay too many. We need oarsmen, too!"

He glared at me, aroused, the blood-lust strong on him. He took a great draft of air.

"Aye—aye, Dak the Cunning. You are right—and do not forget we have a score to settle, you and I."

"Let us secure the swifter and chain down these damned Grodnims and then we may talk."

Only after he had gone roaring back into the fray did I realize he had been hired by and had been fighting for the Grodnims. But if he came from the northeast corner of the inner sea, as he said, the chances were he did not worship Green Grodno in quite the same way as the Grodnims of the Eye of the World. Anyway, I was in no state to accommodate him no matter what his inclinations.

The light had dimmed after the false dawn. But as the sounds of combat flared over the swifter so the light strengthened. Soon Zim rose in a crimson glory, at which all the Zairians yelled mightily. "Zim! Zair! Zair!"

And, inevitably, when green Genodras rose, and we waited for the shouts of Grodno to echo around the ship, and none sounded, we roared our good humor.

Rukker stormed among the released slaves, cuffing them out of his way, giving them orders, bellowing. . . .

Duhrra was not sure what to do, so it fell to Fazhan to see about chaining down the new prisoners, those who had been spared.

I prevented a mob from tearing apart a couple of Grodnim sailors in their rage, and bellowed at them, "Would you wish these two rasts to go up to Genodras, to sit on the right hand of Grodno? Of course not! Chain them down to the benches, make them pull at the Zair-forsaken oars!"

"Aye, aye!" screeched the ex-slaves. "To the thalamites with them!"

So we managed to save a few men to pull for us.

There would be the problem of what to do with the Grodnims who had been enslaved with us. The oar-slaves were mostly Zairian prisoners; there was an element among them of Grodnim criminals. There could be no half-measures, of course.

I climbed up the mast and took a look around.

Green Magodont lay in the mouth of a river, with low vegetation-choked banks to either side. The mountains inland of the island looked blue and floating in the early morning mist. Downstream lay two more swifters. People were running about them. The noise and confusion in *Green Magodont* needed, it seemed to me, little explanation.

We weren't out of the woods yet.

I looked down.

Two large and powerful looking men, both apims, were arguing. They both carried swords, they both had snatched up scraps of clothing to cover their nakedness. They had been slaves, miserably chained to the bench; now they were arguing over who was in command.

"I am a roz and therefore outrank you, fambly!"

"I am a swifter captain, you onker, and know whereof I speak!"

I watched Rukker. He walked toward them. He bellowed.

Other men crowded around on the upper deck. They could be called slaves no longer—or, perhaps, for a space no longer if we did not do something about the other two swifters. Rukker yelled.

"I am in command here! Get about your business!"

The two men turned on him, hot in their anger and pride, a pride so newly returned to them. Their swords flickered out.

One of them dropped with a sword through his guts, the other could not screech. His throat had been ripped out by the Kataki's tail-blade. I sighed.

"I, Rukker, command! If any more of you rasts wish to die, then step up."

Duhrra, at the back, started to rumble and shove forward. I went down the mast with some speed and jumped to the deck.

"What! Dak! And so you wish to challenge me." Rukker waved his tail above his head. The blade glittered.

"If you are in command, Rukker, which I doubt. What do you think we should do about the two swifters that will surely pull up here to retake this vessel? Come on, man. Speak up."

"I do not wish—" he began. But the other slaves—ex-slaves—were running to the rail and pointing at the swifters downstream and caterwauling.

I said, "You may not wish to know about them, Rukker. But that won't make them go away."

"One day, Dak the Cunning, I'll do you a mortal injury."

"You may try. Until then you had best listen to what I say."

"I am in command!"

"You command nothing, Rukker the Kataki. This is no swifter fit to fight. You could not tackle those two. Think, man—" I did not take my gaze from him, and I watched that treacherous tail as a ruffianly sailorman watches a sylvie as she dances the Sensil Dance.

But he was, I felt sure, a high noble of one kind or another, and he could think quickly when he had to. "And what do you, oh wise and cunning Dak the Proud, think we should do?"

It would have been easy and cheap to have said, "But you are in command, Rukker."

The men had broken out the wine now and would soon be helpless. At least, some would, for the supplies wouldn't stretch to better than seven hundred thirsty ex-oar-slaves. I looked downstream again. The oars were moving in the swifters. They would back up to us, and their men would be armed and armored and ready. But drunken men can fight if they have a bucket of cold water soused over them and know that if they do not fight they will be killed if they are lucky, and go to the galley-slave benches if they are not lucky. But it must be done quickly.

In that uproar it was difficult to make myself heard. I turned to Duhrra. "Go and bash on the drum, Duhrra."

"Aye, master."

When the booming banging went on and on the men gradually quieted down and turned to look at Duhrra as he bashed away where usually the drum-Deldar beat the rhythm. I held up my hand. Duhrra stopped banging the drum and the silence fell.

I bellowed. I am able to let rip a goodly shout, as you know.

"Men! We must fight those swifters! There is no other way out for us. We can win easily if we stick together and fight for Zair!" This was mostly lies, of course. We could have run into the island and hidden. That would have been better than slaving at the oars. And as to winning, it would not be easy. But, Zair forgive me, I needed these men and their flesh and blood to further my own plans. I own that this makes me a criminal—a criminal of a kind, perhaps—but there was nothing else I could do, impelled as I was.

Vax shouted, before them all, "Aye! Let us take the two swifters to the glory of Zair!"

So they all bellowed and stamped and then it was a matter of finding weapons and clothes and armor and of seeing that not too many men fell down dead drunk.

We would have to wait for the attack until the last moment.

I said to Fazhan, "You are a ship-Hikdar. Can you organize from these men a crew to run the swifter?"

"Aye, Duk."

"Then jump to it. If we have to man the banks with our own men, they will have to do it. By Zair! They should be proud to row for Zair! We'll cripple those rasts out there!"

I turned to Rukker, who during all this had stood glowering, with his tail waving dangerously. I felt he would not strike just yet. He was too shrewd for that. "You want to be in command, Rukker. But you know nothing of swifters. Let Fazhan run the ship. Once we have those other two, we will have three alternatives."

He started to say something, thought better of it, and swung away. I bellowed after him, "Go and command the prijikers, Rukker. That is a post of honor."

The two swifters made no attempt to turn in the narrow mouth of the river. They could have done it. No doubt their captains wished to get up to us as fast as they could. I fancied they erred in this. I hoped I judged correctly.

The water rippled blue and silver, with jade and ruby sparks striking from it as the suns rose. The birds were busy about the trees. The day would be fine. I sniffed and thought about breakfast.

No time for that now. Men were arming themselves from corpses and from the armory. I went down and had to push my way through a throng crowding along the quarter-deck and so into the cabins. Men gave way for me, for they knew I was Dak, and Dak had freed them. They had been told this by Duhrra, although some still thought Rukker had organized the break. It did not concern me.

We could find no red cloth anywhere, and no one seemed overkeen to wear green. Not even the Grodnim criminals, who kept very quiet, with good reason.

With seven hundred men or so to arm there was no chance of my equipping myself with a longsword to match the Genodder, and any man with two weapons had, perforce, to give up one to a comrade who had none. I bellowed for bowmen and soon all the men who said they were archers clustered on the deck where all the bows we could find were issued. As for arrows, these were brought up in their wicker baskets and likewise issued. There were insufficient bows to go to all those who clamored for them.

I saw Nath. He had a piece of cloth. He saw me and waved and then stood on the bulwarks and dived cleanly into the water.

One or two men yelled and they would have started an outcry.

"Silence, you famblies! Nath the Slinger goes to collect pebbles."

A few other men turned out to be slingers and they went off to collect ammunition. Rukker turned up again; he was growing tiresome, but I wanted to humor him, for not only did he intrigue me, I needed his bull-strength in the bows as a prijiker when the attack came in. And that would not be long now. He wore a mail shirt and a helmet. He carried a longsword. He looked exceedingly fierce.

"I do not know why I suffer your impertinence, Dak. But after we have taken those ships—"

I turned to Vax.

"Why have you not put on a mail shirt, Vax?"

"Because they are all taken already."

That was the obvious answer to an unnecessary question. But Rukker took the point. His face went more mean than ever, and he began to bluster. I pointed forward. "They are almost here."

He swore—something about Targ and tails—and stormed off to the bows. He had selected a strong prijiker party, those stem fighters who were the cream of a crew.

Again I went a little way up the mast. Grodnim swifters still had only the one mast, apart from the smaller one for the boat sail forward. I studied the oncoming swifters. Their tall upflung sterns towered. Men clustered their quarter-decks and poops, armed and armored men, anxious to revenge their fellows in *Green Magodont*.

I called down to Fazhan standing on the quarterdeck.

"Get under way and aim for the rast to larboard."

He was a merry soul, this Fazhan ti Rozilloi, when not being flogged at the oars.

"I have ample volunteers to act as whip-Deldars, Dak. But not many oar-slaves."

"We do not need a great speed. Just enough to get our beakhead onto his quarterdeck."

"That I will do."

Vax met me as I reached the deck.

"And the cramph to starboard?"

"If Rukker can handle his swifter, I'll take that one."

"Then I will stand with you."

I lifted an eyebrow, but did not comment. Truth to tell, at that moment I was pleased to have him with me in the fight. Rukker had his party poised, and I saw he had about twenty Katakis with him. Again the incongruity of Katakis actually being slaves, instead of slavers, struck me.

We could all hear the steady double drumbeat from the oncoming swifters. Their helm-Deldars kept them sweetly on course, going stern first, and I fancied they would both be smart ships. This was not going to be as easy as many of the ex-slaves seemed to think, screeching their joy at freedom and their malefic hatred of the damned Green Grodnims.

Duhrra said, "The one to starboard is *Vengeance Mortil*. Duh—just let me get aboard of her. . . ."

Vax lifted his handsome, fine-featured face, with the blood staining under the skin. "It will give me exquisite pleasure to chastise her whip-Deldars."

I said, "And each time you strike you will strike at your father, no doubt."

He flung me a scorching look.

"It is likely, for he and they have much in common. He has done me a great injury and I shall never forgive him."

"My old man," said Nath the Slinger, walking up dripping wet, carrying a leather bag filled with stones, "used to knock the living daylights out of us kids. But he meant well, the old devil."

"Back in Crazmoz," said Duhrra, fussing with his hand, "my father was always chasing the women. My mother used the broomstick on him right merrily. Duh—how we all ran!"

My father had died of a scorpion sting, back on Earth; but now was no time to consider how that had affected my life.

"Just so long as we get onto the deck. By Zair! We hold the Grodnims in play and the men slide below and release the slaves. That's the only way we'll win."

It was not the only way, of course; but it would be the easiest. And I wished this fight to be over so that I might resume my tasks in the Eye of the World.

A brief inquiry among the men as the two swifters hauled up to us established the second galley as *Pearl*. She was smaller, a two-banked six-four hundred-and-twenty swifter. She was not a dekares of the *Golden Chavonth* type. I eyed both of them as they backed up. Fazhan had those men of ours who had not found weapons at the upper bank looms. A little byplay had ensued there, for a group of ex-slaves without weapons had protested vigorously at taking their places on the rowing benches. I strode up, mighty fierce, not happy but knowing what I did was right.

"Give us weapons!" bellowed the men. "We will fight!"

"You will row," I said. "That will be your fighting."

I did not say that by not already snatching up weapons they proved themselves less able than their comrades who had. But I glowered at them, and spoke more about the glory of Zair, and shook the Genodder, and finished with, "And two last things! Once we strike the damned Grodnims you will have weapons in plenty. And if you do not row I shall beat you most severely."

They were convinced.

My friends, even, say that sometimes I have a nasty way with me. This is so. And even if I deplore my manner, it does get things done in moments of crisis. As I went back to the station I had taken on the quarterdeck, Vax gave me a dark look, sullen and defiant.

"You are a right devil, Dak."

"Yes," I said, and went off bellowing to a party of men to sort themselves out, with the bowmen in rear, a great pack of famblies, asking to be slaughtered.

Rukker looked back. The gap narrowed.

I yelled at him: "Get your fool hands down! They'll be shooting any moment."

As I spoke, the first shafts rose from the two Green swifters.

"Get the ship moving, Fazhan!" I swung about and roared at the two men who had taken the helm positions. "Bring her around to starboard! Put some weight into it!"

Green Magodont's wings rose and fell. We could put out only a few oars; but these gave us sufficient way to take us out into midstream. I judged the distances. Arrows struck down about us. The helmsmen looked at me, hard-muscled men, hanging on to their handles, waiting my orders.

"Hard over! Larboard!" I bellowed at Fazhan. "Every effort, Fazhan! Make 'em pull! Speed! Speed!"

The oars beat raggedly and then settled and the swifter's hard rostrum swirled to larboard and cut through the blue water. We surged ahead, aiming for the starboard quarter of the larboard vessel, *Pearl*. Our stern swung to starboard. We formed a diagonal between the swifters. Arrows crisscrossed now. I saw Nath leap up and swing his cloth about his head, let fly. I had the shrewd suspicion his stone would strike. The swifters neared. Any minute they would strike.

"*Ram! Ram! Ram!*"

The bull roar bashed up and men tensed for the shock of impact.

We struck.

The bronze ram gouged into *Pearl*. Both vessels shuddered and rocked with the impact. Men were yelling. I bawled out to Rukker; but there was no need. With his knot of Katakis about him, a compact force of devils, he leaped onto the swifter's deck. Instantly a babble of brilliant fighting ensued. Our stern swerved on, still going.

"Rowed of all!" I screamed at Fazhan. Our oars dropped. The stern hit.

Somehow I was first across, scrambling over gilding and scrollwork, hurling myself onto the deck of *Vengeance Mortil*. Like a pack of screeching werstings my men followed. The blades flamed and flashed in the light of the twin suns, and then we were at our devil's tinker work, hammering and bashing, thrusting and slicing.

Vax followed and Duhrra leaped at my side. We swept a space for ourselves and then flung forward; for to stand gaping was to invite feathering.

"Below!" I yelled and men darted off to drop into the stinking gloom of the rowing banks and begin the task of freeing the slaves.

A monstrous man in green and gold fronted me, swirling his longsword.

This kind of work demanded a longsword; but I made shift with the Genodder, dropped him, and with no time to snatch up his sword engaged the next man with a clang. Swords flamed all about me. Men screamed and dropped. The rank raw tang of blood smoked on the morning air.

"Grodno! Grodno!" rang the shrieked battle cries.

"Zair! Zair!" the answering screams ripped out.

Mailed men boiled across the quarterdeck. For the next few murs the mere strength and solidity of packed men would tell. I cursed the damned shortsword, for its premier advantage in the thrust availed little against mailed men, although I gave a couple of fellows sore ribs before I got the point into their faces. I swung the Genodder in a short blurred arc and bashed through a mailed shoulder. A longsword hissed past my ear. It was a case of duck and twist and to the devil with the so-called dignity and art of fighting. I chunked a Fristle's eye out and slashed back at a Rapa, who spun away, screeching as Rapas do screech. The very fury and frenzy of the fight pushed us back and forth across the deck. But we had men, many men, and soon more swarmed up from below as their chains were struck off.

Chapter Five

———◆———

Vax

The sheer pressure at our backs drove us on. The hideous sounds of mortal combat shocked into the sky. Blood ran greasily across the deck and men coughed or screamed or said nothing as they died. In the press the shortsword proved of value; but I caught a distorted glimpse of Duhrra swinging his longsword and clearing men from his path as a gardener hews weeds. Vax drove on with him. I cursed and beat away a spear-point, thrust short and sharp, and brought the blade back to catch a longsword sweeping down at my head and felt the jar smash along my muscles.

I made a grab with my left hand at the longsword and after one fumble, during which I kicked a fellow in the guts, the longsword was mine. It was a common one with a small hilt; but it would serve. I swapped with a feeling of release.

In the next mur I had leaped after Duhrra and Vax. Together we cut a triple furrow through the Green ranks. Duhrra fought as he always did with a sword, using tremendous sweeps, enormous bashes, and mighty slashings to hew down his opponents. I felt vast relief that he had found and donned a mail shirt, for he left himself dangerously exposed. Vax fought with the trim economy of the trained swordsman. I saw the way he handled his blade and again I wondered if, at his age, he could be a Krozair.

We reached the double doors leading from the quarterdeck into the passage under the poop. *Vengeance Mortil* was a longer vessel than *Green Magodont*, rowing thirty oars to a bank against the latter's twenty-one. The poop over our heads was now the scene of fighting. We could hear shrieks and the thumps of feet on the deck. Most of the cabins were empty and we tore straight on toward the captain's cabin.

He was not there, and I recalled the large man I had felled at the instant of boarding. If he had been the captain, then his crew fought well without him. Satisfied that the cabins here were all empty, we turned to dart out and finish the fight. I stopped stock still.

Duhrra and Vax halted in the doorway.

"Come on, Dak!"

A glass case stood against the bulkhead. A shaft of mingled light struck through the aft windows and illuminated the contents of the case. Crimson blazed. A long blade of steel shafted back gleaming light.

"Trophies," said Duhrra. "Some poor devil of a Zairian—"

I swung the sword at the glass and smashed the case open.

I took the longsword into my fists. It balanced beautifully.

A Krozair longsword. The genuine article. I saw the etched markings, the Kregish letters in flowing script: *KRZI*. So this was a longsword of the Krozairs of Zimuzz. The red cloth was a flag. I ripped it down and swathed it about me. I drew it up tightly between my legs and tucked in the end. I picked up the Krozair longsword.

"Now I'm ready to finish this little lot."

We belted back down the passage. Our backs were secure. We had only to surge forward along the swifter and take or slay all the Green and the ship would be ours.

A dead marine lay at the corridor entrance. I bent and ripped off his belt and buckled it up about the red flag I used, without blasphemy, in all honor, as a loincloth. We went into the fight like leems. I felt rejuvenated. How ridiculous and petty it must seem that a piece of red cloth could wreak so great a change! But the true change was wrought by the Krozair longsword. The blade flamed. The balance was perfect. I felt the power in my fists and I battled forward, bellowed for my men, and together, yelling, "Zair! Zair!" we catapulted the Greens from the quarterdeck, drove them along the upper gangway. More and more slaves poured up from below, whirling bights of chain.

The uproar continued.

I took time to step back as a Grodnim dropped under the blade and darted a quick and savage look at *Pearl*. Yes, the

"I swung the sword at the glass and smashed the case open."

fighting there flowed forward, as did the fighting in *Vengeance Mortil*.

A perverse desire grew in me to clear this swifter before Rukker cleared his. I shouted again and roared on, cutting into the last resistance. The Krozair brand sheared through mail where the shortsword would have bounced. We tore into the dying remnants of the resistance and, suddenly, we were on the forecastle with the beakhead lifted, and there were no more adversaries to taste our steel.

The men in the swifter at my back began cheering.

I looked across the gap of water at *Pearl*. Fighting boiled across her forecastle where a knot of men in the green resisted to the end. I saw the Katakis—fewer of them now—battling in the front of the struggle. Rukker was there, a giant figure striking with sword and tail-blade.

Springing onto the bulwark, I put my left hand to my mouth—my right was bloodier than my left—and I lifted up my voice and shouted in right jocular fashion.

"Hai! Rukker! What's holding you up?"

He heard.

The Kataki devil heard. I saw a Grodnim head fly into the air and Rukker stormed onto the starboard bulwark, springing up to glare across at me.

"We have cleared all! There are no skulkers at our backs!"

"And no slaves to pull the oars, either."

He didn't like that.

"We have taken this Takroti-forsaken ship! That is what matters."

"You may have taken her—but have you slaves to man her?"

"I do not wish to discuss that."

I heard a gurgling laugh and looked back and there was Vax holding his guts and laughing. Well, it was funny, of course; but I had no desire to be stranded without oar-slaves by that Kataki idiot over there.

Anyway, there was every chance that our ram had done *Pearl* too serious a mischief underwater to make her seaworthy. That must be looked at, at once, and the man to do the looking was Fazhan ti Rozilloi, ship-Hikdar. I bellowed to Duhrra to sort out the men here, told Vax to see about chaining up the new slaves who had so lately been sailors and soldier-marines of Grodnim, and took myself off aft. Fazhan was cleaning his sword. I had had no time. The beautiful Krozair blade gleamed red in the lights of Antares.

"Hai Jikai, Dak!" Fazhan greeted me.

I pondered for perhaps a half mur. Was this a Jikai?

Perhaps.

It was most certainly not a sufficiently high enough High Jikai to enroll me once more in the Krozairs of Zy, that was for sure.

"Is *Pearl* seaworthy, after we struck her?"

He saw my face. "I will see, at once." He ran off.

In the nature of things there was a great deal of confusion. Released slaves, all naked and screaming, surged about, and I knew there would be no Grodnim whip-Deldars to chain down to the rowing benches. I saw men I thought must be of some importance—or, rather, men who had been important before they'd been captured—and tried to bash some sense into them. Our own slaves from *Green Magodont* had by this time some idea of what was needful in this situation. Soon all the men of Zair would come to an understanding. For the moment sheer exuberance and wild release of fettered spirits would make of the three swifters hell-holes.

So I will pass quickly over the ensuing scenes. I took myself off back to *Green Magodont* and met Rukker storming back. He looked savagely delighted with his morning's work. He saw my red breechclout and the sword, and he made a face and began to make some kind of snarling remark; but he did not. His tail quivered and shot erect over his head, the tail-blade gleaming, for he had cleaned it off.

"The ships are ours, Dak. You have served me well. Now I will resume full command."

The Katakis formed a bunch at his back. He had them well cowed. They were extraordinarily formidable. I hefted the Krozair longsword. I opened my mouth and Vax appeared at my side, laughing, saying, "Give me your sword, Dak, and I will clean it off for you. It is a beautiful blade."

"I clean my own sword."

He looked offended.

Rukker bellowed, "Now we carouse and make merry."

The released slaves would do that, anyway.

Some onker was bellowing that *Pearl* was stuffed with wine. He carried an armful of bottles, waving one above his head, the rich red wine spilling out over him. He was already half-seas over. I did not consider long. Maybe I could have halted the debauch that followed. Maybe not. I did not try. I wanted to talk to Rukker and see if the way I planned to handle the Kataki devil would work.

He had taken a good long look at the three swifters. Fazhan reported that *Pearl* had taken a nasty crack, but that the sharp sheer of her stern had been enough to prevent our ram from driving home, and that she would be fully sea-worthy when the planking had been repaired. So Rukker could tell me in his lofty way, "I will take *Vengeance Mortil*. She is the largest. You may have either of the others."

I said, "Bring a few bottles to the cabin. We can talk there. If you wish to fight, here and now, I shall accommodate you. Otherwise, no fighting until we have decided what to do."

Now that he had won and was in a strong position, he no doubt thought to show a facade of magnanimity. I do not think I do Rukker an injustice if I say that because he was a Kataki he was, by his religion and customs and mores, what other people would call an evil man. He could not help that; like the scorpion, it was in his nature. But I found that he had a gift denied to most other Katakis. He had a streak of humanity in him that, at first, because I did not believe it possible, I found disconcerting.

"Surely, Dak the High-Handed. We will drink together. But there is no question of our deciding." He emphasized the "our." "I have decided what we will do."

I did not answer but barged off to the cabin, snatching up a couple of the bottles the idiot from *Pearl* had dropped—for he had passed out, beaming idiotically, on my quarter-deck.

My quarterdeck.

Ah! How we arrogate to ourselves, arrogant in our pride!

Nath the Slinger appeared. He wore bits and pieces of finery, and carried a Genodder as well as his sling. He saw Rukker. He started to say something, but Rukker chopped him off.

"We talk, Nath the Slinger. Afterward, I may take from your hide payment for your insolence."

Nath said, "I think the people may set fire to the swifters."

That was a very fair chance.

Rukker bellowed at this, and in a twinkling, a dozen of his Katakis ran out along the gangways, roaring. That was one thing I could count on. Rukker would command obedience from his own people, and I could trust them to stop a parcel of drunken ex-oar-slaves from foolishly setting fire to the swifters they so much hated.

"Tell 'em to make sure they don't kill too many Grodnims," I said to Rukker, sharp.

He bawled it after them. Then he took a bottle from a man near him, who did not argue, and rolled off to the aft cabin, swinging his tail in high good humor.

Fazhan looked at me, uncertain.

"You did very well, Fazhan. Now come and have a drink."

"We should set a watch—there were three other swifters in the squadron."

"The Katakis will do that. Or Rukker will have their tails."

As I went along aft I admit I felt it most strange that I should be working in collaboration with Katakis. But, there it was. Those of us who had been architects in the escape gathered in the great aft cabin of *Green Magodont* to talk about our futures.

I will not go into all the discussion, although to a student of human nature it proved fascinating, revealing not only the desires of frail humanity but revealing very clearly the different traits of the differing racial stocks. The problem could be broken down into one of allegiances. The released slaves fell into four main classes. There were the Zairians who wished only to return to their homes of the southern shore. There were the Grodnims who, as criminals, could go neither to Zairia nor to Grodnim. There were the mercenaries who didn't care who they fought for so long as they were paid and who, because they slaved for them, must have fallen foul of the overlords of Magdag. And there were the Zairians who, for one reason or another, could not return home.

Of the two latter classes, Rukker and I were representatives.

Long were the arguments and sometimes bitter the wrangling. But, in the end, it all boiled down to a decision by Rukker and most of the others, to join the Renders. These pirates infested many portions of the inner sea, of course; but they were particularly strong in the southwestern end, where many islands gave them shelter. As for the Zairians who wished to return home, they might take a swifter that Rukker did not want.

I said, "That does not dispose of all."

"There is no one else, fambly!" Then Rukker, sprawled in a gilt chair, an upended bottle to his lips, roared out, "By the Triple Tails of Targ the Untouchable! No one would wish to go to Magdag!"

"I do," I said.

He gaped at me.

"There is a certain matter I have left unfinished there."

"Well, you will find not a single man to go with you." Then he squinted at Duhrra—enormous in the corner, watchful—and grunted, and said, "Except that mad graint, of course."

"And me," said a young, firm voice, and I turned, and Vax stepped forward. "I wish to go to Magdag, for I have business there, also."

Well, I fancied whatever his business was, it boded no good for some poor devil.

Vax had been drinking. His face flushed heavily and he did not walk steadily, even though *Green Magodont* remained still.

Nath the Slinger had been drinking, also, and he snarled, "No doubt it has to do with your rast of a father."

Vax turned sharply, and nearly fell. I do not like to see young men the worse for drink—or any man, come to that. Vax spoke in a cutting, nasty way. "Yes. For my father has done me a grave injustice. He has finished all my hopes in the Eye of the World. Yes, he bears a part, the cramph. But it is not for him I wish to go to Magdag, but my sister—"

"Well, go to the Ice Floes of Sicce for all I care!" boomed Rukker. He roared his mirth. "Three of you, to run a swifter! Ho—one to pull at the oar, one to beat the drum, and one to steer! Ho—I like it!"

Certainly, the image was a lively one. But I did not smile.

Vax looked as though he would be sick at any moment, if he did not fall down. I judged he was not used to heavy drinking. I stepped over to him and sniffed. I looked down at him.

"You young idiot! Dopa!"

Duhrra said, "Duh—dopa! I know, master—I know."

Dopa is calculated to make a man fighting drunk; Vax had not yet drunk enough to turn him berserk. I saw the bottle in his hand, and I took it away. He tried to stop me. I broke the bottle over a handy table and showed him the serrated edge. "This is what you deserve, you gerblish onker."

He staggered and would have fallen. I grabbed him and propped him upright.

"You're coming with me to a cabin where you can sleep it off. I have work to do." I dragged him out. "I'll see about you, Rukker, when I've seen to this hulu."

I half carried him along to the ship-Hikdar's cabin and tossed him down on the cot. As I say, cots and hammocks had previously been unknown in swifters, because they usually came ashore at night. No doubt the war was changing many things since the genius king Genod had taken over in Magdag. Vax snorted and tried to rise and I pushed him back and the hilt of the Krozair longsword slid forward. He blinked at it owlishly.

"I was to have been a Krozair," he said. He was growing maudlin. "Yes, I trained. Not Zimuzz, though. I worked and all I wanted in this life was to be a Krozair like my brothers."

"Yes," I said, lifting his legs onto the cot. "Get some sleep and you can talk about this later."

He grasped my arm and glared up into my face.

"You don't understand. No one here does. How can they?"

He enunciated his words carefully, as a near-drunk sometimes does; but he made sense in what he said. He was pretty far gone, and he just didn't know he was saying what he was saying.

"My father—"

"Look, son. We all had fathers, and they all failed us at one time or another." That was not true; but the intensity of this lad's hatred for his unknown father hurt me, thinking of my own father and the love I bore him.

"My father failed my mother. He ran away—ran away—"

"You said he died."

"I always say he is dead, out of shame. But he was alive, all the time. All the time. He ran away and left my mother in mortal peril, and she was carrying me at the time, and he ran away and left her. They nearly got her—she told me, and she laughed—but—but I knew. He wouldn't answer the Call, the Azhurad, and it is im-impossible for a Krozair not to answer the Call. So they made him Apushniad. And serve the rast right. And I was training to be a Krozair of Zy—and they— they— So I left them, ashamed. My father, Apushniad—

destroyed me. Destroyed me! Me, Jaidur, Jaidur of Valka, ruined my whole life, and if I find the kleesh I shall surely slay him."

I just gaped, stricken.

Chapter Six

Renders of the Eye of the World

The Renders of the western end of the Eye of the World made us welcome. They welcomed reinforcements of tough and ruthless fighting-men. They were not so sure of the three swifters we·brought, for they habitually used small, fast craft, which could slip into a convoy and cut out the fat prizes. They said they could no doubt pick up enough oar-slaves for the swifters. But we would to a great extent be on our own. Rukker boomed his great laugh and swished his tail and said he'd show these people what real rending was about, what a fighting Kataki could do in the piracy business.

He had found a competent ship-Hikdar among the ex-slaves to run *Vengeance Mortil* for him. I ran *Green Magodont*, and a tough and experienced swifter captain, a Krozair of Zamu, took command of *Pearl*. Once we filled with oar-slaves we would be a hard little squadron, and carry some punch in the Eye of the World. The Krozair of Zamu, Pur Naghan ti Perzefn, would sail *Pearl* back with all the Zairians who wished to return home.

These Renders were a cutthroat lot. Consisting of escaped slaves, criminals, men who could find a home neither north nor south of the inner sea, they carved out their own destiny. If ·you ask why I was with them, instead of pursuing my schemes in Magdag, the answer is surely plain.

My son!

Jaidur—that same name that Velia had spoken, and I had not understood, when she had been dying in my arms. So my Delia had been pregnant when we'd flown off to chastise the shanks attacking our island of Fossana, where the damned

70

Star Lords had sought to make me do their wishes. I had refused out of stiff-necked pride and fear for Delia, and so had been banished to Earth for all of twenty-one miserable years. There had been twins again, twins of whom I had known nothing. The girl, Dayra, the boy, this same Jaidur who called himself Vax out of shame.

He had rambled on a little more before falling into a drunken stupor. He was quite unused to dopa. He had known that any son of Dray Prescot, the Lord of Strombor, would receive scant shrift from the overlords of Magdag, and he had been on his way there because his sister, Velia, had been missing, reported captured by a swifter from Magdag.

Velia had, indeed, been captured. But she had been captured by Gafard, the King's Striker, the Sea Zhantil, and they had fallen deeply in love. I believed that to be true. I believed it then, and I am sure of it now. Gafard owed complete allegiance to King Genod, and even when the king sought to abduct the Lady of the Stars, the name by which Velia was known, for the same reasons that Jaidur called himself Vax, Gafard had been unable to blame him; for the king possessed the yrium, the mystic power of authority over ordinary people.

King Genod had, in the end, taken Velia. And because Gafard's second in command, Grogor, had shafted the saddlebird the king flew, and because the king was abruptly in fear for his life, the genius king had thrown Velia off, to fall to her death. Yrium or no damned yrium, when I caught the cramph I'd probably have trouble stopping myself from breaking his neck before I dragged him off to justice. I know about men who possess the yrium. As I have said, I am cursed with more than one man's fair share of the yrium.

All this I, alone of our family, knew.

I could not tell Jaidur—or Vax.

I could not tell him.

I had not told him I was his father.

How could I?

There had to be a kinder, better, way of breaking that horrendous news to him.

He was in very truth a violent young man. How could I lift a hand against my son in self-defense? And yet how could I stand and let him slay me? For I thought he very well might try. That would be a sin not only for him but for me, also.

His hatred was a real and living force.

Mind you, if I told him and then invited him to try to carry out his avowed intent, and so foined with him and disarmed him—no, no, no. . . . That would shatter his self-esteem, would turn hatred for me into contempt for himself. And, anyway, he was a remarkably fine swordsman. He might finish me. I share nothing of this silly desire to call oneself the greatest swordsman of the world—or, in my case, of two worlds. That way lies not only paranoia, but a mere killing machine without interest or suspense. Each fight is a new roll of the dice with death, a gamble of life and death.

I had decided to go to join the Renders with Rukker because had I gone to Magdag, Vax would have gone with me, and in evil Magdag he might all too easily be slain or enslaved. I did not want that and would stop it. So I had turned aside from my purpose.

A scheme occurred to me whereby I might turn Vax from his path, also. It would give him pain; but nothing like the pain he would be spared.

We sailed out on a few raids and caught Magdaggian shipping and so fought them and took them and built up our stock of oar-slaves. Our base lay up a narrow and winding creek in the lush green island of Wabinosk. When I say *green* I refer to the vegetation. The island boasted a large population of vosks; but they were kept down by an infestation of lairgodonts. I had no further wish to meet any more lairgodonts, for the risslacas had caused problems before and, anyway, the things were the symbol of King Genod's new Order of Green Brothers. The islands in this chain were, in their turn, infested by pirates, and we had one or two set-tos with Renders who fancied our prizes. But with Rukker booming and bellowing away we kept what we took.

One day Duhrra started talking about Magdag to Vax, who was most anxious to learn all he could. I listened.

The people we had released from oar-slavery had settled down into a pattern, taking up tasks for which they were suited. Those Zairians who wished to return home had gone in a captured broad ship. Now we had smallish crews, but we were building, and our motive power was almost up to strength. I planned to leave at the earliest moment I could; I had to be sure of Vax first.

"Zigging Grodnims," Duhrra was saying, sharpening up his

sword on a block, taking care over the work. "All they do is build monstrous great buildings. Rasts."

Vax egged him on to talk about Magdag. And as I listened so I caught an echo of the way Duhrra saw the rousing times we had spent as pretended renegades. "The king in Sanurkazz has our names down on his roll of infamy—and we innocent."

"When King Zo hears what you did, Duhrra, I am sure he will pardon you. Was the Lady of the Stars, then, so beautiful?"

Duhrra spit and polished meticulously. "Indeed she was!" Duhrra rolled his eyes. "No maiden more fair graced the earth, they said."

I felt a pang. Roughly, I said, "Did you ever see her face, oh Duhrra of the waggling tongue?"

"No, master. But I know she was. Duh—everyone said so."

Here was a chance. I felt a pain in my chest.

"Yes, she was beautiful. Gafard loved her truly, and she loved him truly." I did not look at Vax. "I think that does mean something important." I leaned closer. "And here is something Gafard told me that must go no farther than the three of us." I turned and glared directly into my son's eyes. "Do I have your word?"

"Yes, Dak. I will not speak of it."

"Good. Then know that this Lady of the Stars was the true daughter of Pur Dray, the Lord of Strombor."

Before I had finished the great word *Strombor*, my son Jaidur, whom I must think of as Vax, leaped up. He let a terrible cry escape him. Then he turned—I saw his face— and he ran to the ladder at the stern and fell down it and so raced like a maniac into the bushes of the shore, vanishing out of sight.

Duhrra stared after him, a powerful frown crumpling up that smooth, seemingly idiot face. "Duh, master! What did I do?"

"You did nothing, Duhrra. And I am not your master."

"Yes, master."

I walked away, feeling the desolation in me. This was not my idea of family life. But, then what did I know of family life? I had been privileged to know my eldest twins, Drak and Lela, for periods off and on until they were fourteen. My second twins, Segnik and Velia, had been three when I'd been so mercilessly hurled back to Earth. And now Segnik was Zeg and a famous Krozair of Zy, and Velia was dead.

Of Dayra I knew nothing, and of her twin, Jaidur, I must see him every day and speak with him, and call him Vax, and bear the agony; for he hated the memory of his father, a father he knew nothing of—or, at least, knew nothing good of.

I did know one thing of Dayra. Delia had told me she had been giving trouble at school, with the Sisters of the Rose, of course. And I remembered old Panshi talking of the young prince and of my assumption he meant Segnik, when he meant Jaidur. Old Panshi had had a little frown of puzzlement. Why couldn't I be just an ordinary simple man? But then, if I were that, I would never have won Delia, the Princess Majestrix of Vallia, at all.

We sailed out on a raiding cruise the next day, hopping from island to island, and I was exceedingly beastly to the Magdaggian shipping we caught. The three swifters acted together, for it seemed the natural thing to do, and Rukker was getting the hang of sea fighting. On this cruise we took a small swifter by a ruse, and boarded her and slew or enslaved her Magdaggian crew. Her slaves joined our ranks. She was sailed back to Wabinosk in triumph.

That night we caroused as Renders do. I had run through all my memories of carousing the nights away with Viridia the Render on the Island of Careless Repose, in the Hobolings. She had been youngish then, and with the normal two-hundred-year life span of the Kregan, I had no doubt she was still at her piratical tricks. Would I ever see her again? Would I ever see any of my old comrades—and enemies—again?

The coveted High Jikai appeared to come no nearer.

But my words with Vax—I must think and talk of him as Vax—bore fruit.

Fazhan, who acted as my ship-Hikdar, told me the swifter we had taken was of Sanurkazz. She had been taken by the Magdaggians and converted to their use. As in the wooden navies of the eighteenth century of Earth, the ships of the contending nations were of so similar a type they were fully interchangeable. She had the name arrogantly painted on her bows and under her stern—the sailors of Kregen follow this fashion more often than not—and I read this aloud. "*Prychan*. A suitable name."

"Yes," said Fazhan. He reached out with his knife and scraped at the green paint. "Yes, as I thought. See, Dak, underneath. Her real name, carved as is proper; but blocked up with this damned green paint."

We remove the offensive paint and saw the original name of the galley.

"*Neemu.* Yes, I see." You know that a neemu is a black-furred, near leopard-sized killer, with a round head, squat ears, slit eyes of lambent gold, and runs ferociously upon four legs. A prychan is a very similar beast, sharing the same characteristics, but having fur of a tawny gold. I studied the lines of *Neemu.*

She was two-banked, a four-three seventy-two. Although she had only eighteen oars to a bank, they were concentrated in the usual way of swifters, giving her an exceptionally long forecastle and quarterdeck. She was narrow in the beam, so narrow I ordered her oars kept in the water to keep her upright. She was fast. I tried her in maneuvers and found her cranky so that she did not respond as well as—for instance—*Green Magodont*, which was a much larger craft, a three-banked hundred-twenty-six. *Green Magodont* was of that class of swifter designed to sail in the front rank in a battle, agile so that she might spin about and deliver the diekplus, shearing away an opponent's oars. Then the second line would come in to take on what was left. This *Neemu* was clearly a scouting vessel, designed for high speed, yet powerful enough to tackle reasonably heavy opposition.

Vax said, "I would like to take all those who will come and sail back to Zandikar."

There was now a fresh batch of rescued Zairians wishing to go home.

I said, "Why Zandikar?"

He said, without shame, "There is a girl—"

"Oh," I said.

So the brutality of my ruse had been worth it. Vax had decided not to go to Magdag to search for his sister Velia. He knew she was dead; he did not know the manner of her dying. I had told no one that I had held Velia in my arms as she died, and of how the overlords had trampled up to take me. They had not caught Grogor, Gafard's second in command; but he it was who had shot the arrow into the king's fluttrell; he it was, they thought, who had slain the stikitches employed by the king. I was a mere pawn, Gafard's man, and me they had dispatched to the galleys.

"Very well—" I started to say, when I was interrupted by a harsh and ominous screeching.

I knew exactly what that raucous shriek from the sky was, and I did not look up. The Gdoinye, the great golden and scarlet raptor of the Star Lords, the magnificent bird of prey they used as a messenger and a spy, had sought me out once again. Duhrra was talking to Vax about taking *Neemu* back to Zandikar, and trying to urge him to go on to Sanurkazz, for that was nearer Crazmoz. Vax cocked up his head.

"What is that bird?" he said.

Duhrra looked up, also, his idiot-face peering.

"Duh—I see no bird."

I glanced up, casually.

The confounded Gdoinye was up there, planing in wide hunting circles, screeching down. The thing spied on me for the Star Lords, that was sure.

"Up there, Duhrra, you fambly!" said Vax. He pointed. "Surely you see it? A great red and gold bird."

"Vax—you've been at the dopa again."

Vax shouted hotly at this and swung to me. "Dak—you see it?"

I looked up at the Gdoinye circling up there, watching me, telling the Star Lords what I was about.

"No, Vax. I see no bird."

"You're all blind!" shouted Vax, and stamped off. I felt sorry for him. I wondered what he was thinking.

But I thought this must be an omen. I must stir myself, or I might be thrust back across four hundred light-years, to Earth, and never get out of the Eye of the World. First, I must make sure my son Jaidur, who called himself Vax out of shame, was safe.

Chapter Seven

We strike a blow for Zairia and for Vallia

On a fine Kregan morning as we pirates swaggered down to the swifters hauled up onto the beach, I said to Duhrra, "You want to talk to this young tearaway, Vax. Probe him about his father." I saw Duhrra glance across at me. "It is not good that a young man feels this way."

"I agree. But it is a powerful hatred he bears."

"Talk to him."

"Duh—master—it will be all too easy. He will deafen my ears with his anger."

Our plans for departure had been interrupted by this capture of *Neemu*. There was no question of the ship being given to Vax. He was far too young and inexperienced on the Eye of the World. I did not say this. It was freely spoken of by the other Renders. Among their ranks were men who knew the inner sea, men who had fought for many years upon the sparkling blue waters, men who understood the ways of the Eye of the World. Pur Naghan ti Perzefn had not taken *Pearl* back. Those Zairians who wished to return home had sailed in a broad ship. Pur Naghan, Krzm, realized he could strike resounding blows for Zair in thus rending with us. As a Krozair of Zamu his vows impelled him to struggle with the Green at every opportunity. Our plans called for us to sail back together, *Pearl*, *Neemu*, *Crimson Magodont*, as a squadron.

No Krozair, not even an ex-Krozair, could command a swifter with *Green* in her name.

Green Magodont was now *Crimson Magodont*.

Rukker, waving his bladed tail in a typical Kataki fury, had bellowed, "I spare no oar-slaves! If you wish to fill your banks you must take the rasts yourselves. And *Vengeance Mortil* sails with me." He was in a right old fury.

I recall this particular day with some brisk satisfaction as demonstrating a neat double-hander in my dealings on Kregen. Occupied though I was by affairs and mysterious dealings in the Eye of the World, I was still aware of the vaster problems awaiting me in the lands of the Outer Oceans. Out there that great and evil empress Thyllis planned to hurl all the military resources of her empire of Hamal against my island of Vallia. Out there intrigues and treachery and double-dealing blossomed like the black lotus flowers of Hodan-Set.

So, on this day, when our squadron sighted sails on the horizon, and the whip-Deldars flew about with ol' snake licking, and bellowing, "Grak! Grak!" and the swifters flew over the waters, I found a profound joy in me as I saw those sails resolve into the typical shapes of the canvas of argenters from Menaham.

Menaham with her argenter fleet was used by the empress Thyllis of Hamal to trade with the overlords of Magdag. She sold them airboats and saddle-flyers. Judging by the course of the argenters, which bore on bravely with their three masts clad in plain sail straining, I would find out what King Genod paid the empress Thyllis in return.

I pushed away disappointment. I would have preferred to have captured the argenters on their way to Magdag. Then I would have taken vollers and flyers. As it was, this blow would more directly damage Hamal. But that mad genius Genod would suffer, too. . . .

In any kind of breeze the swifters would never have caught the argenters. But the Eye of the World, like the Mediterranean, is a fluky place for wind. Oared vessels reign there except—and this I say with pride, for the pride is not for me—for the great race-built galleons of Vallia. We pulled in for the kill.

Sails billowed and fluttered as the breeze fluked around. The argenters wallowed. We could see their people running about the decks and a pang struck through me, for I remembered when Duhrra and I had stood in an argenter and watched the Renders pulling in for us. That made me make sure that lookouts with keen eyes were aloft to spot the first hint of Green slicing toward us over the horizon.

"They scurry like ponshos before leems," observed Vax with bloodthirsty satisfaction.

We stood on the quarterdeck. I looked at my son.

"Do you so hate them, then, Vax? They are not of Magdag."

"I have reasons for hating them. You would know nothing of my reasons. But, believe me, they are very real."

Much though I was dismayed at my boy's bloodthirstiness, I was cheered by his evident concern for the affairs of his own country. And, anyway, on Kregen a modicum of good honest skull-bashing is often the only antidote to poison. I deplore this; but while it remains true I prefer to have other people's skulls bashed. The truth also is that I have done a great deal on Kregen to lessen the incidence of skull-bashing and bloodthirsty fighting in these latter days. I speak now of a time when the famous old Bells of Beng Kishi regularly rang in many and many a thick skull over the length and breadth of Kregen.

Just to get Vax going a little more, I said, "And these marvelous reasons, Vax. I suppose your cramph of a father is mixed up with them—oh, but he's dead, isn't he?"

He shot me a murderous glance. I did not know how much he remembered of what he'd maundered on about to me; I fancied he had precious little idea of what he had said.

"My father—" He scowled and gripped his sword-hilt. "He did fight the Bloody Menaham. I will give the rast that."

Duhrra was looking at both of us with an expression that on his gleaming idiot-face looked most comical.

"So you have something good to say about your father, then?"

"By Vox! No! I believe he fought only through others, that his friends did the fighting, while he—"

"Rukker's going ahead!" bellowed the lookout.

I was rather glad of the interruption.

Fazhan bellowed down to Pugnarses Ob-Eye, our oarmaster, who might boast only one eye but who ran a taut six oar banks.

We heard Pugnarses' whistle blow and then his full-blown voice telling the whip-Deldars interesting facts about their physiognomy and antecedents and probable destinations in the hereafter, and the beat of the oars quickened. No one on

the quarterdeck or on the forecastle thought overmuch of
the pains of the oar-slaves. We knew exactly what they
were going through. Exactly.

As Mangar, our drum-Deldar, increased the beat in response to the commands from Pugnarses and the oars
thrashed faster, so we began to pull back the distance Rukker
had surged ahead.

Three swifters ravening down on four argenters. I found
by chance that I would line up on the third ship from Menaham. Rukker would hit the lead ship, and Pur Naghan the
second.

There would be time. I said, "It's surprising to me, Vax,
that any man with a father like yours would bother to get
born at all. I suppose you will spend the rest of your life
hating him?"

"And if I do, it will be spent gladly."

The first varter shots were coming in. Our varters up forward replied. Soon the bows would sing. I could not leave
well alone.

"Of course, if your father died before you were born, you
have only the words of others. You don't know yourself."

"I know enough! I know what being Apushniad means—"
He checked himself there, and glared about. He wore mail
and a helmet and he looked young and bold and vigorous
and—and frighteningly vulnerable with his flushed face and
scowling lips. He whipped out his longsword. "I fight with
the prijikers today and show the world I am not as my
father!"

"*No!*" The word was shocked from me. I could not stop it.

He glowered at me, half turned, ready to storm off to the
forecastle and be among the foremost of the prijikers who
would swarm along the beakhead when it thumped down
onto the argentner's deck.

"No? I am a fighting-man. I am—I was, nearly— What
do you mean, Dak; *no?*"

I couldn't explain. He was my son. I didn't want him in
the forefront of the most dangerous part of the attack. A
prijiker, a stem-fighter, joyed in his honor and glory and
danger. I reckoned they were all more mad than other sailors. They bore the most wounds; from their numbers the
most men made holes in the sea.

"I want you to be at my side."

"But why? Do you deny me the glory?"

"There's no damned glory in getting killed in a stupid render affray!" I roared at him. "It's only loot out there. Are you so greedy for gold you'd throw your life away?"

He drew himself up in that faintly ridiculous way a young man indicates that he is grown up in his own estimation.

"You cannot stop me from fighting with the prijikers. If I get killed that is my affair." He swung his sword violently at the argenters. "Anyway, they are enemies of my country."

We were closing now and the arrows were feathering into the palisade across our forecastle. The beakhead swayed with the onward plunge of the ship. Men crouched up there, ready to spring like leems onto the decks, ready to smash in red fury to victory.

"And is that your marvelous reason?"

"It will do for now!"

And he swung off along the gangway. I glared after him. I knew practically nothing about the way he would act. He was a headstrong and violent youth, suffering under a sense of shame and outrage, carrying a heavy burden of hatred that ate at his pride. But as the fight developed and we smashed into the argenter and the beakhead went down and we roared across her decks, I had to understand that I could not do as I had unthinkingly sought to do. I had acted, I conceived, as any father would act. I did not want my son to go off fighting. But I could not hold him back. His own instincts, his pride, his youthful folly, all impelled him to rush headlong into the thickest of the fight.

Can any father thus shield his son from reality and expect to produce a man?

Sometimes the burdens of fatherhood are too heavy for a simple man to bear. Sometimes, I think, nature should have invented some easier way to carry on the generations. I did not enjoy that fight. I drew the great Krozair longsword and I went up the gangway after Vax, and I bellowed back to Fazhan to conn the ship, and I plunged into the fray like the madman I am, striking viciously left and right, thrusting and hacking, carving a bloody path through those poor devils from Menaham. We took the argenter all right. I had known we would take her. Everyone knew we would take her. It seemed idiotic to me that my son should imperil himself in so obvious a way over so obvious a fight.

But he did.

He was my son.

He was just as big a fool as I am.

When it was over and the flag came fluttering down in a blaze of blue and green and the shouts of "Hai!" rose, I saw that Vax, although splashed with blood, was unharmed. He had fought magnificently. I had been near him and there had been no single time when I had had to intervene. He could handle himself in a fight, that was plain. I knew he had been under training with the Krozairs of Zy. Their wonderful Disciplines had molded him well. He must, I guessed, have been very near to the time when he would have been accepted into the Order as a full member and have been allowed to prefix that proud *Pur* to his name.

But, all the same, despite his prowess, I was mighty glad when the fighting ceased.

Vax it was who spotted the danger to *Pearl*, ahead of us. He sprang onto the forecastle of the argenter and waved his sword.

"*Pearl!* Pur Naghan's in trouble!"

The swifter had wallowed around and broken a number of her starboard oars. The fighting on her decks looked confused. Men were spilling over into the water. There was no time to be lost.

We pulled up and launched ourselves afresh into the fray, battling up with *Pearl*'s men to take the Menaheem by surprise and so overpower their last resistance.

"Thank Zair you appeared, Dak!" panted Pur Naghan. His mail had been ripped and blood showed on his shoulder. "They fight well, these Menaham sailors."

"Bloody Menahem," said Vax. "I owe them."

"You owe a lot of people, it seems, Vax," I said.

He scowled at me, his brown eyes bright, his face flushed.

"Do you mock me, Dak?"

"Mock? Now, why should you think that?"

"If you do—"

Duhrra appeared, immense, his idiot-seeming face creased.

"You do—uh—seem to poke fun, master."

I knew that Duhrra regarded Vax as an oar-comrade, and this gladdened me. I realized I had gone far enough.

I glanced over the side.

"And while we prattle Rukker has boarded the last argenter."

The cunning Kataki had taken the first ship, and then

pulled out and dropped down to the last. Now he had two prizes.

Pur Naghan said, "We will share this one, Dak, of course."

Vax favored me with a scowl and took himself off. I bellowed the necessary orders and we took possession of our prizes. There were only three. Rukker's first impetuous attack with the ram had so holed the argenter that she was visibly sinking. A great deal of hustle took place as the goods were brought up and whipped across to the swifter. Chests and boxes, for they contained treasure, were favored over merchandise.

Soon the three swifters and the three argenters began the voyage back to the island of Wabinosk. We called in at our usual island stopovers and met with no untoward incidents.

We pulled with a fine reserve of manpower.

The argenters were sailed by scratch crews and we held fair winds almost all the way, only having to tow the sailing vessels twice in calms.

At the island hideout we inspected our spoils. The ship taken by *Pearl* and ourselves contained mostly sacks of dried mergem, whereat I felt greatly amused. This seemed to indicate Thyllis was in want of food for her people. Our ship contained a quantity of the fine tooled and worked leather for which Magdag is famous. As well there were sacks of chipalines and also, to my surprise, many wicker baskets loaded with crossbow bolts. These were uniformly of fine quality. I guessed they had been manufactured by the slaves and workers of the warrens, those people who, downtrodden and accursed, I had attempted to free, only in the moment of victory to be whisked away by the Star Lords and to leave them to defeat and continued enslavement. I picked up one of the iron quarrels and turned it over in my fingers. Yes, this was a fine artifact, and it should by rights be driven from a crossbow to lodge in the black heart of an overlord of Magdag. Had we not intercepted it, the bolt might well have battered its way into the heart of a Vallian.

Of the cargo carried in the ship Rukker had taken we were concerned only with the treasure.

It seemed fitting to me that all gold and silver and precious gems should be heaped into a great and glittering pile and then be shared out equally, portion by portion according to the Articles.

Maybe I was naïve in this belief. Rukker's ship had carried the majority of the treasure paid by King Genod for the Hamalese fliers and flyers. The saddle-birds and vollers had fetched extraordinarily high prices. I lifted a heap of golden oars and let them trickle through my fingers back to the glittering mass within the iron-bound lenken chest. This was what Thyllis needed. Her treasury must have been sorely used by the war and now, twenty-odd years after, she was busily building up her reserves so as once again to send sky-spanning fleets against Pandahem and Vallia.

With these thoughts in my mind I went to the meeting with Rukker and the others of our people in positions of authority and found myself not one whit surprised that the Kataki claimed all the treasure he had taken for himself. I was not prepared to argue. I wanted to place my son Vax in safety and then see again King Genod. Only after that could I begin to think again about what to do to free myself from the prison of the inner sea.

"You may keep what you claim, Rukker. If you can maintain your hold on it. For I do not renounce either my claim or the rightful claim of my people."

He did not sneer at me; but his look, brooding and dark, held calculation. "I take note of your words, Dak the Proud. But I think you will be hard pressed to take what you claim."

Vax bristled and shook off Duhrra's hand and barged forward.

"I do not renounce—" he began.

"Keep quiet, Vax," I said.

"By what right do you—" he blustered.

I looked at him.

Duhrra said, "The master speaks sooth, Vax." And then the old devil added, "I think you needed a father to teach you the ways of life—duh! You will get yourself spitted if you go on like this."

"Should I care, Duhrra?"

When my son said those words I felt the hand of ice clench around my heart.

Rukker broke the awkwardness, booming out in his coarse Kataki way, "You sail for Zandikar. Well and good, for, by Takroti, I am sick of all this quibbling." He glared around, yet he was in a high good humor. "I will sail with you and from thence back to the Sea of Onyx. With this treasure I can alter certain events at home."

So it was settled. The local Renders were only too pleased to see us go, for not only had we beaten off their attacks on us, after the first flush of welcome, in our operations we had shown them up almost humiliatingly. The four swifters and the three argenters made a nice little squadron, sailing east, cutting through the blue waters of the Eye of the World, sailing for Zandikar.

Chapter Eight

———◆———

Rukker does not speak of his seamanship

A man who has but two score years and ten to look forward to, and perhaps a little longer for good behavior, is filled with the thrusting desire to be up and doing—or he should be if he has any sense. To a Kregan with about two hundred years of life to use to explore experiences on his wild and wonderful planet, the desire to be up and doing burns no less strongly; but the Kregan can contemplate with equanimity the passing of a few seasons in doing something outside the mainstream of his life. Rukker the Kataki, as vicious and intemperate a Kregan as they come, made nothing of spending the time we had among the Renders of the inner sea. These little side excursions transform life for a Kregan. I, too, with a thousand years of life to use, shared much of that attitude, even though I had not thrown off the ways of the planet of my birth.

This trip to Zandikar to see my son Vax safe was a mere side-jaunt. I did not forget that in this jaunt Delia, Vax's mother, would concur wholeheartedly with what I was doing.

So we sailed past those mist-swathed coasts of mystery. The Eye of the World contains many areas that remain unknown, shores of faerie and romance, as well as shores of danger and horror. We pulled across the blue waters, from island to island, dropping down to coast most of the way in easy stages, venturing out across wide bays where the portolanos told us we would fetch the opposite headland in good time. I felt no sense of frustration. I was fascinated by Vax.

This journey would have been a good time to become acquainted. How I longed to ask him for all the details of his life!

Even the man I was then understood that children have their own secret areas sacrosanct from their parents' understanding. But I hungered to know more of Vax, and through him, more of my other children. And, of course, most of all, to hear about my Delia.

I might explore the Eye of the World. I was debarred from exploring my son's life.

Duhrra did as I asked and would often regale me with tidbits of information he had gleaned. I slowly built up a picture. Vax would freely admit he did not come from the inner sea, and once he had indicated to Duhrra that he had learned much from the Krozairs of Zy and would soon have been admitted to membership of that august Order; he did not tell anyone he came from Vallia and Valka.

"Whatever his father did, Dak," said Duhrra, pulling the fingers of his right hand into the right shape to clasp a flagon of Chremson, "Vax felt he could no longer continue with the Krozairs. Duh—anyone who gets that close must be remarkable. The Krozairs—" He picked up the flagon but did not drink, looking thoughtful, as is proper when mention is made of the Krozairs of Zair. "Duh—they put ice and iron into a man, by the Magic Staff of Buzro! No wonder he detests his old man."

"No wonder," I said, and turned away.

A commotion boiled up in Rukker's *Vengeance Mortil* and we all looked across the bright water. The sail billowed and crackled and then blew forward. The mast bent and bowed and came down with a run. We could hear the passionate yelling over there. I said, quite gently, to Fazhan ti Rozilloi, my ship-Hikdar, "Put the helm over, Fazhan. We must make a beaching. Rukker has proved once again that he is no sailor."

"Aye, Dak," said Fazhan, with a laugh. Rukker might be a ferocious and malevolent Kataki—with yet a spark of common decent humanity surprisingly in him—but, all the same, an old shellbacked sailorman would laugh at him for his woeful lack of seamanship and understanding of the sea.

Vengeance Mortil might quite easily have continued under oar-power and certainly Rukker would have no thought for the well-being of his oar-slaves. We had ghosted through the islands and were now making southerly toward the south-easterly sweeping arm of the inner sea past Zimuzz. Astern we had left Zy, that famous extinct volcanic island cone set boldly within the jaws of the Sea of Swords. The coast here was seldom visited. A triangularly lobed bay southward received the waters of the River Zinkara, running from the Mountains of Ilkenesk. On the Zinkara stood the city of Rozilloi. Fazhan had heaved up a sigh when our calculations showed us we passed that longitude special to him. Zandikar lay some sixty dwaburs farther to the east. We could hope for a wind. So we set about beaching the swifters and anchoring the argenters and removing the weights. We made camp and prepared ourselves for what might come.

Far inland, low rolling hills showed that purple-bruise color of distance, and on the sandy plains between only straggling trees grew. A party would have to push some way before they found a tree that would yield timber suitable for a mast. The made-masts of my own old Terrestrial navy were known here on the inner sea; but usually a single stout tree trunk was employed in swifters.

We had stationed a lookout and he bellowed down.

"Swifters! Green! Six of 'em!"

The curve of the bay where we had beached concealed us from seaward observation—an elementary precaution—and the lookout could see without being seen. The nearer headland under which we sheltered contained a mass of ruins, ancient stones, time worn and weathered, tumbled columns and arches, shattered walls. Up there I had a good view. There were six swifters, medium-sized vessels plowing in line ahead with their oars rising and falling in that remorseless beat. They pulled into the wind, long, low lean craft, evil and formidable. We waited carefully until they were past.

Rukker said, "I will stand guard on the camp and the ships."

"Very well," I said. "It will be a nice task to select the proper tree for your mast."

So it was decided. If those six Green swifters returned or if we were beset by unexpected foes, then Rukker and his men would defend the camp with ferocious efficiency. I took my sailors and a gang of slaves to drag the timbers, and set off inland.

We spent the rest of the day as the suns declined searching for the right tree, and when we found it and cut it down and dragged it back, two of the lesser moons sped past above in their crazy whirling orbits, and She of the Veils smiled down in fuzzy pink radiance. We had seen no signs of life apart from the spoor of mortils and the bones of their prey, and the high circling of warvols, the vulturelike winged scavengers waiting for the mortils to finish. Once upon a time—or, as Kregans say, under a certain moon—this land had been lush and fertile, filled with the busy agriculture and commerce of the People of the Sunset. Now they had gone, and the land gleamed sere and empty under the moons.

The moment we arrived back in camp we were greeted by news that filled me with amusement and filled Vax and the others with heated fury.

Old Tamil told us—a cunning rascal, quick and sly, who had appointed himself Palinter in *Crimson Magodont*. As our Palinter, our purser, he could be relied on to wangle extra supplies for us in his accustomed tortuous dealings with the common resources; in looking out for himself he looked out for us.

"That cramph of a Kataki!" spluttered Tamil, his off-center nose more than ever like a moon-bloom in the pink radiance of She of the Veils. "Took the treasure and sailed off!"

Howls of execration broke out at this. But then those howls changed to jeers of derision as we looked where Tamil pointed.

Less than an ulm offshore *Vengeance Mortil* lay becalmed in the water. She was down by the head. She stuck there, solid and unmoving, clearly held fast by fangs of rock piercing her bow.

"So the rast took our treasure and sailed off and ran himself aground!" bellowed Fazhan. He looked as offended as any of them there. They were running down to the shore and waving their arms and brandishing weapons. It was a fitting sight for a madness. It was, also, somewhat humorous—at least, it seemed funny to me at the time.

The treasure meant nothing, of course. It did mean something to these ragged rascals with me, and so that made it important to me because of them. But, all the same, the idea of a great and ferocious Kataki lord sweeping up all the treasure and loading it into his ship and sailing grandly off, only to get stuck on a rock, struck me as ludicrous and something to raise a guffaw.

The old devil had cut down his own mast, of course, to get us ashore in this lonely spot and send us sailormen off on a wild-goose chase. When he had run aground—what must his thoughts have been? He had been thrown by his own varter, as the Kregans say. Boats were ferrying his men back. There was a sublime amount of confusion and argument; but no one came to blows. The first flush of anger dissipated in the sense of the ridiculousness of the Katakis.

I said to Fazhan, "I will wager Rukker's words will be: 'I do not wish to discuss this' or 'I will not speak of this again.' "

"No bet," said Fazhan, being a wise man.

Pur Naghan was highly incensed, although seeing the humor of the situation, for he was bitterly annoyed by the evident lack of honor in Rukker's actions. Honor—aye, the Krozairs set great store by that ephemeral commodity.

Rukker stormed ashore in high dudgeon. At least, that seems to me an avocative way of describing his malevolent scowls, the way his tail flicked irritably this way and that, the dark glitter of wrath in his evil eyes. He was on the verge of a killing mad.

He said in his surly hoarse voice, "I shall not speak of this in the future."

At this a howl went up. And, thankfully, among those howls sounded many a guffawing belly-laugh. I felt relief. I watched carefully. But I think the sheer ludicrousness of it all saved an eruption, for plenty of men there would have chopped Rukker given half the chance. But the heat evaporated from the moment. Wine went around. We ate at the camp fires. We were, after all, a bunch of daredevil Renders, comrades in arms, for the time being. Tricks like this must be expected in such company.

The Maiden with the Many Smiles lifted and flooded down her golden light and we sat and drank and some of us sang. On the morrow we would fashion a new mast for Rukker and so sail off with the breeze toward Zandikar. We sang "The Swifter with the Kink," of course, and "The Chuktar with the Glass Eye," for they are fine carefree songs full of opportunities to expand the lungs and bellow. The firelight leaped upon our faces, on gleaming eyes and teeth, on mouths open and lustily bawling, on long bronzed necks open to the air. The red southern shore is populated by apims almost exclusively, and these apims, I had noticed, were contemptuous and intolerant of diffs. But it takes all kinds to make a world. Here some of the Zairian apims found that for all the tricks of the Katakis the other diffs of our company were human men, after all, and not mere menagerie men.

A little Och sang "The Cup Song of the Och Kings," sending the plaintive notes welling out into the light of the moons, a yearning song telling of great days and great deeds, filled with the throbbing reasonances of nostalgia. Then, as seemed always to happen when an Och sang that song, the moment he finished he pitched forward on his nose, out to the wide.

We all roared and cheered. At the other fires others of the Renders caterwauled to the skies. A Gon leaped up, his skull shaved clean of all that white hair of which Gons are so ashamed, to their misfortune, and started in to sing a wild skirling farrago, filled with spittings and abrupt, deep reverberations, of hints of horror, all accompanied by dramatic gestures evident of extreme terror. This was the song sometimes called "Of the Abominations of Oidrictzhn."*

A man—an apim, a Zairian—leaped clear across the fire, singeing the hairs on his legs, and screaming. He tackled the Gon with a full body-cracking charge, smacked him in the mouth, and so knocked him down and sat on his head.

"You get onker!" screamed the apim, one Fazmarl the Beak—for, in truth, his nose was of prodigious proportions. "You wish to destroy us all!"

We hauled him off and the Gon, Leganion, sat up, highly indignant. "It is a good song and will make your flesh creep."

"Yes, you rast! Do you not know where we are?" Fazmarl the Beak swung his hand violently to point at the moonlit ruins crowning the headland, frowning down above us. "You prate that name—here! Onker!"

One or two other men challenged Fazmarl, and he spluttered out a long rigmarole of weird doings and nightly spells and sorcery, there in the ruins of the Sunset People. He would not bring himself to repeat the name. But he made it very clear that the ruins harbored some malefic being in whom he believed and yet whose existence he must deny in the pure light of Zair.

---

*Prescot spells this name out carefully. He pronounces it *Oydrick-t-shin*. However he may recount his experiences here, there is no doubt they made a profound and uneasy impression on him. A.B.A.

"Superstitious nonsense!"

"Fairy tales for numbskulls!"

Oh, yes, those fierce Renders caterwauled bravely enough as the pink and golden moonlight flooded down and we sang and drank around the camp fires. But I saw more than a few of them cast up a quick and surreptitious glance at the pale stone-glimmer of the ancient ruins.

In the very nature of these men, for there were no women with us, fights broke out. These must be settled according to whatever code of honor and conduct was acceptable to both parties. I have not mentioned the detailed protocols involved in challenges and combats of Kregen, outside of a few remarks on the obi of my Clansmen, and the formal dueling of Hamal. But now, and with horrific suddenness, the finicky demands of honor and the protocol of fighting became of supreme importance to me.

It began with Vax, who had sworn off the dopa, swearing away, as was his wont, about his cramph of a father. One of the Katakis, no doubt as bored by Vax's obsession as the rest of us, bellowed some remark and tossed back his wine. This Kataki was Athgar, called the Neemu, and it was whispered he chafed under the yoke of Rukker's authority. Vax stood up, limber and lithe, and I caught the flare of madness in his eyes.

"You said, Athgar?"

No one had heard what Athgar had spoken; the moment could have been allowed to lie, and so dwindle and die.

But Athgar, wiping a hand across his face, bellowed out a curse to Targ the Untouchable. His low-browed, narrow-eyed face, as malignant and devilish as are all Katakis' faces, even the dark face of Rukker, bore down on the slim erect figure of Vax.

"If your father was the rast you claim him to be, then your mother must be a stupid and unholy bitch to have married him in the first place and so give birth to—"

That was as far as he got.

There was no heroic posturing from Vax. He did not bellow out; he did not request Athgar to repeat his words. My son Vax, who was Jaidur of Valka, Prince of Vallia, simply lashed out with his fist and knocked Athgar the Kataki, called the Neemu, head over heels into the fire.

When the uproar subsided and Athgar was held by Rukker's Katakis, and Vax was held by Duhrra and Nath the

Slinger, the ritual challenges and responses were gone through, the lines drawn and the demarcations between edge and point, between death and maiming, the rules and observances were finalized with all due solemnity. The rules of Hyr Jikordur would apply. I stood still and silent, watching, for the matter was passed from the hands of mortal men and lay now with the gods. Honor and passion ruled all. Words had been spoken. A blow had been struck. Now the answer, in the whims of the gods, must be found in steel and blood.

Moon-mist lay over the camp and the fires flared strangely. In the sand the lines were drawn out.

Men ran from the other fires to form a great circle of intent staring faces. A Jikordur happened every now and then and gave fuel for gossip for sennights thereafter. The matter was grave and full of a prestigious death-wish, filled with blood and death.

Instinctively, in the very moment a challenge had become inevitable, I had stepped forward to take Athgar the Neemu on and so shield my son. But that was impossible. Ideals and honor, however misplaced and distorted, now dictated all actions.

This was to be a Hyr Jikordur. I made an effort. I said, loudly, "Let no life be taken. Let the result be adjudged in the first blow."

Athgar sneered back his thin Kataki lips. "If it be first blood, Dak the Tenderhearted, then I will take the cramph's head off."

And my son said in his ferocious way, which a calmness made all the more vulnerable and bitter, "Let it be to the death, for, by Zim-Zair, I do not care."

At that Krozair oath all my defenses went down. I must stand and watch my son fight a predatory member of a feral and cruel race, vicious, fully armed and accoutered, equipped with a deadly bladed tail. I must stand and watch. To do anything else would impugn the strict codes of conduct, bring the Jikordur into disrepute, and as well as insuring my own death, bring my son humiliation and disgrace.

The Jikordur meant nothing to me. My own death little more. And I would so contrive my interference that Vax was spared that humiliation. . . .

Rukker checked his man. He favored me with a slow glance that I felt meant more than he cared to say. I stood before Vax. I drew the great Krozair longsword. I tendered it hilt first. Vax looked up, and something got through to him, for his lips compressed. Then he smiled.

"I thank you, Dak."

A sword-blade struck a helmet like a gong. The combat began.

Chapter Nine

———◆———

Blood in the Hyr Jikordur

Pachaks have been blessed by nature—or the dark manipulations of genetic science—with quick and lethal tail hands. Katakis must strap their steel to their whip-tails. I am partial to Pachaks, as employed mercenaries, as friends. In long talks with them around the camp fires on the eve of battles I have learned much of the art of tail-fighting. There are tricks. As the gong note clanged with grim promise from the sword-struck helmet, I leaned down to Vax and said, "His tail may be numbed by—"

"I know," said my son.

They always seem to know, these cocky youngsters. I stepped back. I did not waver from my resolution to court personal dishonor and destruction if they were necessary to save my son. The chances were he would know. Planath Pe-Na, my standard-bearer who carried Old Superb into action, must have known Vax as the lad grew up into manhood. Along with all my friends of Esser Rarioch—Balass the Hawk, Naghan the Gnat, Oby, Melow the Supple, the Djangs who were a regular part of the people there; all must have contributed their knowledge toward the education of Vax no less than they had to Drak and Segnik—no, I must call him Zeg now. And, of course, there were Seg and Inch and Turko the Shield. If Vax had taken in what they had to tell him then the combined knowledge should make him a formidable fighter—and he was, indeed, as I had seen, a bonny lad with a sword.

Planath must have told Vax of the tricks an apim might

get up to with the tail of a Kataki. Planath would have relished the telling.

With no more relish in myself at the idea of this fight, but with some feeling of relief, I watched as Athgar stalked forward—arrogant, completely confident—to knock over and slay this slim and supple apim lad.

I cannot do justice to that fight, for I was far too intimately concerned for my own good. I had picked up the look from Duhrra and he had slipped me his longsword. I held it ready, and I must give thanks that the fight occupied the attention of the men there, for had they seen my face in the firelight glow and the radiance of the moons, they would no doubt have run shrieking.

Athgar launched himself, his sword blurring, his tail-blade high and deceiving. Vax lunged right, checked and reversed, came back. The two combatants passed. Now was the danger! The tail hissed around. Vax jumped. I let out a grunt of relief. Vax dropped down hard. He made no attempt at that cunning tail-numbing trick. Athgar had expected him to duck, as would be the instinctive response to the threat of that arrogant high-held blade. Athgar struck low. Vax jumped. And the great Krozair longsword flamed.

Athgar shrieked.

The tail spun and looped away, the strapped blade glittering, flicked like a limp coil of rope into the fire. It sizzled.

Blood pumped from Athgar. He stood disbelieving. He stood for perhaps two heartbeats.

Rukker yelled, "Athgar the Tailless!"

The Neemu screeched and swung his sword in a ferocious horizontal sweep. Vax met the blow, slanting his brand, and let the blades chink and screech in that demoniac sound of steel on steel. His broad back muscles tensed and bunched, drew out in a ripple of massive power. The blade struck forward. The point burst through Athgar's throat above the mail, smashed on to eject itself in a spouting gout of blood.

Without a word, Vax withdrew and stepped back. He looked on silently as Athgar dropped his sword and gripped his crimson throat, his eyes glaring madly. He choked, trying to say something. Then he fell. He pitched down to sprawl at Vax's feet.

Vax looked down. He was my son. Without a word he spit on the corpse. Then he walked away.

No one said a word.

It was left to Vax, turning to speak over his shoulder, to say, "I will clean your sword, Dak, before I return it."

I wanted to say—how I wanted to say!—the words hot and breaking in me . . . I swallowed. I said, "Jikai—keep the sword, Vax. It is yours."

For a moment he stood, silent, limber, lithe and young, staring at me. The firelight painted one half of his face ruby; the moons shone fuzzily pink and gold upon the other. He nodded. Again he did not speak. He just nodded and lifted the sword, and saluted, and so walked into the darkness beyond the fires.

I handed Duhrra his sword. "Take Nath. Follow."

"Yes, master."

Duhrra and Nath melted into the moon-drenched shadows. Other men of my crew followed. They would see that Vax came to no harm. They were good fellows. If I do not mention them overmuch, surely it is obvious that concern for my son dominated all my thoughts.

Rukker said, "There is no need for that, Dak."

"No."

He looked down at the corpse. "He was my man and yet he was not my man. I think this Vax Neemusbane is your man and yet not your man. It was a Hyr Jikordur. There is no blood between us."

"None," I said. "And you are right about Vax. I think he has done you a favor."

"Probably. But I do not wish to discuss that."

It amuses me now to think how Rukker regarded me. He treated the other Renders sharply enough, and they respected or hated him for it, according to their natures. But he must have come to terms with his own ruthlessness in his dealings with me, or so I think. Maybe he did not forget our first meeting, or the way he would have been flogged on the oar bench had I not spoken. As I say, Rukker possessed a scrap of humanity.

All the same, I meant to repay him for his trick when he had loaded all the treasure aboard his swifter and attempted to sail away. He might not wish to speak of that in the future; I had a few words on the subject—and these words would not be spoken but acted on.

In any company on Kregen one feels naked without a sword.

A weapon is needed most everywhere. Even the unarmed

combat skills developed by the Khamorros of Havilfar, and the Krozairs of the Eye of the World, cannot fully compensate for the lack of a weapon if the unarmed combat man goes up against an opponent skilled in his weapon's use. And it does not have to be a sword, of course; but legends and myths cluster about swords.

In our reiving over the western end of the inner sea we had built up an armory and in my cabin in *Crimson Magodont* a useful array of weapons I had taken a fancy to awaited my inspection. As I went up the ladder I turned and saw in the moons-light Vax and Duhrra and Nath walking back to the fires, and already Vax was working away at the blood on his new sword. Satisfied, I went into the cabin. There was no real choice before me; just the one sword I fancied. There had been no other Krozair blade come into our possession; but I had taken a fine Ghittawrer blade. The Grodnims produce fine weapons and, as in the case of the Zairians, the finest are made by and for the Brotherhoods of Chivalry of the Green. This Ghittawrer sword had borne the device of the lairgodont and the rayed sun and I had had them removed. I picked it up and swirled it a trifle, feeling the balance as being good but not as perfect as the Krozair brand I had given my son, honoring his jikai.

That thrice-damned king Genod, self-styled genius at war, had instigated his Ghittawrer Brotherhood, the lairgodont and the rayed sun. The blade was good. It would serve to lop a few Green heads and arms.

A shouting on the beach, and a distant calling from higher up, drew me to the deck. The night lay calm and sweet under the stars and moons; yet mists trickled down like thickened waterfalls from the headland. I looked up. Lights speckled the ruins. Many torches flared among the aeons-old walls and columns.

"What is it, Sternen?" I shouted at the watch.

"I do not know, Dak. But whatever it is, men have gone up to find out." He shivered. He was a tough apim with a scarred face and quick with a knife. "By Zogo the Hrywhip! Those screams never came from a human throat!"

About to check him roughly, I paused. The shrieks from the ruins sounded unnatural. Sternen made several quick and secret signs. These were rooted in a time before Zair and Grodno parted into enmity. I slapped the Ghittawrer blade into the scabbard, for the Grodnims attempted to copy the dimensions of a Krozair blade, and rattled off down the ladder. Many men were running up the steep track in the cliff toward the ruins, carrying torches, bearing weapons, Renders out to prove they feared not a single damn thing in all of Kregen. I followed.

Panting up at my side Nath the Slinger said, "The lights up there aren't ours."

I halted. Duhrra and Vax appeared. Some way beyond them a knot of men I knew would be loyal not only to Zair but to me pressed on. I shouted at them, intemperately, and they clustered around. Before I spoke I looked up. In the lights of the moons the mass of Renders ascending into the ruins looked apelike, crowding up, bearing torches. The Katakis were there. I looked at Vax and Fazhan and Duhrra. I told them what I wanted them to do. I did not mince my words.

"And if there's a watch," I said, most unpleasantly, "knock him on the head and spirit him away. Do not kill him, though."

Duhrra rumbled a hoarse chuckle.

"Duh—master! A fine plan!"

"Aye," said Fazhan. "Just rewards, by Zair."

"And if there is a fight," said Vax, half drawing his beautiful new sword, "I shall joy in showing this boastful Kataki Rukker he may join the cramph Athgar."

"You will not fight him unless I tell you." I looked hard at Vax in the streaming moons-light. "He will not succumb so easily as Athgar."

"Yet is he a Kataki, and Katakis have tails."

"And with them they rip out throats of young coys."

He was beginning to know a little of me, enough to understand that I might argue with him in some matters, and in others he had best obey, schtump. All the same, he looked daggers at me.

"Take Tamil the Palinter with you. He is adept at weighing and measuring."

"Aye, master."

"I shall entertain Rukker until you signal. Now, jump!"

I intended to be scrupulously fair. What I intended was perfectly obvious, of course; but if my men did not do a quick clean job there would be a fight. Renders habitually quarrel and fight; it is all a part of their image, Articles or no. As they took themselves off I wondered if I was doing this out of mere irritation with myself, out of a sense that time was rushing by and I had made no progress, and played this trick not so much out of evil boredom as out of self-contempt.

Then I ran lightly up the trail in the cliff toward the ruins of the Sunset People and the mysteries that might await me there.

Chapter Ten

———◆———

Among the ruins of the Sunset People

From the concealment of a screen of bushes we looked upon a scene at once hideous and horrific. The Renders had extinguished their torches and they did not speak above an awed whisper. The lights illuminating those time-weathered stones were not our lights. The flaring torches wrapped tendrils of golden brilliance about the old columns and arches, lit gray walls and time-toppled cornices. Shattered domes like eggshells smashed wantonly glittered starkly in the pink moons-light. We crouched silently and we stared upon that pagan scene.

Next to me crouched the trembling form of Fazmarl the Beak. I could feel his body shaking against my shoulder.

"I warned them, the fools," he whispered to himself, and I could feel the tenseness in the words he scarcely knew he uttered aloud. "It is Oidrictzhn himself! The Abomination!"

I nudged him. "Silence, you fambly. Is this all you know?"

He glared mutely at me and shook his head.

I drew him down farther into the shadows.

"Tell me. And speak low."

"Oidrictzhn!"

I clapped a hand across his mouth and shot a glance over the bushes. The figures prancing in the torchlights were concerned over their own pursuits and we did not appear to be observed; but I fancied they'd have someone on the lookout. I shook Fazmarl the Beak.

"You bear an honored name. These Abominations. Is that what they're up to out there?" I released his mouth.

He drew in a whooping gulp of air. "Yes. It is old, older than anyone knows. Long before Zair and Grodno, whose name be cursed, separated out of—"

"Yes, yes. I know that. Will they slay the girl?"

"Assuredly. They have come from many little villages inland and they would travel to the west of us. I know, for I lived in one of those small villages, like a vosk in swill—and all knew the old stories of Oidrictzhn and his Abominations."

"You do not mind saying his name now."

He did not laugh; but he emitted a sour grunting kind of cough. "No—for it is too late. The evil one has arisen from his sleep. He has been conjured. Do you not see his gross form, there, where the shadows cluster, although the torches shine the brightest?"

There *was* a puzzling splotch of shadow against an ancient gray monolith where the torches shone, where one would expect light and the reflections brilliant against the masonry.

"How?"

"Who knows? No one owns to knowledge. Yet all know there are those who possess the secret powers. The Abominable One has risen and he will not return until he is sated."

I was not prepared to dismiss all this as fear-induced madness.

On Kregen as on Earth there are the darker myths, hideous stories of hideous beings from out of time and space. Normally one gives no credence to them. But to hear of them among tumbled and time-shattered ruins, ancient before ordinary man ventured to tame fire and crouch at his cavemouth brandishing a stone hand-ax, with the shifting light of the moons streaming across a scene of naked savages—for rhapsodic belief had turned these people savage—screaming and chanting, circling a stake whereon hung the bloody corpse of a ponsho, closing nearer and nearer to a raised stone slab on which lay a young girl, ripe for the sacrifice . . . as I say, to hear these horrendous myths of demons and devils in circumstances like those is to make belief all too easy.

The Abominable One had been driven away when the true light of Zair had risen in the land. But he was not dead. He slept and awaited his call. He could be raised up and he would not be satisfied until he had drunk of the blood of a virgin. That it must be a female virgin was not specified; but it seemed appropriate. I had to hold on to the levity that wanted me to rush out there and lay about with the Ghittawrer blade. I do not totally condemn these feeble-minded stories; a little care for one's ib is as proper as care for one's flesh-and-blood hide.

"The Zair-forsaken cramphs of Grodnims advance from the west. They destroy all who oppose them. King Genod's army is invincible. Soon they will be here. All the little villages to the south will be enslaved—aye!—and the great cities also."

"You may be right, Fazmarl. But I think you wrong. And these deluded fools seek to raise up a long-dead god of evil to protect them? They are mad."

"Yes, they are mad. But madness is easy in these times."

Rukker crawled over. He looked as fierce as ever; but I sensed he was unsure. Why else did he crawl?

"What is this onker chattering about, Dak?"

I told him that out of fear of the Grodnims the locals were raising from his long-sealed vault a monster of evil, out of time and space, a being who might sweep us all away with the power of his breath. Rukker grunted and stilled the impatient swish of his tail.

"If the ancient god is in the likeness of an apim—"

Fazmarl let rip a hysterical giggle at this, a tiny sound of horror in a greater scene of horror.

"His shape is more awful than anyone—"

"Yes," I said. Fazmarl quieted. "It is not of our business, Rukker. Do you agree?"

"I agree. I think I shall not speak of this later."

"Yes," I said. "Yet the girl . . ."

"She is apim," said the Kataki.

"Oh, assuredly. Had she been a Fristle, or a numim, a sylvie, or a girl from Balintol, I do not think it would make overmuch difference."

Fazmarl, quaking, said, "They would mean nothing."

I did not hit him. I must come to terms with this detestation of diffs that was so widespread among the apims of Zairia. I had hardly remarked it during my previous sojourn on the inner sea. I had changed, not the Zairians, that was all. And, anyway, Fazmarl and Rukker would have no idea where Balintol was. I lifted a trifle and peered over the bushes. The blasphemous ceremony drew to its gruesome climax.

Couples were dancing out there in the streaming torchlight, going widdershins, letting abandon carry them away in frenzy. The dread weight of evil bore us down. The sense of evil among the stones shivered through the torchlight, and a coiling mist melted the gold and pink moonbeams. Fazmarl shivered. He began to crawl back, away, shaking his head, his lips slobbering.

I let him go.

I said to Rukker, "It seems to me a little jikai might be created here, Kataki."

"You may. By the Triple Tails of Targ the Untouchable! This is no business of mine."

"You would not trust your Targ against this Oidrictzhn the Abominable?"

"There is nothing supernatural there. It is a man, dressed in a skin, with a chimera for a head."

"So why hang back?"

His tail started to twitch. I drew my sword. He saw it. He said, "You may get yourself killed if you wish. Do you not see the archers?"

"Aye. That proves they fear physical as well as occult powers."

"Then, by Takroti, you may test them yourself."

He would have left then, calling his people about him. I could feel the evil in that place. It is a difficult thing to say. There was some suppurating spirit of demonology flaunting itself against the gray stone wall, drinking the light of the torches. I held Rukker. The people out there, abandoned, most half gone on dopa probably, clustered close to the stone slab.

"Would it not be a jikai to go out there and deprive them of their enjoyment? Would not depriving other people appeal to you, a Kataki?"

Under my hand his arm quivered. I could feel the bunch of muscle below the mail. He hissed the words as a Kataki can hiss. His face was demonic as any devil's, almost as devilish as my own. "Take your hand off me! I shall spit you for this, apim!"

"Then you will have to catch me, Kataki," I said, and stood up, and ran forward into the torchlight toward the stone slab of sacrifice and the girl bound helplessly upon its scarred surface.

Hideous yells burst from the corded throats of the people dancing and clustering about the slab of sacrifice. They were possessed. Drugged on dopa or any one of a variety of narcotics, or on sheer fear-driven hysteria, they capered and screeched and sought to drag me down with clawed raking fingers. I pushed them aside. There was no time to feel either anger or pity for them. I got in among them with vicious speed and the archers perched on the crumbling lichenous walls shafted two poor devils instead of me.

The aura of horror swelled nearer that splotch of utter darkness on the gray wall. In a tangle of naked arms and legs I pushed forward toward the slab. I did not use the edge of my sword; the flat sufficed.

The girl was not unconscious. She lay on her back, strained over by thongs from wrists and ankles that were knotted to iron rings stapled into the stone. She wore stockings that reached to mid-thigh and were banded by red-glinting gems. The stockings were black, a fitting counterpoint to the darkness that hovered over her. Her body gleamed pink and golden in the moons-light, looped with gems, strings of jewels chaining her breast-cups of gold and twining around her stomach and legs, linking her ankles and wrists. Her hair of that midnight black of the Zairians of the inner sea glistered with gems and silverdust. Her face seemed only a pale flower, her mouth and eyes mere dark bruises.

A man leaped on my back and I bent and hurled him away. The sword slashed the thongs of her ankles, sliced the right wrist-thong. I moved to reach the left thong and someone grabbed my ankles. I kicked. A screech like a lost soul in torment cheered me. The sword licked out. I put my left arm under the girl's head, lifted her, slid my arm down to her neck, her back, and took her up as one might hoist a sack of cereal.

She felt light and soft and warm, and she trembled all the time with a fine shivering that tingled against my hand.

Now I would use the edge, if I must.

An arrow splintered against the slab. The scarred surface showed ancient evils stains. Just beyond the slab a pit in the ground covered by an iron grating drew my alert attention. People were dragging the grating up, screaming in ecstasy and fear, throwing the iron grille down and then running, running. . . .

Anything could squirm out of that dank pit. . . .

"Slay him! Strike him down! Immolate him!"

The shouts grew in frenzy. With the girl caught up to me

and dangling her strings of jewels and chains of gold, I began to run back. I looked over my shoulder, just to check my rear, as was my custom—and I saw the dread shadow against the stone move.

At that moment of impending horror an entanglement at my feet brought me pitching to earth. I held on to the girl and as we both slammed into the ground she did not cry out. Her eyes were wide and brilliant and fixed on me hypnotically.

I looked up.

A Thing moved among the shadows.

A Shadow moved among the things.

The screeching and shouting died to a whimper and faded. The breeze stilled. Mists coiled before the moons and the light changed with dread subtlety from gold and pink to a drenching shower of blood-rubied radiance.

I looked up.

Something ancient and evil slithered against the stones. Something . . . There was only one name that could be given this bestial monstrosity from out of the dead ages of time—Oidrictzhn—Oidrictzhn the Abominable!

The Shadow rose and lifted and became monstrous, huge, blotting out vision and reason. A chilling slithering, a hissing, a feral, hateful mind-numbing hissing whispered from the shadows clustered about the Shadow.

The Beast from Time slithered out from the shadows to devour me.

Chapter Eleven

The Beast out of Time

Apim, the thing was, fully ten feet tall, gray and leprous of skin, marked by the splotches of foul disease. Its skin hung from it loosely, fold on fold of repulsive gray mantling, dripping with the festering slime. And its head! Domed of head and yet with leprous crawling skin patches supplanting all hair, with deeply sunken eyes that glared now as mere red slits. Red, red, those eyes, twin pits of fire, burning down on me. I rolled over above the girl. I saw the thing's mouth. Arched and black, it gaped obscenely, and from its upper jaw tendrils of slime hung like oozing living stalactites. Green ichor dripped. The thing lifted gaunt arms from which hung like living gray curtains the hideous folds of flesh. Skeletal the fingers, curved, harsh, bony webs of taloned destruction. Now I was on my feet. The girl lay in her tawdry jewels and gold, winking flashes of fire in the torchlights and that dropping blood-red light, splendid against her flesh in that moment of horror.

The thing advanced farther from the shadows. The slithering hissing of its progress sounded from nameless horrors hidden in the shadows thickly pressing around its legs and feet. Its arms lifted like bat wings, its skeletal talons reaching forward. The red eyes blazed from their deep pits of hate, and the green slime dripped from its mouth. The fetid odor of the thing near drove me back; but I gagged and lifted the sword.

The girl spoke.

"If it touches you with its claws, you are doomed."

"Then, my lady, I shall have to see it does not touch us."

Her gasp was a pretty diversion; but the horror moved on and the contrasts of the moment must be forgotten. This was no mere mortal monster. I did not think a mere mortal man hid behind this obscene facade. This was a real true and *live* ancient evil one, from beyond Time, summoned up and demanding his sacrifice.

How old was this ancient thing? From what pits of hell had it been raised?

The slime dripped from its ghastly mouth and its head bent forward, so that the ruby eyes sank into mere furnace slits.

How could I spare pity for it? It should have died long and long ago, no longer needed by mankind, forgotten and allowed to sink into its tomb. But superstitious humanity had dabbled blasphemously in the black arts of Kregen and had drawn forth this horror. So a simple mortal man must drive it back from whence it came.

"It is Oidrictzhn the Abominable!" The devotees had regained their voices. They were shrieking in rhapsody, falling onto their knees, their arms uplifted in supplication. They prayed in an obsessed fervor to this Abomination. "All praise to thee, Oidrictzhn! Lahal and Lahal to the Abominable One!"

The thing slithered nearer.

And the lassitude and the weakness crept up my sword arms. I held the Ghittawrer blade with both fists, one unhandily near the other, for the hilt was not a full Krozair hilt. I struggled to think of the Krozairs then. Of Zair, of Opaz, of Djan. I tried to form words and hurl them at the Beast of Time. I wanted to shriek out that it should return to its ghastly haunts in the name of Zair; but I could not croak a word.

The sword felt impossibly heavy. My arms trembled. My calves shook. My head drooped. I struggled savagely to lift my head, to lift my arms, to still the agonized trembling of my body.

And the thing spoke!

Serpentlike, the hissing words garbled out through that obscene mouth.

"Puny mortal man! Foundling of Time! I demand my due!"

Only my body betrayed me. I knew what I was going to say. Oh, yes, I knew what I'd shout at the obscene thing.

But it had the power, it possessed the ancient evil powers out of time and it held me in a stasis so that all my muscles could not move my body, my arms could not uphold the sword.

The blade drooped and sank.

The girl struggled to her knees, her golden breast-cups jangling against the golden chains, the gems over her body glittering. She clasped my knees. But I was of no use to her.

I think then, I really think, that I, Dray Prescot, lord of many titles and many lands, would have marched on my last long journey to the Ice Floes of Sicce. I really do. . . .

I fought against occult powers that I dismissed as being the enfeebled ravings of children and idiots. But who may say what festers in the past of Kregen? Who deny the reality of that moment of horror?

The sword drooped and the point struck the ground and I leaned forward. In moments only I would topple helplessly to the ground.

And all the time the ruby fires of the thing's eyes glared furnacelike upon me and the green ichor dripped from the gapping arch of its mouth.

I could not speak; but my mind formed words.

"Sink me!" I burst out. "A stinking slimy half-dead monstrosity with all the black arts of Tomborku to see me off with my own thirty-two-pound roundshot for company! By Zair! A fine fool I'll look when the gray ones greet me among the Ice Floes!"

I felt the tremble in my arms. I remembered what a lady had said. The Star Lords—well, they would probably laugh to see me in this plight, for all that they could have aided me had they wished. So I thought then. As for the Savanti, they were mere mortal men, even if superhuman in their powers. They would not aid me now. Only I could aid myself, so I thought, in my usual blind arrogance and pride.

And the tremble persisted and I felt the sword's weight again and I lifted. The hilt felt incredibly good in my fists. I raised my head. The thing did not advance. Against the shadows a radiance grew. A yellow light. A yellow light that limned that ghastly head with the dripping fungoid growths depending in place of hair, that shone upon the gray walls and drove away the black shadows. Yellow. A yellow radiance.

"By God! Zena Iztar," I said. "But you are very welcome."

And I lifted the sword against the tearing shriek of my muscles and I struck at the leprous shape before me.

It stumbled back. I caught it a glancing blow and it keened a shrill whine. The shadows writhed and coiled and lambent blue sparks spit from the darkness. But they spit and recoiled as that glorious yellow glow strengthened. Again I lifted the sword and took a pace forward and struck. The thing shrieked again and stepped back and back. I could feel nothing, now, in my arms. Twice I had struck and twice I had missed. I, Dray Prescot, swordmaster, bladesman, Bravo-fighter, had missed this shuffling, lumpy, ichor-dripping obscenity not once but twice.

I knew then that Zena Iztar could aid me only in some way, some not-so-small way, that lifted the occult power of the force that enchained me. But I could not move forward. I was held by unnameable powers. The sword glittered in the mingled lights; it could not be impelled against that hideous shape of horror.

"By Zair! Give me but the strength for one last blow!"

Willpower, the striving, the desire, the determination, by these I might stand against the Star Lords, Zena Iztar had told me. I must summon up all my willpower and force my reluctant muscles to power my body forward.

Oidrictzhn the Abominable leered upon me with his furnace eyes of ruby fire. He saw. He moved forward and his claws raked around. One touch was death. One touch of these webbed and taloned claws would doom me for all eternity. This I knew.

I burst the bonds even as the claw raked at my face. I swung the brand and the steel shrieked and bit and green slime spouted.

The thing screamed. It staggered back.

I have scoffed at the word eldritch. But in that moment I knew what an eldritch scream sounds like.

It sounds with the insane terror of pure horror.

The yellow glow began to fade.

The worshipers of this vile thing had dared not to approach. The archers had not dared to loose. The Beast from Time lurched. One claw still made feeble raking passes as it staggered back. The other claw lay on the ground at my feet and even as I looked so it gathered itself to it, and like a webbed scorpion scuttled for the shadows against the gray stone. I let it go. I know about scorpions.

"You have failed me!" the thing's voice whispered now, weird and out of Kregen and altogether blasphemous. "I shall leave you to your fate. Oidrictzhn returns to the Abominations from which it came."

The shadows rushed together as bats swoop about a church steeple. A noxious odor made me retch. The shadows paled and wafted and there were left only the shadows flung from the torches and streaming behind the moons' radiance.

An arrow flicked past my ear.

I hoisted the girl. I was myself again.

I ran. That was a fair old run, a scamper across the sand and sward between the ruins until I had reached the tumbled columns and so run on, safely now, into the bushes.

Only one man stood there to welcome me.

I said, "I salute you, Rukker. And the others?"

His booming laugh rang somewhat hollow. "They scuttled."

"Then let us go down to our ships and push off. This is an evil place."

Chapter Twelve

———◆———

News of the Red and the Green

The mingled streaming radiance of the Suns of Scorpio filled the Eye of the World with light and color. Our little squadron bore on over a sparkling sea, with the wind in our canvas and the spray lifting whitely from our forefeet. Often I have spoken of that glorious opaz radiance of the twin suns of Antares, but seldom have I so luxuriated in the brilliance of the Suns of Scorpio as on the morning following that ghastly nighted encounter with Oidrictzhn of the Abominations.

That part of the southern shore of the inner sea is called the Shadow Coast. The name is apt. Of all the men who had climbed so boldly up to the ruins all but one had fled away. Now I stood on my quarterdeck and watched *Vengeance Mortil* as Rukker urged her along. The new timber for the mast had been pitched aboard and no one had questioned our sailing before the new mast was stepped.

The plan was for us to beach up well away from the Shadow Coast and then step Rukker's new mast. But the Kataki lord had other ideas. Fazhan commented acidly, and Duhrra let fall a few astonished Duhs. Vax looked on Rukker's swifter with compressed lips. For *Vengeance Mortil* and the argenter Rukker claimed as his prize and manned with his own men curved away to larboard. Our course to the east carried us on with the wind. Rukker bore away to the northeast.

"Does he mean to leave us, then?" said Fazhan, peering under his hand.

"It seems so."

Vax laughed nastily.

Duhrra said: "Duh—when he finds out!"

My men had done a good job, so Fazhan said. With old Tamil the Palinter there to weigh and assess, we had deducted our shares of the treasure. Rocks had been placed at the bottom of the chests, with canvas over that and the fair proportion of treasure belonging to Rukker spread artfully to conceal all. Rukker, believing he carried all the treasure, bore away from us. I wondered if he questioned why we did not follow.

One of the hands began laughing. He was a prijiker and stood on the forecastle now in his accustomed place, leaning against the overhanging bulk of the beakhead. Others of the men began to laugh.

"Nath the Berkumsay!" I bellowed. "Belay that caterwauling."

He looked back and I saw the puzzlement chasing the laughter in his face. I turned to Portain, the ship-Deldar, and said with some irritation, "Go forward and tell Nath the Berkumsay to shut his black-fanged winespout. If he wishes to bring Rukker back tell him to swim after *Vengeance Mortil* and tell the Kataki personally."

"Quidang!"* bellowed the ship-Deldar. He bustled forward and very shortly thereafter no one laughed at Rukker as he sailed away with his fair treasure shares, and the rest merely rocks.

"When he finds out," said Fazhan, with some glee, "I am wondering if he will summon the calmness to say that he will not speak of this in the future. Ho—it is indeed a great jest."

These men had not been up in the ruins of the Sunset People, they had not witnessed the Beast from Time; I felt glad they had been spared that. But, all the same, I wondered if they'd be quite so merry and carefree this morning had they seen what I had seen.

Rukker's two ships disappeared over the horizon rim and we settled down to the haul to Zandikar.

Toward evening as we began to look out particularly for our expected landfall for the night, a tiny island called the Island of Pliks, the lookout sighted a sail and hallooed down.

---

*Quidang: At once. Equates with "Aye aye, sir!"

We flew red flags.

The vessel, a small coaster, bore a red flag, also.

We made the Island of Pliks together and after all had been seen to in our camp a party from the coaster came across. They were either incautious, brave, or they did not care. Red flags may be flown by anyone in the inner sea.

After we had drunk tea and sat in the light of the moons eating palines, the coaster captain heaved up a sigh and said, "If you sail to Zandikar, dom, you sail to destruction."

"What?" Vax's lean hard face looked exceedingly dangerous in the ruddy fire-glow. "Spit it out!"

The coaster master, a weather-beaten old salt with a massy beard and a face graven by wind and wine, cocked an eye at this highly strung stripling with the wide shoulders and lean powerful look of the fighting-man.

"Be careful they do not spit you out, son, if you venture there."

Duhrra put his steel hand on Vax's arm. The touch seemed to calm the lad. Maybe it was Duhrra's hand, maybe Vax was learning tact and discretion; whatever it was, he said, "I would like to know what passes in Zandikar. There is a girl—"

"Ah," said the master, who called himself Ornol the Waves. "A girl, is it? Well, King Zenno is partial to young girls."

"King Zenno? Who is he? King Zinna reigns in Zandikar."

I listened, as we all listened. This was news.

"King Zinna is dead, slain by the very hand of King Zenno. Since the siege the city is—"

"Siege? Zandikar is under seige?"

The coaster master, Ornol the Waves, flicked a finger of palines into his mouth, and grunted as he chewed, speaking offhandedly. "You are strangely ill-informed, doms."

"We have been faring in the western sea, taking Grodnim devils. Tell us of the siege and of King Zenno."

"As to the siege, there is little to say. That rast, Prince Glycas, sits down before Zandikar and throttles the city."

There rose sounds of disgust and of anger from the ranks of my men, who were red Zairians. This news was bad, very bad.

"And King Zenno, who was a reiver called Starkey the Wersting, slew the old king and with his paktuns took the city and dubbed himself Zenno—out of mockery or politics, it is all one."

Pur Naghan ti Perzefn started up at this. He looked incensed.

"The rast dares to arrogate the 'Z' to himself? No man may take the letter unless he is born with it already, or unless he creates a hyr Jikai. No one!"

Men were calling out, demanding to know more; others were blaspheming away about Prince Glycas and the Grodnims; others cussing away about the paktuns. I did not smile; but I felt the nudge of amusement that Pur Naghan, a Krozair of Zamu, should feel more concern over a man taking to his name the letter "Z," which as an initial letter is hard come by, hard won, given seldom without a hyr Jikai.

An idle thought occurred to me that the Krozair Bold who had ousted my friend Pur Zenkiren for the position of Grand Archbold, this Pur Kazz, did not proudly own the initial "Z," that he was Pur Kazz and not Pur Zakazz. Well, he had done what he had out of a fanatical belief in his power and authority and in the Krozair-given right to judge. He had judged wrongly, and because of that I was expelled from the Krozairs of Zy, was Apushniad. I had not thought of this matter for some time, and now I rose and shook the black thoughts from me, and went walking quietly in the fuzzy pink moons-light, pondering.

If Zandikar was besieged, would our plans have to change?

There was further information I must have. At the fires Ornol the Waves expatiated on the plight of Zandikar, the city of the Ten Dikars. Prince Glycas had the city in a death-lock. His Grodnim army defeated all who sought to stand against it. It was only a matter of time before he took the city. The Grodnims, led by the overlords of Magdag but drawn from many cities and towns of the northern lands, had leap-frogged once more. They had avoided certain fortress-cities of the southern coast and had landed before Zandikar. They had, in particular, avoided a head-on confrontation with Zy. I could visualize the position with a clarity made all the more awful by the directness of the threat. In this the hand of the genius king Genod was clearly apparent.

Pur Naghan had the gist of it, also.

"I am a Krozair of Zamu!" Here was no time for a strange and mystic reticence, a blanket of aloofness that is usual with Krozairs in non-Krozair company. Here was a time for strong leadership. "Zamu lies a mere twenty-five dwaburs from Zandikar, by the land route. By sea there are many islands and the coast curves strongly in the Nose of Zogo and the way is difficult for an attacker. We must sail to Zamu and join the army that will march to the relief of Zandikar."

Ornol the Waves had finished his palines and was drinking our wine. He swallowed, the wine wet on his lips above the beard, and he said, "I told you. Prince Glycas and his army are invincible. The relief expedition from Zamu is destroyed."

Pur Naghan sagged back, stunned.

The hubbub increased. All now understood the peril.

"The rasts can march from Zandikar and take Zamu. The cities will fall, one after the other. And from Zamu they can march across the base of the peninsula of Fenzerdrin, across the River of Golden Smiles."

"Aye!" shouted others. "And before them lies Holy Sanurkazz itself!"

Holy Sanurkazz!

The sea journey is laborious, and in the name of Zair rightfully so, for in this lies devious protection to Sanurkazz, the chief city and holy place of Zairia. But Prince Glycas and the Grodnims would be marching with their invincible army, securing their rear with Zandikar and Zamu, marching across the base of Fenzerdrin, to attack Holy Sanurkazz from the land.

It was a plan that would work, given the deadly tool with which King Genod would put it into operation.

And—a few dwaburs east of Sanurkazz lay Felteraz, beautiful Felteraz, the home of Mayfwy, the widow of my oar-comrade Zorg. I had done much, I would do much more, to protect Mayfwy.

I stood up and glared upon that ruffianly assembly, all gesticulating and arguing and thumping balled fist into hand, and gradually they looked up at me and fell silent.

"We sail for Zandikar. It is there we can smash the kleeshes of Grodnims. We sail with the dawn."

I walked away. I did not wish anyone to argue, for I would have had to cut him down.

Later I sought out Pur Naghan.

"Yes, Dak, I agree with the plan. I would dearly love to go to Zamu for— But you are right. We must stop them at Zandikar."

"Yes, Pur Naghan."

"You are a hard man. Yet the men follow you. Sometimes I find that strange. I am proud but I am also realistic. I know a man—it is to me the men should look, as an avowed Krozair; but I follow you as willingly as they. It is passing strange."

"If you wish to lead, Pur Naghan, I would not challenge you."

He favored me with a strange, lopsided look.

"I believe you. I do not understand; but I believe. No, Dak, I am content as we are. You are a leader. You have the yrium. As for me—" He moved his right hand in a vague gesture, quite at variance with the man I knew he was. "I am Pur Naghan. I have not yet become Nazhan. I sometimes wonder if I ever will, and the thought of being Pur Zana-zhan eludes me."

"Naghan is an ancient and honored name on Kregen." I thought to snap his spine erect. "And in Zandikar, by Zair, you should find deeds worthy to place the 'Z' in your name."

"Aye, Dak," he said, his hand clenching. "Aye!"

It should be remarked here that the Zairians in their use of that truly honorable name of Naghan softened the hated "G" into a "J."

The coaster skipper, Ornol the Waves, had not put into Zandikar. He had picked up trade among the islands as was the custom and was making for Zimuzz. That great fortress-city, home of the Krozairs of Zimuzz, had been bypassed by Prince Glycas. Before we sailed on the next morning one of his men was brought to me by Duhrra. This man bore the short straight bow of the inner sea; but I noted it was somewhat longer than the average, and stouter. He appeared limber and with the bowman's strength of shoulder, and his nut-brown face creased up around his eyes. This was Dolan the Bow, and I knew a man did not achieve that soubriquet unless he had earned it.

"This man, Dolan the Bow, wishes to go with us," said Duhrra.

There was no need for hesitation. I guessed he was a Zandikarese from the bow. "You are very welcome, Dolan."

He smiled. He did not say much. But Seg would have got on with him, I knew that, and it cheered me.

As we pulled steadily past the last headland of the Island of Pliks we saw considerable activity in the coaster's camp.

Dolan the Bow smiled again, his face crinkling up like a crickle nut, brown and rosy and filled with goodness. "Ornol will be disappointed," he said. Then, "I will show you the safe channels into Zandikar. The Grodnims have wrecked many swifters there, Zair be praised."

We bore on along our easterly and four days later we pulled in for our last landfall. Dolan had suggested we should make a long hard night's pulling of it for the final leg, bypassing the usual stopover. I agreed. Swifters' speeds vary and we had the argenters, subject to the fickle vagaries of the winds if we did not tow them, and the journey was long and tiring. The two men we had chosen to skipper the argenters had by now sufficient experience of them to be able to handle them with reasonable confidence. They were bluff sea dogs of the Eye of the World, and they did not mince their words when they accosted me on the quarterdeck of *Crimson Magodont*.

The gist of their argument was that they would be perfectly happy to drive in, in a swifter; but they doubted the capacity of the argenters. I told them they would be towed for the last dangerous part; but they remained somewhat reluctant.

"These argenters will not answer among the islands off Zandikar Bay. And there will be Magdaggian swifters."

"Aye," I said. "There will be. We shall tow you. I shall tow you, Robko, and Pur Naghan will tow you, Mulviko. If we run into Grodnim swifters we may have to cast you off to fight them. I shall expect you to sail in. We will protect you. It is spoken."

They wanted to argue. They saw my face. They did not argue.

As they went over the stern ladder I called to them.

"Be of good cheer. Before the twin suns rise on the morrow we shall be in Zandikar. Then, my friends, the real business will start."

Passing a towing line at night is always a tricky business; but the wind was with us, a fresh westerly, and I wished to conserve the strength of the oarsmen as much as possible.

Under the canopy of stars we sailed toward the east and Zandikar and ventured into the waters patrolled by the hostile swifters of Magdag. Occasionally the dark bulk of islands occulted the horizon stars. The Twins rose, revolving eternally one about the other. They bear many and many a name over Kregen; but the Twins is what I call them most of the time. They cast down too much light for our purpose; but Notor Zan was not on duty this fateful night, and we ghosted along with our wind under the stars, with the chuckle of water passing down the side and the creak of wood and the slap of blocks an unheard accompaniment to our progress.

Dolan stood with me on the quarterdeck. When the closer time came he would go forward with the prijikers and signal helm orders from there. I, who had sailed impudently through the waters of the approaches to Brest on the unending duties of blockade, felt the keen zest of a seaman's enthusiasm for a difficult technical task. I had no doubts. We would go through.

The time came for the tow ropes to be passed. The difficult evolution went through without a hitch, save that young Obdinon squashed a finger and cried out and was instantly told to stopper his black-fanged winespout, the silly fambly, and get on with the job.

Following my orders against just such a need, we had saved the hated green flags of the swifters. Colors are seldom flown at nighttime; but I had the green bent on and ready, just in case. The sense of mystery and taut-breathing expectancy held us all as we pulled on, going cautiously across the dark and subtly moving expanse of the sea. Night birds passed above us on wings that sighed and creaked like unoiled hinges. We watched the stars and the black bulks of islands and not an eye closed in any of the five ships.

We turned starboard, to the south, and soon the sweet scent of gregarians on the air told us the fabled gregarian groves of Zandikar drew near. Now all those superb groves would lie under the callous hand of Grodnim. We pulled on.

Deeply into the southern shore bites the Bay of Zandikar. South we rowed, and we watched the horizon for the first hint of a long, low predatory outline to tell us we faced instant action and perilous encounter.

When, as I had half known we must, we saw that lean rakish shape of a Magdaggian swifter, I own I felt a stab of disappointment. Magdaggian swifter captains do not relish night sailing. But Zandikar lay under siege, and Prince Glycas was there, I knew, and mayhap the king, also, waited impatiently in the encirclement for the city's fall. Perhaps Gafard, the King's Striker, was there. I felt no recognizable emotions over an encounter with him. I knew very well—or thought I did—what I was going to do to this genius king Genod when I caught up with him, this insane war genius who had callously murdered my daughter Velia.

"Weng da!" bellowed the challenge across the dark sea.

The pink and golden moonlight misted visibility and made accurate vision tricky. I lifted a speaking trumpet to my lips and shouted back.

"Strigic of Grodno! With supplies for the prince."

For a mur or two the silence hung; then the voice from the low quarterdeck of the swifter answered.

"Lahal and Remberee! Grodno go with you."

"And with you. Remberee."

The leem shadow vanished under the moons' shadows and was gone.

Water chuckled from our ram and passed rippling down our sides. The oars rose and fell, rose and fell. We glided on.

"I have sailed to Zandikar before," said Nath the Slinger. "But not by night. But it cannot be too far now. Dolan the Bow guides us well—for an archer."

"I pray Zair," said Fazhan, my ship-Hikdar. "I pray the argenter does not pull the bitts out entire."

"She will not and we will reach the Pharos," I said.

"The lantern will be dark."

"Aye."

A hand ran aft from the forecastle and panted up at us.

"Dolan says three ulms only, Dak."

"Good."

One ulm passed. I swear, although an ulm is about one and a half thousand yards, that ulm seemed to me the full five miles of a dwabur. A shape appeared ahead, athwart our course. One minute the sea shimmered empty in the moons-light; the next the lean, low ram-tipped bulk of a swifter lay there, broadside on, beginning to turn. The water frothed pink from the oars.

The hail, this time, was sharper, harsher.

"Weng da! Heave to! Back water!"

Now the swifter's bronze rostrum swung into line. I yelled

back, *"Strigic of Grodno!* Do not make us lose way—we are towing supplies for the prince."

"Orders of the king! Heave to!"

"But—"

"Heave to or we ram!"

Chapter Thirteen

———◆———

"Ram! Ram! Ram!"

"By Zair!" I said, enraged. "The cramph means business."

Moons-light shone on the bronze ram of the swifter ahead. She had turned directly into line. Her oars lifted and remained level. Our own wings continued to beat on. Once again the hail reached us, and this time there was no mistaking the violence of the shout, the decision taken on that swifter's quarterdeck.

"Your last chance! Heave to or we smash your oars!"

I said to Fazhan, "Signal *Neemu* to come up. Drop the tow."

"Quidang," he said and was off.

I shouted in a voice pitched just to reach Pugnarses Ob-Eye, our oar-master. "At the signal, Pugnarses. Full speed."

We had a few murs' grace. The swifter ahead, two-banked, fast, designed for patrol and scouting duty, still held her oars leveled. In those few murs we must cast off our tow and hope *Neemu* would be able to retrieve it and continue to haul in the argenter. I turned sharply as Vax said, a little loudly, "Tow rope cast off."

"Now, Pugnarses! Full speed! Use ol' snake!"

We all heard the drumbeat abruptly break, then rattle, and finally settle into a swift and demanding rhythm. The oars thrashed and for a moment I thought they'd lost it, and the rhythm had been broken—and then the blades churned the water all in line, level as though on tracks, and through our feet we felt the forward surge of *Crimson Magodont*, that exhilarating onward bounding like a zorca under a rider careering wildly across the plains.

122

"Starboard!" I yelled at the helm-Deldars.

The forecastle of the swifter moved out of line with the swifter ahead. I could see in the moons-shimmer her oars quiver and then fall, all together, and in a macabre counterpointing echo to our own I heard her drum rattling out the time.

For a couple of ship-lengths we surged on and then I shouted to the helm-Deldars to bring her back to larboard. *Crimson Magodont* was of that style of swifter short-coupled, chunky, yet still retaining the long, lean lines of a true galley. She could turn on a golden zo-piece. Her starboard bank continued to pull frenziedly and we could hear through the ship noises the sharp sizzling cracking of whips, the shouts of that hateful word, "Grak! Grak!"

The larboard bank dug into the sea. *Crimson Magodont* spun.

Then every oar smashed into the water, the blades churning, and we leaped as a leem leaps.

"Ram! Ram! Ram!"

We took the Grodnim swifter on his larboard bow. We smashed and bashed down a full third of his length. The pandemonium racketed to the starlit sky. I did not think what was going on among the slave benches of the swifter. We spun into the Magdaggian and we wrecked a third of his oar banks and then we eased a fraction to starboard and so ripped away the remaining two thirds before we turned to free our own blades.

The noises from the Magdaggian obliterated the shouts and yells of our men. Those noises spurted hideously against the pink moons' glow. I held my jaw shut and I could feel my teeth punching into my gums, aching.

Arrows arched. The varters let fly. There would be no boarding. The Magdaggian drifted past, wallowing, one entire wing ripped from her. And here came Pur Naghan! Driving on astern of us, flanking our argenter, he bored on with all his oars thrashing. *Pearl* surged ahead, like a living lance. Her rostrum struck the Grodnim swifter full abeam. The rending sounds as bronze sheared through wood racketed out. What they were doing aboard the argenter that *Pearl* towed I could only guess; but she went clear. *Neemu* had the first argenter's tow secured and was going ahead. I stared around in the moon-drenched darkness.

There were no other Magdaggian swifters I could see.

"She's going!" said Vax. He held the hilt of the Krozair longsword and I knew the young devil longed to dive into the fray and use that terrible weapon.

The Magdaggian wallowed lower.

I said, "We cannot abandon the Zairians in her. Take us alongside."

It was madness. It was folly. The arrangements had been that if attacked *Neemu* would take our tow and *Pearl* would continue on. Nothing had been agreed about what to do with any victim of our ram.

Fazhan said, "If there are other rasts of Grodnims abroad, the noise—"

"Aye, Fazhan. We must be quick."

We were quick. I commanded a crew of men who had been Renders, who knew how to raise a swifter's oar-slaves against their masters. We ravened onto the Magdaggian's deck. Arrows flew. I saw Dolan the Bow calmly shooting from the forecastle, sending shaft after shaft in a flowing rhythm into the ranks of the Greens clustered to receive us. And from the quarterdeck, Nath the Slinger flung his deadly pebbles and lozenges of lead, trying to match the speed of Dolan. I drew the Ghittawrer blade and led the charge that cleared the foeman's quarterdeck. *Pearl* had ripped a ghastly hole in her side. She'd be gone very quickly.

The slaves were pouring up from below, waving their chains, raving. Many a poor devil had been crushed by his loom, those who had neither the knack nor the knowledge to duck under as the cruel ram smashed down in the diekplus. Our successful diekplus had smashed the first third of the larboard banks; from these benches came very few slaves to join us.

There were plenty of others, though, to join us as we dispatched the Grodnims. The freed slaves leaped joyously onto the deck of *Crimson Magodont* as the Magdaggian swifter sank in a smother of bubbles and breaking timbers.

Neemu and *Pearl*, with their tows, had pulled ahead. We followed. I let the scenes of frantic joy blossom on the gangway and forecastle as we pulled in toward the Pharos of Zandikar. Any man released from slavery at the oars of a swifter from Magdag is entitled to leap and cavort, to shout and bellow, to scream his thanks to Zair.

Many men fell to their knees and banged their heads against the flibre of the deck in utter thankfulness.

I did not tell them, yet, that they were entering a city under siege, that when their bellies hungered they might yearn for the slop and the onions and crusts thrown to them on their oar benches.

Among the sailors of the inner sea the saying runs: "Easier a thorn-ivy bush than the Ten Dikars."

Truly, the maze of channels threading between islands and headlands leading to Zandikar are confusing and treacherous. We had come safely through, thanks to Dolan, and now as we reached a broad calm stretch of water the city rose beyond and patrolling Zandikarese swifters nosed in to attack. Now we did not mind heaving to. The swifters assured themselves we were who we said we were—well, who some of us said we were at the time—and very soon scenes of riotous joy spread from our decks and gangways to the battlements and quays and streets of the city itself. Torches burst into flame as hundreds of emaciated people flooded down to the quayside. I frowned.

"Fazhan—anchor out in the center of the harbor."

He nodded. If that lot of crazed and starving people sought to board we'd be done for. Now the mergem carried in the argenter proved of inestimable value. The ship carried enough to supply Zandikar's normal population for a season, possibly; the war and the siege had wasted away at the people; they would not starve now. As well, the chipalines would prove of great value, and the corps of crossbowmen welcomed the bolts. I told my men to let the provender go freely into the town. No one could argue over that. If it flushed out rasts, I would be happy.

The Todalpheme who lived in a small stone house by the Pharos came aboard and were fervent in their thanks. These wise men who monitor the tides are protected by protocol and taboo from any harm from another man. They were indignant that in the siege Prince Glycas had starved them, too. We gave them mergem and sent them away, praising Zair, although I was coming around to a belief that the Todalpheme of Kregen worshiped no gods that other men worshiped.

The rasts were duly smoked out.

They came aboard on the following morning as the business of unloading went on. Fazhan and Pur Naghan had organized well. Boats pulled to the shore loaded with sacks of mergem. On the shore my men and the harbor cross-

bowmen formed a hollow space with the crowds pressing outside, shouting and screaming and raising a dust and tearing
their clothes—but all with joy upon their faces. The sacks
were handed out. All who asked were supplied. Any boats
approaching the argenter were kept off with pointed bows. I
knew that everyone of besieged Zandikar would eat well
this night, even if it was only mergem, and no one would
starve.

The rasts came aboard, having shouted their own importance, and strode across my quarterdeck.

I looked at them. Oh, yes, they were familiar faces, their
bearing was familiar, their manner of talk. I did not know
one of them; but I knew what they were. I had met in my
career on Kregen aragorn, slave-masters, overlords, great no-
bles, masters of the arena, Manhunters—in them there
glowed the same self-satisfied and preening knowledge of
self-importance.

Their leader, a Ztrom,* flashily attired, adorned with
many gems and much gold lace, carrying a Krozair longsword, marched up and I noticed how his right hand crossed
his body among the ruffles of gold lace to rest on the hilt of
the longsword. There was no doubt in my mind he could use
the weapon, gold lace or no damned gold lace. His face, as
I have indicated, showed quite clearly he was for Cottmer's
Caverns when he was at last put where he belonged. I own
I am intemperate in these matters.

"You are the master of this vessel?"

"Aye."

"You address me as *jernu*. We shall take over now."

A commotion began on the quay. Armed men, mail clad,
bearing swords, were beating the crowds away. They were
not overlords of Magdag; but from their demeanor and behavior they might just as well have been.

There were six of them on the deck, and in their boat
alongside waited a dozen more with the oarsmen. I turned
back as the Ztrom snarled—very adept at snarling are these
people, the high and mighty of the land—and drew that great
sword. The blade flamed before my eyes.

"Cramph! Answer when I speak to you!"

---

*Ztrom: Zairian equivalent to Strom—count. The Grodnim title
is Grom.

I said, "If you do not send your men away, you are a dead man." I did not draw my sword.

He gaped. He just did not believe his own two ears.

"Rast! I am Ztrom Nalgre ti Zharan, the king's councillor! All Zandikar does my bidding."

He swung about to order his five men. He stopped, abruptly, as a foolish ponsho stops when it butts its head against the wall. A dozen archers, and chief among them Dolan the Bow, drew their shafts back and held their glittering points upon the five.

I said, very gently, "Secure them all. Bind them well. You, so-called Ztrom Nalgre, I do not believe are a Ztrom at all. You are a jumped-up devil, a sewer-rat, a cramph who steals food from starving people."

He struck then.

I slid the blow, stepped forward, and drove my fist into his belly. As he fell I took the sword away. One thing was for sure, he was no Krozair.

He retched on the deck. I stirred him with my toe. "Him, too." Over the side the men in the boat were shouting. I walked calmly to the bulwark by the quarterdeck varter. A rock rested in its beckets, like a shot garland, ready. I leaned over and shouted.

"Go back to your cramph of a king and tell him if he touches the food for the people, his Ztrom Nalgre ti Zharan will be hanged in the sight of all. Schtump!"

One of the fools loosed a shaft. I moved my head. The arrow flew past. They just did not believe anyone would cross them, deny their wishes. They had to be shown, and shown quickly. I lifted the rock over my head in both hands, bent back, and then catapulted forward. It was a nice little throw. It took the bottom out of their damned boat.

The next second they were in the water all caterwauling and yelling. We threw ropes down to them and hauled them out and ran them down to the lock-up, a tiny brig that soon filled, and so we had to chain them down on the gangway of the thalamite tier. Some of the oarsmen swam for the quay. I bellowed my words after them. But so far, not so good. I had not done enough.

"No more sacks ashore, Fazhan—tell the argenter."

Very soon thereafter the crowds dispersed. The mail-clad riders dismounted and stood watching us. They were mostly apim, although a few Rapas and Fristles were in evidence.

The walls of the city here along the shore remained firm, at the least. Those walls, all of a grayish-white stone, gleamed under the suns. The jumbled red roofs of the city, the spires and towers, clustered behind those walls. I could not see the farther walls inland; but that was where the siege was going on. If this newly appointed king did not make haste my own patience would be gone. I had not come here to act as a Palinter, important though that was.

Pur Naghan had himself rowed across and came up onto my quarterdeck looking somewhat perturbed. I reassured him.

"Normally a central rationing point is essential. But we have so much mergem that is not necessary. We must get the people and the warriors fed and back in health and heart again. I must get up to the walls."

"This king will not take kindly to you."

"I've already taken unkindly toward him."

"Aye," said Pur Naghan, who was a man not averse to a hearty chuckle, like any Zairian. "I had noticed."

Presently a party of sectrixmen cantered down to the jetty and there was a deal of flag-waving and shortly thereafter a fat and sweaty Pallan was rowed out to us. He stood on the quarterdeck, panting, patting his face with a lace kerchief—prepared to be nasty, as I saw, or prepared to be reasonable, as I hoped.

"The king bids you attend him in his palace at once."

"Does he not inquire if Ztrom Nalgre is dead or alive?"

"Let us not be hasty—give me your name and style and we may talk."

This fellow's robes, although originally of red, were so smothered in gold and silver and chains and tassels as to make of him a tapestried object of ridicule. He wore a wide flat red cap, much folded, sporting feathers secured by a gold buckle. He stood and I let him stand. His pouched eyes rolled in search of a chair.

"You are the visitor in my ship. It is for you to open the pappattu."

His fat and greasy face regarded me and I saw something there I had not expected. He made a small bow.

"I am Nath Zavarin, Battle Pallan to his most exalted and puissant majister, King Zenno, on whom—"

"Yes," I said with coarse rudeness. "I suppose like any jumped-up paktun he adorns himself with titles." I own I knew I smiled away inside my skull like any fambly—me, Dray Prescot, badgering on about amassing titles! But there are ways and ways. I had decided what to say. "I am Dak of Zairia."

That said all and said nothing, and this Zavarin knew it.

"Do you think, Captain Dak, I might sit down? I am not as agile as once I was, and my stomach makes inordinate demands on my ib, demands I own I fail more often than not."

"You will oblige me by stepping into my cabin, where I have a wine I would value your opinion of, Pallan Zavarin."

Again he cocked those poached-egg eyes at me. He nodded. So we went into my cabin and he tasted the wine and pronounced it better than the muck they were forced to drink since all the best had been consumed and that cramph prince Glycas sat down before their walls. He had seen that a period of bargaining lay ahead. As to the idiot Ztrom Nalgre ti Zharan, well, Zavarin said, the king valued him as a fighting-man. That was all.

"And you?"

He smiled and drank, wiping his plump and shining purple mouth most prettily. I had expected to have to browbeat the messenger from the king. That I was not doing so pleased me.

"I served King Zinna long and faithfully. I know Zandikar. The treasury—" Here he shrugged in a way more French than I cared for. "The king holds that with his own key. His paktuns took the important offices after Zinna was murdered—I mean, after King Zenno ascended the Roo* Throne. And for me—" Here he turned his lace-ruffled wrist meaningfully. "I know much of Zendikar. I am Battle Pallan, and thankful for it."

I knew what he meant. Battle Pallan is a somewhat lurid way of saying Secretary of War, or War Minister. I imagined Nath Zavarin had not willingly wielded a sword in earnest for many a long season. King Zenno had him under his thumb, and could draw on his knowledge of the city's ways, and, confirming my judgment, Zavarin said he personally enjoyed much popular support.

"The people must be fed," I said. "That is the first concern. The king's men have interfered with that."

*Roo. Eleven.

"I agree. But the king holds all food under his hand."

"I agree that to be a sound method. We have mergem and to spare. I do not wish the king to charge money for my food."

"The king will do what the king wishes."

"And you remember King Zinna?"

He drank again, and I saw he did so to stop himself from speaking what boiled in his brain. He was very frightened. That was clear, yet he put a bold front on it, this fat ridiculous man.

To divert that line of talk, he swallowed and said, "I am fat. I have always been fat. It is a misfortune. In time of siege it can be fatal."

"Yes. I can see that."

"The king commanded me to bring you to his palace."

"Did he not stop to think why his onker of a Ztrom had not done so?"

This fat Pallan looked at me, searchingly, and made a face, and said, "The king did not expect him to. Ztrom Nalgre was under instructions to slay you and take all the food."

"I am not surprised."

"You are a strange man. There is artillery on the walls. They could sink your ships."

"Seawater and mergem can be mixed. I do not recommend it."

The sweat shone on the immense rounded surfaces of his cheeks. He wiped his brow again, taking the red hat off and laying it upon the table. His fear had ebbed a little and puzzlement was beginning to replace the terror and revive his natural instincts. A political, this man. To my own vast surprise I found I was quite taking to him, fat and all.

"Now that King Zenno rules in Zandikar," I said, "and the people live under his hand, you must be proud that you assisted him to ascend the Roo Throne. I could understand that."

He sucked in his breath, making all his chins wobble and his cheeks abruptly hollow. "I did not strike a blow or instigate one scheme against Zinna!"

"Ah!" I said.

He glared at me. "You are a cunning rogue, Dak of Nowhere. I cannot open my heart to you. Suppose Zenno uses his arts of torment upon you?"

I ignored that unwholesome thought and put questions to him about the siege and the state of the city. The Grodnims had put in three major set-piece assaults and had been beaten off, each time with increasing difficulty. The food we had brought would put heart and strength into the soldiery. Yes, said Zavarin, the soldiers were loyal, for they fought for the city. As for Zenno and his pack of hangers-on, they made hay while the sun shone. Paktuns, employed to fight for hire, they had seized the throne and now lolled about in comfort. It was all one to them. The siege went on apace, for they wished to appear to keep faith with the city. In the paktun philosophy of living in the immediate present, they took what they could and let tomorrow take care of itself. "But—" said Zavarin, and paused, sweating.

I finished it for him. "But this cramph Zenno—or Starkey the Wersting—will strike a bargain. As soon as he feels safe from the anger of the people, or as soon as they are beaten down enough, he will parley with Glycas, and open the gates. Yes, it all fits."

Anyone of the city—citizen, sailor, soldier, refugee farmer—who attempted to object to Zenno was mercilessly put down by the mail-clad riders. A siege existed outside the walls, and a reign of terror swept everyone within.

I felt this conversation had not gone far enough. From my first vague stirrings of schemes I had now reached certain conclusions. They seem obvious enough now. But this was like wading through a marsh by the light of Drig's Lanterns, every step treacherous. This Nath Zavarin caught my drift at once when I said, "How many men has Zenno in his pocket? His paktuns?"

"You must understand, I am no party to anything. My concern is for Zandikar."

"I do not blame you if you do not trust me."

"You are unknown. You arrive with five ships and food, you chain up the king's councillor, you utter threats, you do not treat the King's Pallan with deference—not that I am concerned over that. You act as though you were a king yourself, or a Krozair."

"A Krozair of Zamu commands one of my vessels."

His puffy lips let his little gasp past with a plop.

He recovered himself. "We of Zandikar are famous for our archers, our gregarians, the difficulty of finding the open channels, and for the songs made by King Zonar five hundred seasons ago. Although I daresay it was the king's minstrel, in truth, who composed them. But—we have no Red Brotherhood. I have often desired an Order of Crimson Chivalry. I love Zandikar."

Before I could speak, for I own this fat and no longer ridiculous man's words affected me, Duhrra burst in. I swung about in the chair prepared to be nasty to him; I saw his face and with a flung word to Zavarin walked quickly into the side cabin with Duhrra. He was excited and annoyed, twitching his steel hand.

"Master! Duh—I do not know—"

"Spit it out!"

"It is Vax! The young onker! He dived over the side and has swum to the city. We saw him, running past the ship sheds into Zandikar."

Chapter Fourteen

Of a conspiracy and of Queen Miam

The news appalled me.

"The young rip said he wanted to come here because of a girl, master. I did not think— But we are anchored here, doing nothing."

"We do a great deal, Duhrra. But this makes me think I must do a great deal more."

"Aye, master." He did not know Vax was my son, Jaidur of Valka, Prince of Vallia. But I was sure he guessed that there was something more in my feelings for the rascal Vax than he could fathom out.

I went back to Zavarin. He saw instantly my changed demeanor. I did not beat about the bush.

"I do not suppose I could bribe you, Zavarin. I would try if I thought I could. I do not do so. That is not because I do not wish to insult you, but because I recognize your integrity. I tell you, Battle Pallan, the Grodnims will not be cheaply allowed to walk into Zandikar. There is more at stake here than the foul lives of a bunch of miserable foresworn paktuns. If this Zenno has to die, then he will die, and none to mourn him. Go back and tell him what you will. But add that if he makes a pact with Glycas and opens the gates, he will surely be hanged and drawn and quartered. This is not a threat. It is a statement of fact."

He rose, somewhat unsteadily, and groped for his hat.

"I will tell him what I think politic, Dak, as you know. I think I shall embroider a little. By Zair! I think I shall enjoy

133

something for the first time since— Well, he will be working himself into a rage. I must go. I thank you for the wine."

"Take a few bottles with you. See my Palinter. I have work to do—and when I call on you, Nath Zavarin, I shall expect a prompt and purposeful answer."

"Aye, Dak of Nowhere. I think you will."

The crafty old devil went out. He didn't commit himself. In his position, of course, no man would.

The suns beat down on deck with soothing warmth. The day would be fine. Men worked about the ship and some slaves had been released to haul up buckets of seawater and hurl them down over their fellow-sufferers on the oar tiers. Everything appeared normal, for Fazhan ran a taut ship. I looked at the four other vessels and saw nothing that appeared amiss. Well, I was going to alter all that. I shouted at Zavarin as he walked along the gangway bearing two bottles clasped to his pudgy chest.

"Wait a moment, Zavarin." To Duhrra I said, "Bring out that fine golden mixing bowl we took from that Grodnim broad ship—the one with a captain like a vosk."

"He pulls with the thalamites now," said Duhrra, and ran back to the treasure storehouse by my cabin. When he reappeared the golden krater winked and gleamed magnificently under the suns. I held it out to Zavarin.

"Give this to the king with my compliments. Your man will handle it with care, for it is of great value. Tell him we can discuss the disposal of the mergem as soon as he wishes."

Zavarin's jaw did not drop. But he looked at me as though I had been stricken with lunacy before his eyes.

"I do not understand, Dak."

"There are reasons. Three hundred, you said? A fair force to keep order."

He shuffled his feet as his men took the wine and the krater away to his boat. He lifted that bulbous face of his and looked at me straight. In a low voice, he said, "We have had news, secret and sure, that Prince Glycas intends a fresh assault on the day after tomorrow. We have spies. The day will be hard for the soldiers. That might be a time of opportunity."

I said, "I cannot wait all that long."

He looked bewildered.

Then, "The people believe Zenno, for I have told them he

is the true king, after Zinna. This I was forced to do. They will fight well against the cramphs of Grodnim."

"They had best do so, for the sake of Zair. Take this fool Ztrom Nalgre with you, him and his men. I do not want them fouling my ship."

By the time the Ztrom and his party were over the side, and Zavarin with much wheezing and puffing had been manipulated down the ladder and into his boat, I had prepared. Dolan the Bow had said, simply, that he would follow me. He knew Zandikar. It was his home. Duhrra and Nath the Slinger would not be dissuaded. So I told Fazhan to take over. He would consult with Pur Naghan and the other skippers. They were to do nothing until they heard from me. With that the four of us went down into a boat with half a dozen sacks of mergem and pulled gently across to an inconspicuous wharf that Dolan said was used to ship in animals' intestines used in tanning.

The city appeared to slumber in the warmth. The gray-white stone and the red roofs glittered with a soft brightness, many points of light combining into a brilliant yet gentle haze. Towers and domes floated over the golden mist of colored rooftops. On one of the arms of land embracing the outer harbor the massy pile of the seaward fortress, the Helmet of Buzro, glowered down, and yet for all its vastness and grimness appearing only a fairy-story castle, flaunting its red banners against the blue radiant sky.

"He said she lived in a place called the Ivory Pavilion," said Duhrra. "And her name is Miam."

"The Ivory Pavilion," said Dolan as the boat touched the stones and I leaped out. "Yes, I know it. A palace on a hill, grand and beautiful. Of course, I have never been inside."

"You will today," I said.

I felt the hurt in me. My son could tell these things to Duhrra, who was his oar-comrade, things he had not cared to tell me. Why should he? I was a comrade and his captain. Had he known I was his father he'd no doubt have told me with a sword.

We had been through adventures together and I knew, from what Duhrra told me, that Vax regarded me as a good captain and a good warrior. He had, so Duhrra said, a high regard for me and my prowess. As to affection, that remained an imponderable. Duhrra suggested that Vax went in some awe of me, which thought I heartily disliked. Yet he copied my ways, I knew, and that must mean something.

The look Nath Zavarin had given me as I lifted and handed the golden krater across had apprised me that he recognized my strength. Duhrra had strained a trifle to lift the golden mixing bowl. Perhaps Vax merely envied my strength. Well, if he was his father's son he'd inherit that, particularly after his stint as an oar-slave. I tried not to think of Delia, for I had harsh and unpleasant duties to perform. The little girl we had taken from the sacrifice to the Beast of Time remained fast shut in the ship, a source of temptation to lecherous sailormen. I had barely spoken to her, save to learn her name was Lena, and that she came from a dusty and forgotten little village called Fairmont and that she was truly a virgin and thus fit for the sacrifice. I had told her that so long as she remained in my care she would preserve her virginity. She was illiterate, as so many poor folk are on Kregen, and was dizzied by her experiences, having been snatched away from home and stripped and loaded with gold and gems and lashed to a sacrificial stone block.

I must think only of the fate of my son Vax. The streets and alleys of Zandikar wound and wended in the usual haphazard way of most Zairian cities. Dolan led on, carrying one sack of mergem. Duhrra and I carried two each, and Nath the last. The houses showed evidence of the siege, many having been pulled down to provide stones for the catapults and varters. A dim murmur like bees in summer rose from the inland walls where the siege went on. Nothing much would happen until the onslaught of the day after tomorrow. The suns burned down and we padded swiftly along the cobbles, mounting between tall gray-white walls to the hill on which stood the Ivory Pavilion.

No one paid us much attention. We looked desperate enough, Zair knows, and the mergem we had earlier landed was now being mixed and cooked and eaten.

Parties of soldiers were rarely to be seen; they would be moving between their billets and the walls. A fire began past the hill and we could see only the ugly waft of black smoke.

Presently, panting, Dolan said, "The gate ahead."

A long gray-white wall flanked the top of the hill. Much vegetation grew beyond, and flowers depended over the walls. The gate was barred by iron, and inside a man carrying a spear stood guard. To him I said: "Llahal, dom. We have food. Let us in."

"Who are you?" He squinted, and turned his head in the bronze helmet from side to side to get us in his sights.

"Friends of the lady Miam."

He sniffed at this; but Duhrra let his two sacks down and extended his left hand with a golden zo-piece glittering on his palm. "We come in friendship with food. Do you think your mistress would be pleased if you sent us away?"

"You are from the king?"

Duhrra opened his mouth and I said, harshly, "No. Open up."

As I had chanced the throw, so that remark reassured him and the iron gate swung open. We were escorted by three guards, men who all looked unfit for fighting on the walls, up to the palace. Whatever happened, I was prepared to wait until I saw Vax. What happened then would depend on how he had fared.

A considerable bustle had just subsided as we entered the porticoed way and marched into the antechamber. The place was a palace right enough, with quantities of marble and statuary, a fine balcony, tall windows, and with intricate mosaic pavements cool beneath the feet. I dumped my mergem down as a tall, elegant middle-aged man stepped toward us. He bore the stamp of authority; but he bore it as though he understood the responsibilities as well as the perquisites of power. His robes were of white, dazzlingly clean, trimmed with red, and at his side he bore a scabbarded, golden-hilted sword of the solaik variety.* He looked to be a man I could talk to.

He said, "What do you here? We have naught left—"

I said, "I have brought food for the lady Miam. I would like to see her. I am Dak. There is not much time."

He bristled; but he was intrigued. At his side a shadow moved and a man stepped out. He was a dwarf. He had a finely shaped head; his body was stunted but strong. He held a crossbow and the quarrel centered on my heart. His clothes were an incongruous mixture of reds and golds and mail.

I looked at him. I did not smile. He was deadly.

"No one comes here for the lady Miam without a ready explanation."

---

*Solaik: threequarter.

"Send for her and you will have your explanation."

He hesitated and the dwarf cocked an eye up at him.

"You say you have food for her? You are from the ships in the outer harbor?"

"Yes and yes. Now—whoever you are—send for the lady Miam, or I shall have to penetrate the women's quarters myself."

A nasty scene was spared by the entrance of the lady herself.

I have seen many beautiful women. I have seen many women lovely in the sight of men. There have never been any women to match in beauty my Delia—and, at this time, my dear dead Velia—yet this Miam bore herself with beauty and with demureness, her color high, her long braided brown hair glowing in the lights through the tall windows. Her white dress moved over her bosom with an agitation I did not connect with my arrival. The young devil! Mind you, I was wrong. . . .

"I am here, Uncle—if this fierce warrior is Dak—"

"He is, niece."

"Then all is well. I have had news—such strange news— that Zeg wishes to be remembered to me. That is all."

I gaped. Zeg! Zeg was the Krozair name my son Segnik had taken, and he would fight anyone who added the "nik" to his name. I looked at Miam and I burst out—I, cunning, canny, cynical old Dray Prescot—I burst out like any callow youth, "But I thought it was Vax—"

She laughed. The tinkling, refreshing, superbly rational sound drove all the cobwebs away. Naught of evil could live in the sound of that laugh.

"Vax brings me news of his brother and assures himself I am safe. He does not love me."

"In that, my lady Miam," said Vax's voice as he stepped into the room, "you wound me sore. You do me an injustice."

"Oh, yes, Vax, I know! But you know what I mean."

"I do." He looked at me and had the grace to look suddenly confused and to look away sharply.

I said, "If you do anything stupid like this again I'll tan your backside myself."

He bridled. His hand whipped to his sword—to that superb Krozair brand I had given him. His lips pouted into a sullen droop, and his head snapped erect, his eyes glaring.

"Do not think I would not, Vax, for all you are a great warrior now. Anyway, you did not think to bring any food for your friends."

"Come, come," said this Miam's uncle, spreading his arms. "It seems we are all friends here. Let us have no more unpleasantness." He turned to me. "Lahal, Dak. I am Janri Zunderhan, Roz of Thoth Zeresh. We have no wine fit to drink to offer; but we have a little tea left."

"Tea is better than wine any day. I will have supplies brought up from my ships. I thank you for your hospitality. Lahal, Roz Janri."

He looked quite pleased, no doubt expecting some uncouth paktunlike remark. We all went into an inner room and soon the confusion was sorted out. This lady Miam was the great-granddaughter of the dead king Zinna. She hadn't even been a gleam in her father's eye when last I'd been in the Eye of the World. She and Zeg, I gathered, had more or less decided to set up house together. He was off corsairing on the inner sea and she was shut up here under siege. I had an idea Zeg didn't know that. And here was I, sitting with one son and talking about another son, and denied all the heart-burning words I longed to speak!

I turned the conversation the way I wanted it to go and learned that Nath Zavarin was regarded not as a fat fool, or even a fat hulu, but as a man desirous of serving his city who was being forced into bad company and bad ways. He was regarded as being clever to have avoided being chopped by Starkey the Wersting. They had a finicky disability over calling Starkey King Zenno in this household. Miam could prove an embarrassment to the new king and she was being kept very quiet indeed. All the fit men were off fighting on the walls; but Roz Janri indicated that all here would fight to the death for the lady Miam and himself. Her relations were all dead, as were his. They had found good comradeship in each other's company.

The dwarf, Roko, bustled about bossing the serving wenches, waddling along on his big flat feet, a cheery, cheeky little man, a man to be reckoned with. I thought the back of his neck must ache with the continual looking up he must do. Still, I supposed he was used to it.

It is not necessary for me to go into every tiny detail of my movements over the rest of that day, or of the plans I formulated almost bur by bur. Everything fell into place with an ease I would have regarded with great suspicion had the circumstances been other than they were. I wondered—true—if the veiled hand of Zena Iztar could be found in this. She could well be manipulating events. Zair knew, she, like the Star Lords, had power enough.

The upshot was that, as the Suns of Scorpio sank in floods of fire and the first stars began to shine out, my sealeems quit the ships in silence, their weapons muffled. The very first star of Kregen was a huge blue fat beauty, shining with a calm refulgence, extraordinarily bright at this time of the approach of orbits. This is the planet Kregans call Soothe. Soothe is one of the more famous Goddesses of Love, and her voluptuous representation is found all over Kregen, in apim or numin, sylvie or Fristle form, in any of the shapes of females most admired by lecherous men. Soothe and Venus—if this was mere coincidence, I did not know.

So, under the fat blue gleam of Soothe, and with the first of the hurtling moons skating low over the city, we rowed ashore. Everything went as Roz Janri and Nath Zavarin had promised.

The paktuns, once they had overcome their initial astonishment, fought well. But there could be no time for finesse. They must be subjugated as fast as possible. In the event as we roared into the Palace of Fragrant Incense—and trust the Zandikarese to call a palace that was a fortress by a pretty name like that!—and drove the paktuns yelling before us, we overcame their last resistance and still over a hundred yet lived.

Starkey the Wersting, who called himself King Zenno, was bundled out of bed and the sylvie with him fled, shrieking in her nakedness. We showed him a bloodstained blade and he was very agreeable to do our bidding. I say *our*, for Vax and Dolan and little Roko were most active in this coup.

Nath Zavarin came a-running and panting in his slippers, pulling on a grave black hat of judgment, gasping with the effort of hauling his bulk into the High Hall of the palace. Torches lit the scene. Roz Janri and his people were there. The paktuns, disarmed, stood under guard along the side to watch. The scene held the starkness of midnight drama, when men are tumbled out of beds, and heads roll, and the fortunes of crowns and cities change hands.

I said to King Zenno, "You may stay as Starkey the Wersting and fight for us for hire. You may take a boat and seek to escape with such of your men as will go with you. You may not communicate with Prince Glycas." He glared at me—this sharp-faced, vicious rast of a fellow—hardly crediting what had hit him. "Or, of course," I said, off-handedly, "if you wish you can be killed, here and now."

"I would dislike that," said Roz Janri. "Yet it might be the most sensible course."

"I am not a man of blood," I said. I saw Vax and the little smile on his face, and through the sudden chill that smote me, I struggled on. Truth to tell, that knowing little smile on my son's face made up my mind for me. "You will sail in a boat. Tonight," I had to add, out of shame or out of a desire to convince Vax I did not know. "I am not a man of blood; but I am not averse to spilling kleesh blood. You have an abundance of that, Starkey."

"May Zagri rot your eyes and liver!" this King Zenno that was burst out, raving. He spit, choking, demented. "May Zagri cave in your chest and soften your sinews, and—" He would have gone on, for Zagri is a most powerful demon and well-called on in times of stress and cursing. Vax stepped up and rapped the fellow on the nose enough to tap his claret, and said words in the ex-king's ear that hauled him up all standing.

"If you say another word, cramph, I shall pull your vile tongue out by the roots."

Everyone there in the High Hall knew that this young tearaway, Vax Neemusbane, meant what he said.

And this was my son.

Just about then strong parties of soldiers from the walls rushed in, demanding to know if the Grodnims had struck here. I realized they had a good reason to suspect the possibility that attack could reach the city-center, and I filed the information away. With a great yell I jumped up—most blasphemously—onto the Roo Throne. The throne is called this because the city is protected by the Ten Dikars, and the throne is the eleventh to guard all. Had Kregen possessed in addition to its seven moons and two suns one more heavenly body, then on the nights of blackness it would not be Notor Zan which rose but Notor Roo.

"Listen to me, soldiers!" I bellowed in my old sailorman's voice. "The usurping dog of a paktun is thrown down! The true lineage is preserved. Queen Miam rules now in Zandikar!

She will lead us all to victory against the Zair-forsaken Grodnims!"

The expected outburst of cheering broke against the high ceiling rafters. If it was grossly unfair to saddle a young girl with such onerous responsibility, I can plead only that I was in a hurry and that, anyway, she was the great-granddaughter of a king and must therefore expect to be thrust forward into positions of power and peril.

"Queen Miam, the true daughter of Zandikar, leads us on to victory!" I glared down on them as they waved their swords on high. Zair knows, I have stared down on mighty warriors waving their swords and shouting the "Hai Jikai!" often enough. But, this time, they were not shouting for me. I rather liked that. "Glycas and his Green cramphs will never take the city! We have food! We have strong arms! And we have a queen! Every man will do his duty for her sake." Then I bashed it out just as in the old days, the old vicious intemperate Dray Prescot bawling his head off to a ravening pack of fighting-men. "And if any man seeks to cower away and fail the queen I'll have his entrails out for varter springs!"

They howled at this, indignant at any suggestion impuning their honor. I quieted them down and told them to pass the word to their comrades on the walls. I mentioned that we had brought food into the city more than once, just to keep the notion fresh in their minds.

The scenes of wild enthusiasm persisted as individual warriors, convinced that they were orators, shouted their own promises of valor and what they would do to the Grodnims. Later in a small inner sanctum we conspirators met. The ex-king Zenno and those men of his who wished to go with him had been taken down and stuffed into a small boat, to be dispatched. I did not think he would seek to join Glycas. Glycas, the mean cramph, would probably hand him over to his tormentors for failing his plans.

In the small room with the lamps burning nastily with cheap mineral oil, for all the samphron oil was long since used, Miam said to me, "I do not know if I should thank you or hate you."

"Many people hate me, Miam. And a few thank me. You must make up your own mind."

Vax bristled; but he was really coming to know my ways, and understood I spoke like this to make the girl see reality.

I bore down the other speakers. We had a great deal to do and precious little time in which to do it. I gave orders. Oh, yes, I gave orders. At first there was opposition, then reluctance, finally acceptance, and, at the end, enthusiasm. I felt the trace of tiredness. But tiredness is a sin, especially when there is a queen to make safe on her throne and a city to save—quite apart from all my own concerns, by Vox!

Early the next day I rode one of Roz Janri's sectrixes on a circuit of the walls. They had stood up to the bombardment very well. The besieging army dug their trenches close and closer. Areas of tents covered the ground where the gregarian groves had been ruthlessly cut down. Smoke lifted from many cooking fires. The infantry out there dug and sweated and the cavalry trotted about looking magnificent. There was no chance of the solid phalanx in this siege. Or, so the Grodnims would think, not until the final breach had been made. Then the cavalry on which they doted would charge in and the mercenary warriors earn their hire. I studied everything carefully. I had had a few burs' sleep; tonight I would sleep longer. Now there was work to do.

At a spot in the inland walls where the cracks looked ominously gaping and the wall had been hastily repaired I stopped.

"Here, Roz Janri," I said. "This is the breach. Here they will break in. This is the spot."

Chapter Fifteen

The Siege of Zandikar: I.

A Savapim holds the gate

Everyone who could be spared worked. We had the oar-slaves up out of the swifters and set them to hauling stones. I took pains to make sure houses of architectural merit were not knocked down; but we took ruthlessly all the stone we needed. What I proposed was no new thing; but if the Grodnims persisted in their high-handed arrogant ways it was a winner. Or so I hoped. I will not go into every detail of the Siege of Zandikar. A great song was made, later, and in it, among a wealth of stirring anecdote and much jikai, the part of Dak is mentioned with some frequency. But, so are the names of all my comrades who labored with me.

If the stunning ease with which we had disposed of King Zenno indicated to me that Zena Iztar had taken a hand, I did not think she gave overt assistance during the stages of the siege itself. Sieges are fascinating. They are also quite horrible. The horror detracts, for my part, from the fascination.

On this day, the day before we expected the next grand assault, an event occurred that made me once again revile the ethics of some paktuns, and to realize afresh that other and greater forces invested effort in this siege, despite the aloofness of Zena Iztar.

Some seventy or so paktuns had elected to stay and fight with us, acknowledging the sovereignty of Queen Miam. Her coronation would have to wait, as Queen Thyllis had waited for hers in distant Hamal. I had ridden over to see how the work on the new wall progressed—as I say, the plan was simple—when a rider flogging his sectrix roared up and screamed of an attack on the western wall. We all turned at once and spurred to the point threatened.

When I say *all* I mean the officers and staff with me and the escort; not the workers. Also, I bellowed at a likely Jiktar who seemed a smart man, to go personally to the eastern wall and check that the attack on the west was no feint.

We arrived at a scene of dust being kicked up as men battled in the open space between the houses and the walls. The Grodnims had scaled the walls and dropped down, howling in triumph, intending to reach the nearest gate and fling it wide to their waiting cavalry. A Hikdar, one ear missing and his helmet a blaze of blood, husked out that some of the paktuns on duty here on the walls had betrayed their post. It had been concerted. The Grodnims would have dropped down and opened the gate. But, said the Hikdar, a warrior appeared and halted them in time for reinforcements to come up and engage them. I looked at the fight, and my anger against the treacherous paktuns was overlaid by conjectures. Surely, I thought, surely I shall see a man who, although I will not recognize him, I will know?

With wild and savage shouts the men with me drove in on the fight. The dust smoked higher. Men on the walls were shooting outward, and I knew they were keeping back the cavalry out there, which were impatient to spur in through the gate they expected to open at any moment. Shrill shrieks rent the air. Dust and blood cloyed on the tongue. Then I was in among the melee and slicing down with my Ghittawrer brand at a red-faced fellow trying to degut my sectrix. With him disposed of, I was faced with others trying to reach the inner gateway. We smashed and bashed around in the dust for a space, working them in to the wall and finally ringing them and so disposing of them. They were of the Green.

When it was all over I mounted to the wall and looked out.

A mass of infantry was drawn up in impeccable formation out of varter shot. Cavalry moved impatiently between, the green pennons flying, the glitter of their war harness brave under the suns. Back and forth they cantered, their swords breaking the light into fragments of radiance, back and forth. But the gate would not open for them this day.

"Bring me the warrior who stemmed the first attack."

"Quidang!"

He was brought. I stood on the ramparts of the wall and looked at him. Yes, I did not know him; but I knew him.

He wore mail, which altered his appearance; but over that he wore russet hunting leathers, and leather harness, and a short red cape descended from his shoulders—just to be on the safe side, I assumed. He wore a helmet over his coif. His face was hard, dedicated, filled with the knowledge that had been denied me.

I did not say, "Happy Swinging, dom." I wished to preserve my anonymity here. I said, instead, "You wear a strange sword, dom." I held out my hand.

He was a proud, fine upstanding young man, as they all are. I heard him say something, half under his breath. He spoke in English. "They warned me," he said, half complaining, half rueful. "They are barbarians. But this fellow—not even a thank you."

I held out my hand and I did not move a muscle of my face.

He let me take the sword. Again I held in my grip a real Savanti sword. Oh, well, it is a long time ago, now, and we were in the middle of a siege and I was in dire trouble with just about everyone except the new comrades with me in the siege. I held the sword and felt that marvelous grip and the subtle cunning of the blade, the balance, the sensuous feel of it, and abruptly I thrust it back at the Savapim.

"You have our deepest thanks for your assistance. The gate would have been lost but for you."

He looked at me oddly.

"You do not ask me where I come from?" He, also, had swallowed one of those magically scientific genetic pills and so could converse in languages. He spoke well and forthrightly.

"No." I eyed him severely. "Do you intend to stay to fight at our side in this siege?"

"Who are you? You speak as though—but, no. . . . Who are you?"

"I am Dak."

"And I am Irwin."

I wanted him off-balance. "Irwin what?"

"Irwin W. Emerson, Junior." He shut his mouth, suddenly. Then, slowly, he said, "The name must mean nothing to you, Dak."

"No," I said. "I do not know anyone of that name. But it is a fine name. It has a ring to it. You come from a proud line."

"I like to think so."

Duhrra loomed up then, still cleaning the blood off his blade, to tell me a Deldar was dying and wanted to talk to me before he went. I nodded to Irwin and clattered down off the wall.

Ord-Deldar Nalgre the Twist lay in the dust, his left arm missing, the rags stuffed to his stump stained in a most ugly and dreadful way, his face white and drawn. I knelt at his side.

"Dak—Dak—I'm on the way to the Ice Floes."

"You are a fine helm-Deldar, Nalgre. I trust you. As an ord-Deldar you have standing; but I would like you to go as a Hikdar. Does that please you?"

His face regarded me gravely, white and suffering, yet understanding I did this thing for myself, not for him.

"Thank you, Dak. In the brotherhood I was known . . . I shall go to Sicce as a Hikdar. It may help me there."

"You will sit on the right hand of Zair in the radiance of Zim. Take the Hikdar and lift up your head."

"Zair—" he said.

He died then, and I hoped being a Hikdar would aid him as he sought his seat among the millions sitting on the right hand of Zair in the radiance of Zim.

When I looked up to the walls again, Irwin had gone.

After that we split the paktuns up, as I should have done in the first instance, and set them with men we knew to be loyal, so that thereafter we had no further trouble from the mercenaries.

The interesting fact was that all the diffs among the paktuns had elected to go with Starkey, the ex-king Zenno. They were as well aware as anyone else of the dislike for diffs of the apims of Zairia. Among the Grodnims who had scaled the wall in treachery there had been a goodly number of diffs. It had been a Chulik who had taken Deldar Nalgre's arm off and broken up his insides as he fell. I saw an omen in this, something very obvious, really. The Savanti, those awesomely mysterious supermen of Aphrasöe, the Swinging

City, had sent one of their agents, a Savapim, to assist in the vital moment when the city might have fallen. I knew this Irwin would moments before he landed here in Zandikar have been in Aphrasöe, being briefed for his mission. The Savanti had sent a Savapim to protect apims from diffs in a tavern brawl in Ruathytu. They must be taking like hands in many places of Kregen. I decided then that the Savanti were definitely fighting on the side of Zairia against Grodnim. This cheered me.

Our preparations continued. As I worked and checked and issued orders so I kept a lookout for Irwin, and sent messengers to find him. They returned empty-handed. I fancied he'd been whisked back to Aphrasöe—wherever the Swinging City was—his mission accomplished.

I could have used a regiment of Savapims just then.

Any fighting lord could use Savapims at any time.

That night we had the inner wall, built in a square against the weakened outer main wall, up to head height. "We must build high enough so the cramphs of sectrix-men cannot jump the wall," I said. "All night we go on. Use wood for the walkways. Tell the archers to get some rest. They will be vital on the morrow." My orders were obeyed.

I made a point of asking Miam, who was now Queen Miam and a trifle dazed by events, to dress in her finest and to ride a milk-white sectrix—an unusual beast, an albino and somewhat weak—around the fortifications with me. She made a superb impression on the minds of all who saw her and the rolling thunders of the acclamations followed wherever she rode.

I told my son Vax to go always with her, her protector and my liaison with her. He was not loath. I liked, more than I had expected I would, his devotion to his brother Zeg. Most young men in a like situation would have tried a little pelft on their own behalf—or almost most. But Vax, I saw with pleasure, had imbibed notions of honor from somewhere as well as from his mother Delia. They had not come from me. The Krzy had most probably done a thorough job on him before my Apushniad had driven him away in shame from their august ranks.

When the lambent blue spark of Soothe appeared in the sky and the stars twinkled out to follow, we began to take down the outer wall. The job had to be done with exquisite care, so that nothing showed from the outside. We carried the blocks of stone and raised our new inner wall with them. The inside of the main wall was eaten away, leaving a mere shell. Zandikar, as I have indicated, was just the same luxury-loving, indolent, careless city as most any other of Zairia. Her people had built a good strong wall around the city and then had knocked off to sing and dance and quaff wine. Well, if Zandikar had been my city I'd have had three walls, at the least, knowing the damned Grodnims as I did.

Sanurkazz boasts seven walls in places.

The Twins rose and by their light we labored on.

Vax, rubbing his eyes, found me bellowing in a whisper, a most fearsome way of putting hell into a workman, on the inner wall. "Dak," he said. "The queen would like to talk to you."

"That's the style, Naghan," I said to the naked workman who was guiding a new block into place, whip in hand, directing the line of sweating naked slaves. "You're building well."

Then I went with Vax to the Palace of Fragrant Incense to crave an audience with the new queen. I put it like that, for the whole affair smacked of the grotesque to me, so conscious of the ravening leems of Grodnims beyond the walls. She received me in all dignity, superbly clad, wearing a crown, the torches smoking down, lighting in flickers of orange fire the gems and the gold and silver, the feathers and silks. Yet she looked imposing and grand in an altogether human way. I could not smile at her; but I did not, at the least, frown overmuch.

She did not waste time on preamble.

"On the morrow we beat the accursed Grodnims. I am the queen of Zandikar. I shall stand on the wall so that all my people may see me."

"And get a quarrel through your pretty head."

She flushed. "If Zair so ordains—"

"Zair would ordain nothing so foolish. Anyway, I forbid it."

"You! I am the queen!"

"You are the queen. You have responsibilities. If you are slain, and slain so stupidly, what will happen to the loyalties of your people? Could you care for them then? And what of my—what of this man Zeg you prate of? Is he Vax's brother or not? Would you spite him?"

Her face blazed scarlet in the torchlight. She fumbled with the golden mortil-crowned staff, the emblem of Zandikar.

"You speak boldly, my lord."

"You call me jernu. I am Dak."

Nath Zavarin, sweating and panting as usual, coughed and said, "It would be meet for the queen, whose name be revered, to witness the fight from afar. But in a place where her loyal warriors may easily see her and be heartened thereby."

"Find such a place out of arrow range," I said. "And I agree. But not otherwise."

Vax scowled at me.

I said to him, straight, "If the queen is slain, what do you say to Zeg?"

He did not answer, but the hilt of the Krozair longsword went down under his fist and the scabbarded blade licked up, most evilly.

Then it was the turn of Roz Janri to be dissuaded from putting himself in the forefront of the fight. I had to be brisk; but I think he understood. I gave him the task, which he accepted, of bringing up our cavalry at the decisive moment. I did not tell him I devoutly wanted the thing done before our sectrixmen became involved. The poor beasts were very tottery on their legs, and a lot had been eaten so that our chivalry was weak.

In the crowd waiting in the High Hall it was easy enough to pick out Dolan. I said to him, "Dolan the Bow. Will you pick me out a bow—a good one—and a couple of quivers? I think I will join you at the breastworks tomorrow. I have not shot of late. I need practice."

"Right gladly, Dak."

He was as good as his word and produced a good specimen of a Zandikarese bow. I know Seg Segutorio would have smiled quietly had he seen it, for it was a puny thing compared to the great Lohvian longbow. But to my misfortune we had not a single one of the Kregen-famous Bowmen of Loh in our ranks. There was a small corps of the red-headed archers from Loh with Glycas. I gave orders about them, not caring overmuch for what we would have to do to them. The main missile strength of the Grodnims lay in their sextets of crossbowmen, working to the system I had devised so long ago in the warrens of Magdag for my old vosk-skulls.

Many imponderables must weigh down one side or the other of the balances; success or failure would be a composite of many disparate events. We did all we could to weigh down our balance pan to success and then, after that, it would be up to Oxkalin the Blind Spirit.

The vacuum in the higher commands left by the evanishment of the paktuns meant that my own men could be employed, and there were many good men of Zandikar. Zena Iztar had aided us then; in the siege and more particularly in this coming fight we were on our own. Unless the Savanti decided to send more Savapims, of course.

It seems scarcely necessary to mention that all day the incoming hails of warning went up. The boys on the ramparts would beat their gongs and the yells of "Incoming" would shriek out and we'd all either duck or stand stoically until the spinning chunk of rock had found a billet inside the walls. The Grodnims used catapults for this general mayhem; they had gigantic varters designed as wall-smashers lined up against the point of the breach. The catapult throws with a high trajectory; the varter with its ballistalike action hurls with a low trajectory. Glycas had at least six fine engines, not as sophisticated as the gros-varters of Vallia; but big. They played on the point that both Glycas and I had selected as the point d'appui, and very early in the morning the first stones tumbled free and the evident cracks, visible from outside, widened to let daylight through.

A great cry went up from the assembled Greens.

We let them have an answering cheer.

To an impartial observer the decisive moment would clearly be seen to be at hand. As the suns shone down and the varters clanged, huge chunks of rock smote into the wall. Stones chipped into dust and fractured and fell. The parapet vanished. The wall slumped as rock after rock smashed in. Fountains of rock chips burst upward, the dust made men cough, the noise clanged on and on. During the morning two feint attacks were made and disposed of. By midday Glycas had moved all his wall-smashing artillery to this decisive point. From the vantage point of a tower I could see the solid square of his infantry paraded, ready to deal with any sortie we might make. His cavalry waited in long glittering lines. The mercenaries seethed in clumps of never-ending movement. And still the wall was bitten away.

Our work from the inside brought all down with a run as

the suns began their decline. We would have a long afternoon.

So thorough was the work and so sudden the final collapse
that the way was just practicable for sectrixes. But, like a
sensible commander, Glycas sent in his mercenaries first.

Howling and shrieking, waving their weapons, they
poured forward in a living tide of destruction. At least, they
no doubt assumed themselves to be a living tide of destruction. We Zandikarese archers looked forward with calm
confidence to the ebbing of the tide.

Breaking down the walls of fortresses usually takes time
and patience with the battering engines. Glycas had picked
this weak spot and now he saw victory opening before his
eyes, all in a day. The trumpets of Grodno pealed triumphantly above the charging masses as they clambered the
low breach and flung themselves forward into Zandikar.

The lethal horizontal sleeting death awaited them.

They pitched to the dust in droves. The high triumphant
yells turned in an instant to shrieks of agony. Remorselessly
the shafts drove in. More and more men clambered up only
to jump down to death. When they stopped coming we
clambered up in our turn, and jeered and taunted the massive ranks of the Magdaggian army poised beyond artillery
range, and yet still and not moving. The cavalry made one
or two feint advances, and then retired. The varters took up
their bashing work and the catapults began to sing.

Within that square of stone the ground ran red. A shambles in very truth we had created. Now was a time for
clearing up and rebuilding the wall more strongly. The resistance to the Green attack had been decisive, without the
desperate touch-and-go incoherence of the previous assaults,
and it marked a new stage in the siege operations.

That was the end of the beginning of the Siege of Zandikar.

Chapter Sixteen

The Siege of Zandikar: II.

I am short with a Krozair of Zy

I do not wish to dwell overlong on the Siege of Zandikar. From that day of the slaughter of the mercenaries in our trap it was a constant round of repelling assaults, of building walls, of keeping awake, of siting varters and catapults in advantageous positions, of keeping alert, of making the rounds, of maintaining morale, and of building walls and building more walls.

Twice more we caught the damned overlords of Magdag in the same trap. The second occasion was noteworthy, for we used a gateway, the gateway on the east of the city called the Gate of Happy Absolution. Instead of building a square of stone walls within the gate, we build a wedge shape, a triangle of death. One of the paktuns whom I felt I could trust repeated the exploit of his compatriot and betrayed us to Prince Glycas. He must have spoken eloquently for he returned with a bag of golden oars and news that all would go as planned.

So the shooting intensified around the Gate of Happy Absolution, and then as the return shots came in, slackened and died away. We began a great shout within the battlemented towers of the gate, shrieking for: "Shafts! Shafts! In the name of Zair bring up arrows!"

From a rearward tower I watched. This time Queen Miam stood to watch with me, and Vax hovered nearby. We saw the mailed chivalry of Magdag trampling up, proud in their power. They formed before the gate as infantry ran

in with hide-covered rams and smashed in the gate. We had
removed the good stout bars and replaced them with old
beams that were artfully sawed and cut so as to break with a
satisfyingly genuine rending of wood. The gates flew open.
The siege-batterers leaped clear and, heads down, swords
pointed, the overlords of Magdag charged in through the gateway.

We repeated the previous two performances, and this
time we drove our shafts with such an unholy joy that the
hated overlords themselves felt each biting head.

After the second trap we had discovered the bodies of
several Bowmen of Loh scattered on the rubble where they
had been shot attempting to shoot in the attack. So I had a
great Lohvian longbow to my hand. I could not stop myself from going down among the archers of Zandikar and
showing them what a Lohvian longbow might do in the
hands of a skilled archer.

The cruel walled funnel is a bitter trick. The riders rode
boldly through and charged on, yelling, and so the farther
they galloped the more compressed became their ranks. Confusion set in; they recoiled and men toppled from the high
saddles; they shrieked now as the arrow storm sleeted upon
them. The bow of Zandikar may be only puny compared to
a longbow; but it could wreak havoc in these conditions
where the shafts sped so thickly that the air appeared filled
with their whispering death.

Sectrixes screamed and thrashed their six hooves. Men
fell, to be battered to death. The arrows never ceased their
spiteful singing. A handful of mail-clad riders reached the
far wall and I leaped up, placing the longbow down carefully first, and so went at them on a level with the Ghittawrer blade. It was all pulsing and high excitement for a
space; we beat down those who had survived to reach the
end of the funnel. They died unable to fall, so great was the
crush. Men in the gate towers shot into the riders from above,
and great stones fell upon them.

By the time we closed the doors and put the stout beams
back and walled up the aperture, my men were stripping off
the harnesses and mail, leading away those animals that had
not died, carting off the corpses, collecting up the weapons.
Details of archers with wicker baskets picked up all the
shafts. The broken ones would go back to the factories,
where women and girls would reshaft the old heads, fletch

"The gates flew open."

them with the feathers of the Zandikarese chiuli bird—a deep plum color, most pleasing.

"How long can they sustain such losses?" demanded Janri.

"As long as this genius king orders them to," I said.

Thereafter we maintained a careful watch upon all the walls and beat back sudden attacks, and prepared for grand assaults, and listened for mining operations, and so caved in two tunnels upon the diggers beneath. The siege went on.

I said to the Queen's Council in the High Hall of the Palace of Fragrant Incense, "I think Glycas will try an assault from the sea."

Pur Naghan ti Perzefn, a Krozair of Zamu, leaped up, declaring, "Let me take the swifters and ram and sink them!"

He was given permission and took as well as our three swifters the four smaller swifters the Zandikarese navy had left of those they had begun the war with. On the day the expected attack developed the land operations demanded my attention. Pur Naghan reported in as the suns sank, smiling, blood-spattered, grim, and triumphant.

"We lost *Zandikar Mortil* and *Pearl*," he said. "But we took four and sank three. It was most satisfactory."

"Hai Jikai, Pur Naghan," I said. "The queen will see you."

Queen Miam, without much prompting from me, expressed her thanks to Naghan, and then said, "We feel it right in the jikai that you should be known henceforth as Pur Nazhan. Do you agree?"

"I agree, Majestrix. I thank you."

So Pur Naghan became Pur Nazhan. I was happy for him. The siege went on.

All this time, for all the power I could exercise in the city, I did not forget that, in truth, I was in deep dire trouble in the areas of life that mattered to me. I might bellow orders and send mailed men scampering into action, whip my blade down and so order the release of five hundred deadly shafts from the bows of the Zandikarese archers, I might chivy and cajole and instruct a queen, I might be imperious with Pallans and Chuktars; all the time I remembered I was Apushniad, outlawed from the Krozairs, debarred from returning home to Valka and my Delia.

And, too, I had most certainly not lost sight of my business with King Genod—the genius at war, who had murdered my daughter Velia—and with Gafard, the King's Striker, the Sea Zhantil, Velia's lawful husband.

We knew these two were not with the army of Prince Glycas, and we surmised they were with the Grodnim army of the west, pressing on along the coast, and no doubt thinking about encircling Zimuzz, if they had not already taken that great city. Genod's plans had worked so far, for he had enclosed various centers of resistance as in a nutcracker. We could afford no assistance to Zimuzz. They could not aid us. Zamu, the next great fortress-city to the east, would be the next to fall, and then it would be Sanurkazz—Holy Zanurkazz.

Pur Naghan—or, as he now was, Pur Nazhan—had scored a notable victory and as a result four of the Ten Dikars were open again. This was small consolation to us, penned in Zandikar, for we knew there were no forces at sea waiting to come to our relief. We were wrong in our suppositions, and the correction of our misapprehension came one dark night before She of the Veils rose to flood down in fuzzy pink moonlight. I had just completed one of my eternal circuits of the walls and had thrown myself down in the small room of the palace I used for sleeping when I could. Duhrra snored noisily in the corner. Roko, Roz Janri's dwarf and chief chamberlain, bustled in flat-footed with a girl bearing a torch. He shook me awake.

"A messenger, Dak—a Krozair of Zy! Just come in."

Rubbing the sleep from my eyes and girding on my weapons, I followed Roko to the High Hall. I let Duhrra slumber on. The hall held a narrow cold look and a feeling of meanness in the night as I entered. Numbers of the high officials of Zandikar waited whispering together. The queen arrived shortly afterward and seated herself on the throne, with her handmaidens and guards about her. She had not yet adopted any throne step pets; I'd had experience of neemus and Manhounds and chavonths; I wondered what she might choose when she understood more of her power. Her small elfin face looked sleep-drugged, as did all our faces, for the sake of Zair; but we knew what we were about.

I was prepared for the newly arrived Krozair of Zy to take one look at me and to whip out his sword and bellow, "Pur Dray! The Lord of Strombor! Apushniad!"

But he did not. I did not know him. He looked a proper Krozair, well-built, erect, clear-eyed, with the fierce upthrusting moustaches of a Zairian. We ex-oar-slaves had grown most of our hair back by now, although still somewhat straggly. I looked at the coruscating device on his white surcoat, that hubless spoked wheel within the circle, and I own I felt an ache. He was all business.

"The Grodnims take all along the southern coast to the west. Zy still holds. We have been bypassed. Zimuzz is about to fall. The king is there, may Zair torture him eternally."

I stood half in the shadows at the foot of the throne steps and I did not speak. Roz Janri stood at the side of the throne, a tall and dignified figure, and he it was who said, "You are welcome here, Pur Trazhan. Have you no good news for us in our darkness?"

This Pur Trazhan smiled. "Yes, Roz Janri. I am bid to tell you that the city of Zandikar must not fall. You must hold. An army is on the way. It is a strange army, for it is composed of men who do not swear by Zair, and who fly in the air in metal boats."

There was a quick buzz of surprised comment and conjecture at this startling news. I felt a glow all over my limbs. But—of course!—it was Vax who started forward, eagerly, calling excitedly above the hubbub.

"This army of men who fly in the air, Pur Trazhan! Are they of Vallia?"

"Yes, they are." Trazhan was clearly not quite sure what to call Vax or how to address him.

"Then, by Vox!" exclaimed Vax. "It is Prince Drak and the army of Vallia, with fliers! It must be!"

"That is so," said Trazhan. "It is Pur Drak, a great and renowned Krozair of Zy, who leads them. Long have we awaited their coming, since the Call went out. And now Pur Drak has answered the Azhurad, as he promised he would when he was given permission to go to his home country, wherever that may be."

So that explained what Drak had been up to. My eldest son had answered the Call in a typically Prescot way. He'd sought help from his own. I learned that he had brought vollers by sea from Vallia, vollers loaned by his grandfather, the emperor of Vallia. They had sailed all the way in those marvelous race-built galleons of Vallia. I knew why they'd sailed and not flown. The same reason had prompted Rees and Chido to sail and not fly. And, it also meant that the emperor, the tightfisted old devil, had not spared first-quality vollers. He'd let his grandson have those fliers bought from Hamal and therefore suspect, not safe for long aerial journeys. I did not blame Drak for sailing. This way, he brought all his men and fliers into the Eye of the World instead of leaving them stranded all the way across the Sunset Sea, the Klackadrin, the Hostile Territories and The Stratemsk. Soon, he would be here and we would be relieved!

"I have heard of Pur Drak," said Roz Janri. A frown crossed his face. "He is the son of Pur Dray Prescot, the Lord of Strombor, once the most renowned Krozair upon the Eye of the World. But that was long ago. Now this Pur Dray is Apushniad. It is common knowledge."

Vax did not say a word.

"Certainly Pur Drak is the son of this accursed Dray Prescot," said Trazhan. "But Pur Drak is an honorable man. He is well worthy of the trust of the Krozairs of Zy and the respect of ordinary men."

That was a clear and chilling reminder that Krozairs were not as ordinary men. Nor are they, by Zair!

Vax did not step forward, and his voice was almost steady, as he said, "And his brother, Pur Zeg?"

"At sea, upholding the glory of Zair for the Brotherhood."

"Do these two brothers speak of their father?"

I heard a noise and saw that Duhrra had rolled into the High Hall, yawning. He gazed around sleepily, puffy faced.

"They say of him that what has been ordained is just." Trazhan peered into the shadows at Vax. "Why do you ask?"

Before Vax could answer, I said, "Do these brothers hate their father as much as this young man Vax hates his?"

I own I wanted to stir it a bit, feeling vicious; but at the same time I wanted to know the answer to my question.

Trazhan put his left fist onto his sword-hilt. "Who can say? They do not speak of him to others. He is Apushniad and therefore less than nothing. Now I would like to rest, and—"

"You are, Pur Trazhan," I said, trying not to sound too cold, "I trust, empowered to stay and fight with us?"

"Well—" he began.

I admit, with only a little shame, that I wanted to hit out. I owed the Krozairs nothing at this time. One of their number was fair game. They had done what they had done to me, and I was going to prove them wrong; but right now I would make this high and mighty Krzy wriggle a trifle.

"After all, Pur Trazhan, you have admitted that Zy is not attacked, therefore your duty cannot lie there. Zimuzz is about to fall, and so to go there is useless. Here in Zandikar we successfully resist the cramphs of Grodnims and will never surrender. I would have thought a man's duties lay here. Particularly if he happened to be a Krozair of Zy."

He took a half-step, and paused, and peered belligerently into the shadows.

"Who are you, who speaks thus to a Krozair?"

"I am Dak."

"Dak," he said. "I think the name is familiar—"

"Oh, there may not be as many Daks as there are Naths and Naghans and Nalgres; but there are a lot of us." I shot the last words at him like crossbow bolts. "Are you staying or not?"

He swung his head at me, and then looked at Miam.

"Who is this man?"

Before she could speak I took a pace or two forward and planted myself in front of him. I glared at him evilly.

"You may be a Krozair of Zy. But you address the queen of Zandikar in a proper and respectful fashion, or, by Zair, I'll pull your damned tongue out!"

He wanted to start on me, then and there, but I would have none of it, not with poor Miam looking on distressed, and I backed away and bellowed for everyone to calm down. I finished, "And this great and famous Krozair, this Pur Trazhan, will be happy to stay with us and fight for Zandikar. He will honor his oaths. And, anyway," I ended with gruesome levity, "we have ample mergem to feed him and his crew."

After the fuss Trazhan agreed to stay and fight. Of course, poor devil, he could do nothing else.

Mind you, I was not altogether happy about his performance. No Krozair I had known, for all we put no great store by kings and queens, would have flung up so brusque a question to a young queen like that. To some fabled Queen of Pain, perhaps . . . Maybe standards were lowered in the Krozairs and they were being forced to let in a rabble. I own I can be most arrogant when it comes to those people and institutions in which I put value. But I had, at this time, still to remember I was an outcast, Apushniad.

Just before we all left about our business, Queen Miam lifted her hand and we fell silent. She said something that was unnecessary and yet, at the same time, it made me feel warm to her. I figured Zeg would be a lucky fellow.·

"This man Dak," said Queen Miam, "is the heart and soul of the defense of Zandikar."

While it was not true—well, not altogether—it had a pretty ring.

I bowed to her, and from somewhere deep in the bowels of Cottmer's Caverns, I shouldn't wonder, I scraped up a smile for her. She smiled back, so I fancy my face indicated some grotesque caricature of a smile.

"We shall hold Zandikar, Queen Miam," I said.

"I wish to talk to you privately for a crooked mur, Dak."

By "a crooked mur" Kregans mean a minute or two. We went into the small luxurious room behind the throne where she might doff the heavy robes of state and the crown and mortil-headed staff. When she was clad again in her own simple white gown she shooed out her handmaidens and turned to me, one hand to her breast.

"I wanted to ask you, dear Dak, of your goodness, not to mention that you know Prince Zeg, Pur Zeg, to be Vax's brother. It is a thing he would not wish known."

"Why does he not ask me himself?"

"I rather think he does not realize what he has let slip to you as to me. If it is known . . . Is this Dray Prescot, then, so terrible a beast?"

I looked at her in the lamplight. She was beautiful. I felt for Zeg, not envying him, but feeling happy for him.

"I think most young men take against their fathers at some time in their lives. When they mature they come to a better understanding—if their fathers are worthy, of course."

"You do not answer my question."

"No, Miam, I do not. I do not know. I have heard stories. I think it probable he was unjustly stricken from the Order of Krozairs of Zy. To be made Apushniad is a horrible fate."

"Oh, yes!"

"He will be your father-in-law. I think you would make any man see reason."

We passed a few more words, then she said, "And you will remember about Vax and his father?" and I said, "I will," and we parted.

The name of Dray Prescot, the Lord of Strombor, once Krozair of Zy, could arouse as passionate a response here in Zairia as it inevitably could in Green Grodnim. I had heard more than one old soldier curse and spit and say he wished to Zair that Pur Dray was not Apushniad and could be in the forefront of the battle with his comrades in his accustomed place in the struggle against the rasts of Magdaggians. I was there, although they did not know it. But I wanted the Krozairs to reinstate me, not so that I might fight on for Zair, but so that I might go home to Delia.

A few days after that, as the siege dragged on, Prince Glycas tried a new trick. He must have had the beasts landed from animal-carrying broad ships and driven them up to the walls of the city. The shouts rose as the lookouts bellowed the warning in a misty dawnlight. By the time I was up onto my favorite tower, midway along the inland wall, with a fine varter to hand, I could see the mists coiling and rising, emerald and ruby in the mingled streaming light of Antares, see the huge rounded backs of the turiloths as they waddled ponderously on, see the crowding warriors following these mammoth beasts.

"Turiloths! Turiloths!" the cries racketed about.

Archers began to shoot. Their shafts simply bounced off the hard gray upper hide. The turiloth's hide altered in color to a dark bottle-green along the sides and a grayish streak ran along the belly. Sixteen legs has a turiloth, with six tusks and a tendrilous mass of whiplash tails, a veritable forest of Kataki tails at his rear. He has an enormous underslung mouth equipped with suitable fangery, and he is keen scented and he has three hearts. If this description sounds familiar, I assure you it is; the turiloth of Turismond is very similar to the boloth of Chem. I had fought a boloth on a notable occasion in the arena. Now we had twenty of these gigantic beasts plodding along to smash down the gates of Zandikar and let the swarm of warriors in to an orgy of destruction.

A paktun near me screamed, "All is lost! We are doomed! Doomed!" He scrambled madly down the tower, running away. The panic spread.

Chapter Seventeen

The Siege of Zandikar: III.

The turiloths attack

"We are doomed!"

The cries rang out with chilling panic through the early morning mists.

This was a time for instant action.

There was no time to shaft the running paktun, as he deserved. I grabbed a varterist by the ear and ran him up to his engine. I hurled both of us at the windlass, for the varters were kept unspun to save their springs, and began a frenzied winding. "Orlon!" I bellowed at another varterist, who hung over the battlements, gaping. "Shove a dart in! Hurry, man!"

The dart slapped into the chute as the nut engaged and the windlass clanked full. I swung the varter on its gimbals and sighted on a vast bottle-green hide and pressed the trigger.

Praise Zair—or praise Erthyr the Bow, the guiding spirit of Erthyrdrin bowmen—the dart flew true. Its massive bulk smashed into the tough hide where an arrow would break or spin free. The turiloth squealed at first, and then when he realized how deeply he had been wounded, he began to scream. His six tusks whipped about as he tried to reach back to dislodge the cruel barb in his guts. His tendrilous tails lashed in frenzy. But he was not the monster aimed for the gate beneath our feet. I had had to shoot in enfilade to hit a flank. I glared about for Sniz the Horn, my trumpeter, and yelled, "Load another! Get at it, you onkers! These are

163

only beasts and may be slain, the poor hulus! Sniz! Sound the rally! Blow hard!"

"Quidang, Dak!"

I had spared the time to shoot, myself. Now all who looked over the battlements could see at least one monster screaming in agony, and slowly sinking down onto his sixteen knees. Turiloths are usually ponderous and slow; but with their three hearts they can be whipped up into a short and vicious charge of surprising speed. If that happened before we got them all, any one of them could go straight through the timbers of the gate as a swifter's ram smashes through the scantlings of a broad ship.

The watchfires of the night had not yet been doused.

"Torches!" I roared. "Torches to set their tails alight!"

After that first blind, unthinking panic my men rallied. Varters clanged from the towers along the walls. Torches were catapulted out. We had rocks ready, and vast caldrons of hot water that would come to the boil as the fires were stoked. It was a pretty set-to while it lasted. But with Sniz blowing his lungs out and the drums rolling and the air filled with varters and torches, with the boiling water spilling out and down on the last turiloth that lumbered into a charge, we held them. It was a near thing. The last one, bearing two varter darts, four of his six tusks knocked away by a rock, boiling water fuming from his gray back, slumped to his knees before the gate. One of his remaining tusks touched the wood. It made a sound so small it was lost in the uproar of continuing battle.

For the Grodnims charged in, anyway, bearing scaling ladders. Their towers had been set alight many times and still they built more and shielded them with wet hides and sheets of bronze. We smashed them with varter rocks. The scaling ladders were pushed away with forked sticks. Arrows darkened the bright morning as the mists burned away. It was a merry set-to, as I say, and many a good man went down to the Ice Floes of Sicce, or up to sit in glory on the right hand of Zair or Grodno in the radiance of Zim or Genodras, according to his color.

Before the Hour of Mid the last few Grodnims were shafted and sent reeling, the main pack retreating sullenly. Among the attackers there had been men who bore pikes, men with shields, men compact in the grouping of six cross-bowmen in sextets. So Glycas was sending in the new army.

was he? Actually committing men trained to fight in the open in phalanx into the messy business of assaulting a wall? That was a fine omen for our continued holding.

When the excitement had died down Duhrra found me. He did not look pleased.

"Nath the Slinger has been wounded, a shaft through his arm. Oh, and the Krozair, Pur Tranzhan, is dead."

I said, "Fetch me his sword, Duhrra."

Oh, yes, it was callous. But other good men were dead. And I could use the Krozair brand, where probably others could not. If pride had gone to my head, I trust I understood why. I went to see Nath the Slinger and found him cursing away, in good spirits, but very foulmouthed about the Maggians.

"My shots were bouncing off their shields, Dak. A coward's trick, the shield."

He but mouthed the usual opinion in Turismond.

"I got one of 'em, though, a beauty right under the helmet im. And then his mate shot me in the arm."

"Rest and have it seen to and you will be fine."

"Oh, aye, I'll be fine. By Zair! It is not my slinging arm!"

The turiloths were the subject of conversation for the rest of the day. As was my custom I sent strong parties out, well screened, to pick up every weapon they could among the corpses. As for them, we scattered pungent ibroi on them and gradually the smell went away. The boloth of Chem has eight tusks, and is apple-green and yellow; otherwise he is much the same as a turiloth. I thought of Delia, naked, tied with silver chains to the stake, and of the boloth—and of by and Tilly and Naghan the Gnat. By Kaidun! If a man could get out of a scrape like that, with good friends like Seg and Inch and Turko the Shield, then surely I could get out of this one with my son Drak flying to our rescue! The problem here was, as Pur Trazhan who was now dead had said, that Drak's army would most likely relieve Zimuzz first. We just had to hold. So I glared upon the gigantic mute corpses of the turiloths as my men picked up weapons, and debated how to dispose of the monstrous things before they choked us out with their stink.

In the end the clouds of warvols attracted to any scene of death floated on their wide black wings from the sky and settled on the corpses and began the long and succulent job of picking the bones clean. The vulturelike warvol has his uses in nature. I had my eye on the bones, for the meat was not pleasant enough for us to eat, rich as we were with mergem. If we starved, we'd eat turiloth meat and gag and chew and choke, but we'd eat it right enough.

This siege would be decided one way or the other before the mergem ran out. A small teaspoonful of mergem in two pints of water, boiled up, produces a rich and nourishing broth, with all the proteins and vitamins and whatnot a man's metabolism requires. For roughage we ate of the chipalines, and almost everywhere possible in Zandikar the flowers had been replaced by vegetables. Only along walls in those days were flowers to be seen in the besieged city.

No, I will not detail all our sufferings and tribulations during the Siege of Zandikar. That siege was not really one of the great and illustrious defenses of Kregen; for one thing we did not starve. But we fought well. We held the Greens off. They vastly outnumbered us, and for all that we kept on killing the rasts, still they seemed never to decrease in number. Glycas had used a part of the famous new army of King Genod in the assault; so we were hurting them. A frenzy grew in the attacks. They became more and more desperate, lacking in finesse, wave after wave of yelling men hurling themselves frantically at the gray-white walls of Zandikar, screaming, "Grodno! Grodno! Magdag!" We heard the shouts for Prince Glycas, and, also, the shouts for King Genod. But for all the shouting and the onslaughts they did not pierce or climb the walls—unless we allowed them.

On one crucial night attack a brave party of Grodnim managed to make a lodgment on the walls. They held a wall and a flanking tower. We came up, realizing we faced a task of gigantic proportions to force them off. But they did no drop down on the inside. They made a deal of noise, banging drums and blowing trumpets; but we released a series of firepots into the darkness beyond the walls and after a time the Grodnims dropped back outside the walls, abandoning what they had achieved.

Roz Janri and Pallan Zavarin and others of the high officers were puzzled. They had become used to decisiveness in the Magdaggian army. I said, "This is a great and good sign. The rasts believed we prepared a trap for them. They have been caught before. They thought that if they attacked further we were waiting. Well, the mind is often more powerful than the muscle."

The information heartened everyone in Zandikar.

Now we believed we would hold.

Then came the moment that I, alone among all those people with such high hopes in Zandikar, had dreaded.

Yes, I had told the people of the city; yes, we will hold.

But I had not told them that King Genod had formed an alliance with the empress Thyllis in far Hamal. I had not told them that Genod had bought fliers and saddle-birds from Thyllis. I had not told them that as soon as the king arrived he would bring with him vollers and fliers.

We did not know if he had been reducing Zimuzz, or if he had tried a fling at the sacred Isle of Zy. All we knew early one morning was that King Genod, the war genius, had arrived in his camp before besieged Zandikar.

We saw the dots in the high air. People looked up and pointed. Exclamations broke out. They had seen the flier that Duhrra and Vax had brought here with Hikdar Ornol ti Zab. That had long since been smashed and no one knew where Ornol was. So they knew what these fliers were, and they also knew what they portended.

I knew that this day, the very same day he landed here, the genius at war, King Genod, would launch his aerial armada against Zandikar. The walls would avail nothing. Assailed at a hundred points within the city itself, Zandikar must fall.

Chapter Eighteen

———◆———

Pur Zeg, Prince of Vallia, Krzy

Had Miam not been the great-granddaughter of old King Zinna and the rightful heir to the throne, or had Starkey the Wersting realized enough to have had her killed, or had some other reason debarred her from being the pawn in my machinations, I believe Zena Iztar, whose supernatural powers were of an extent I could not comprehend, would have found some other road for me and my comrades to preserve the city of Zandikar. I did not believe she would have plotted as she had only to let all go to waste. No help in the shape of a vast sky army was to be expected from the Savanti. They might transit more Savapims. As for the Star Lords, well, the Everoinye had been very quiet of late and I fancied that was because in this internecine war of the inner sea they backed the Greens.

The damned fliers and flyers of King Genod landed on the flat expanse outside the soldiers' camps. I made myself stand and watch them. I counted. At least a hundred vollers, and perhaps merely twenty fluttrells, turning their headvanes with the wind as they landed with widespread feet and down-turned tails, amid much wing-fluttering and dust. Their riders were ill-trained. That made sense in a society like the one of the inner sea where airboats and saddle-birds were exotic phenomena.

There remained to me now one course of action.

As I prepared, hurriedly, bellowing for Duhrra and Sniz and Dolan, sending them scurrying about the things needful, I wondered if I was to be cast in the role of Pakkad. Whether or not he was merely a legendary figure—or if red

blood had flowed in his veins, and he had been clothed in
flesh, a real man of some distant epoch—neither I nor any
other human of Kregen knew. But poor Pakkad had been
cruelly treated by Mitronoton, the Reducer of Towers, the
Destroyer of Cities, a very devil. Now his story formed part
of the mythology of Kregen, and Pakkad himself stood as a
symbol for the outcast, the downtrodden, the unwanted, the
pariah. Well, I was to meet a latter-day incarnation of
Mitronoton, as you shall hear, during the Time of Troubles,
and if I do not speak often of that man-god-devil I follow
only a general custom. One does not call lightly on Mitronoton, the Leveler of Ways.

Fazhan bustled up, saying, "The swifter is prepared, Dak."

"Then let all repair aboard. We have little time."

We took the swifter brought in by Pur Trazhan, who no
longer needed her, being dead. She was single-banked, with
two men to an oar and fifteen oars a side, of the style called,
in Zairia, chavinter. There are many and many names for
the different sizes and styles of swifters of the inner sea, of
course; I usually refer to them all indifferently as swifters to
save confusion. Every oarsman was a free man, a warrior,
and he pulled with his weapons ready to hand. The narrow
central gangway extended aft into a quarterdeck by courtesy
only, and I stood there ready to command the ship as Dolan
the Bow conned her out through the Dikars.

Nath the Slinger, cursing by Zogo the Hyrwhip, and
fulminating against the zigging Grodnims, raced along the
quayside and fairly leaped aboard, landing in a sprawl and
a bellow of pain as he jolted his wounded arm. He staggered
up, shouting, "And you would sail without me, Dak the
Ingrate!"

"Welcome, Nath—you may observe the fantamyrrh, if you
will."

On the quayside Nath Zavarin and Roz Janri watched us
leave, puzzled even though I had sworn by Zair I was not
deserting them. Queen Miam, attended by her people, came
down to see us off. They all knew I was about a desperate
enterprise, and they wished me well, casting my fortunes into
the hands of Zair.

They would see that the soldiers and warriors fought when
the attack came in. I knew that. And, knowing that, I wondered only a little if I did this thing for Zandikar or for the
memory of Velia.

Since Trazhan had slipped through the channels in the night after Pur Nazhan had opened up four of the Dikars, we guessed the Grodnims would have reestablished patrols and probably sealed up most, if not all, of them again. We had to sail through in daylight. We pulled so as not to lift a sail above the low-lying islands; and past the cliff-sided islands the wind would often fall away to nothing. We glided on and we waited for the attack we all felt certain would come, although I heartily wished to get through the ring without an encounter.

"Mother Zinzu the Blessed!" quoth Nath the Slinger, lowering the goblet and wiping his lips. "I needed that."

"You have a wounded arm," I said, "and therefore cannot pull at the oars. I believe you to be a very cunning man, Nath the Slinger, by the disgusting nostrils of Makki-Grodno!"

"Aye, Dak, that I am." And he belched most comfortably.

I thought of my old oar-comrade, Nath, and I sighed, and watched the openings of the myriad mazy channels as they passed away astern.

The swifter was low and lean, and standing on the deck raised a man little more than four feet above the water. Her name was *Marigold*, and she was a dinky little craft and her ram was short and stubby and sharp, a vicious hacking tooth that would do a ship's business for her. The oars had been muffled and we glided as silently as a vessel ever can glide through chinking water. We crept along stealthily and we watched with alert eyes and even then were nearly caught. No one spoke an unnecessary word and then only in a whisper. Dolan the Bow up with the prijikers signaled with a smashing cut of his hand and we understood. Fazhan gave the signal to the oarsmen—we were not using a drum, of course—and they swung the ship away from the channel on our larboard bow. We glided into a deviating channel to the right and everyone heard the creak of oars and the splashing as a swifter prowled past. We went on, and if a swifter's crew can be said to have bated breath—we did, by Vox!

Very softly, so that only I heard him, Nath the Slinger said, "By Zinter the Afflicted! I would welcome a few handstrokes. My arm pains me."

I did not reply. Dolan came aft, walking along the gangway with the habitual grace of the swifterman. He, too, whispered.

"We approach an area of great danger. An open reach.

We will have to pull at top speed to get in among the rushes to seaward. If we're caught in the open—" He had no need to spell it out. Fazhan caught my eye and I nodded and he went along the benches whispering to the oarsmen. Free men. They would pull.

This Fazhan ti Rozilloi had grown in stature since we had labored at the oar benches in *Green Magodont*. He was an oar-comrade. And yet the did not possess the superficial brilliance of character so many men have; he was quiet and contained, with nothing of the coarse virility of Nath the Slinger. He was a gentleman of Zairia. There are not many of them.

So we dug in the oars and *Marigold* leaped forward. We burst from the narrow channel and a wide and open stretch of water showed ahead, reaching for perhaps three ulms. A damned long way to row. The water glimmered silver in the light as clouds passed over the Suns of Scorpio. There were very few wild fowl, for they had been hunted mercilessly during the siege. The water chuckled and ran past and the oars dug and pulled and lifted and so dug and pulled again. The men threw their backs into it. We foamed along.

Just under halfway I heard Nath shout a short, sharp obscenity and so before I turned I knew.

From the starboard side a channel opened and from the channel leaped a Magdaggian swifter. Lean and feral, with a single bank, she pounced down on us. She had twenty-five oars a side and I guessed four men to a loom. She was altogether bigger than *Marigold*. We swerved as the helm-Deldars threw their weight on the steering handles. Our starboard bank would have gone on pulling, blind and determined in their rowing; but I yelled, high and harsh, "Ship oars! Weapons! For Zair!"

So the two vessels closed and the struggle began.

We could not have escaped being touched had we rowed on, and we risked having our wings clipped. Also, although mail-clad men clustered on her forecastle and quarterdeck, she would be pulled by slaves and so we might outnumber her fighting-men. And, too, we might play the old Render trick and get among her oar-slaves and free them to fight on our side.

Dolan the Bow flowered his shafts from the forecastle and I saw them like leaping salmon hurling into the men packed on the Magdaggian's forecastle. Nath was cursing and slinging

like a madman, screaming to Zinter the Afflicted that his
arm felt like a dish of palines. The Magdaggian hauled off
and tried to give us the ram; but our swerve eluded him and
he fell aboard bow to bow. In moments we were at handstrokes.

The Grodnims took a nasty shock when the oarsmen rose
in fury and snatched weapons and smashed back at them.
But we were after all outnumbered. The Green cramphs
poured aboard and our prijiker party battling back either
went down or hurled themselves along the gangway where
the oarsmen formed a solid wall. This was no time for me to
skulk on the quarterdeck.

"Zair!" I bellowed. "Zandikar!"

The answering yells spurted up, brief and vicious. "Grodno! Magdag! Magdag!"

The beautifully balanced blade of the Krozair longsword
flamed in the cloud-broken suns-light. I whirled and thrust,
and we cleared a space and saw the crossbowmen in the
Grodnim swifter lining up. We had no shields. I would not
have my men stand, however bravely, and be shot down
without a chance to fight back. I yelled, coarsely.

"To the quarterdeck! We smash them there!"

My men understood instantly. With sixty oarsmen milling
in so narrow and frail a craft, we'd all as likely pitch into the
water. In a solid clump we leaped the narrowing gap,
clambering up and using oars and wales as toeholds, and
ravened up over the bulwarks and the apostis down onto
the gangway. The fight spread all along the Grodnims' deck.
There was time only to smite and smite again, and not ever
think, but go on smiting, over and over.

We reached the Magdaggian's quarterdeck in a snarling
mass of venom. We were outnumbered, for the Grodnim was
packed with soldiers as a gregarian is packed with fruit-
juice. I saw our men going down, and I raved on, for all this
consumed time I did not have to spare. Nath and Fazhan and,
miraculously, Dolan were there with me. Other men formed
and fought and now the shafts could get at us. Dolan concentrated on the Green crossbowmen with the few bowmen
he had left. We kept smashing forward into the Greens and
then skipping back, trying both to use them as a wall of
defense and to slay them at the same time.

I fancy we would have come out on top in the end, for
they had not completely cleared our men from their decks

and we held the quarterdeck and their captain was slain. Occupied in the immediate fighting—and, although believing we woud win, becoming concerned over the eventual outcome and the cost of this struggle—I barely noticed the jarring shock and the rocking of the Grodnim swifter. I took a glance at *Marigold;* she still floated and must have swung in to bump the side.

The noise increased.

Back into the fight I went, like a madman. The Krozair brand gleamed redly wet from point to hilt.

The shouts and screams increased, the swifter rocked under the violence of the struggle, and now as the yells of "Magdag! Magdag!" and "Zair! Zandikar!" racketed up, above them all a new and powerful war cry blasted into the overheated air.

"Zair! Krozair! Krozair!"

I had struck down a Grodnim and had just reached out for the next when I saw his face. I saw the tightly clenched jaw, the staring eyes, the black down-drooping Magdaggian moustaches. And I saw the sudden appalled look of horror flash into that face as the fellow heard that deep and menacing war cry. "Krozair!" He never knew what hit him and sent him to Cottmer's Caverns, most likely.

"Krozair!"

I swirled my blade around and deflected a Chulik's blade. He pressed on with vehemence, for, he, like everyone else, could hear those ferocious war cries blasting up at his rear. I clashed blades again, and looked past the Chulik for an instant, took in what I saw, and then went back to work.

Beyond the bows of this Grodnim swifter a larger swifter had eased up, a double-banked vessel. She lofted over the fighting-men, and warriors poured from her—and, they wore the red, the glorious red, and at their head punched a tight and compact knot of Krozairs, their brands living flames in the speckled light.

I took the Chulik with the old underhand and he toppled back, yelling, for even a Chulik may yell when he has been hurt to death. He fell. Now the decks were clearing. Grodnims were hurling themselves overboard. A few more sought to stem this fresh and sudden onslaught, and then saw that the fight was hopeless. Those who did not jump overboard were cut down. A crossbowman took a last shot at me. The Krozair brand, held in that cunning Krozair grip, flicked the bolt away.

Blood ran across the decks. The slaves were caterwauling like men released from hell. Well, they were, of course.

I stood lightly, holding the sword-point down so that blood spread from that sharp point across the deck. I looked at the men—at the man who led the newcomers.

Yes, I recalled that moment with a mixture of pungent emotions. I remembered it often and I remember it today.

They strode through the shambles toward us survivors. They looked magnificent. Their mail shimmered, their white surcoats blazed with the coruscating device of the hubless spoked wheel within the circle. They were Krozairs. Their hard mahogany faces with the harsh upthrusting moustaches, their helmets crowned with flaunting masses of scarlet feathers, their Krozair longswords held still at the ready, they bore down on us blood-covered men as beings apart, dedicated, relentless in their fanaticism, puritan in their Zairian zeal. And, of them all, the man at their head, their leader, most brilliantly illuminated all the superb qualities of a Krozair. This man was fit to lead.

"Llahal, jernus," he said in a strong, though pleasant voice, giving us the courtesy. "It seems we were just in time."

"Llahal," I said. "We had them on the run." I made my voice flat and hard. I could not afford to waste a mur.

"Indeed?" His voice took on the inflexible tone of harsh authority smelling out rank heresy. "Has the city fallen? Do you with the rough tongue flee from Zandikar, like a rast?"

"The city has not fallen—yet." I bellowed to my men. "All aboard *Marigold!* Schtump! Leave the shambles here." The Krozairs went with us, for they sensed treachery. "No, the city holds. That cramph king Genod has brought up an army and flying boats. Your help will be warmly received."

"So you scuttle from the last fight?"

"Fambly," I said, for I was anxious to press on and there was much to do. "Gerblish fambly! We go to prevent Genod—"

His sword whipped up in a smoky flash of light and the tip hovered at my throat. His handsome face, young, strong, brilliant, glared in fury. His brown eyes bore down on me.

"I am a Krozair and do not relish being called a fambly by scum who desert a despairing city."

The sword could be slipped, Krozair though he was. I

know more tricks than even the Krozairs teach. I stood. I
said, "Your swifter—the golden chavonth as figurehead. I
salute you as a great Krozair captain."

I remembered how this Krozair vessel, *Golden Chavonth*,
had so plagued Gafard, the Sea Zhantil, burning his broad
ships and fleetly avoiding his war swifters.

This young man looked resplendent in his youthful power.
Strength and authority flowed from him. I knew he possessed a goodly share of the yrium. Resplendent . . . resplendent. . . .

"You address me as Krozair, jernu or sir. I ask you again.
Do you flee from Zandikar?"

"No," I said. "And I would like to know your name." I
thought I already knew, and the ache bit into me, bit hard
and fearsomely, like a cancer in my breast.

He did not move the longsword. He wore a solaik sword
scabbarded above the scabbard of the Krozair longsword. He
looked at me, and he looked puzzled.

I said, "I am Dak. I would know your name."

He shook his head. The sword did not tremble.

"I am Pur Zeg."

I hardly heard the rest. Pur Zeg, Krzy, Prince of Vallia,
whom I had last seen as a shouting, laughing, tumbling
three-year-old in far Esser Rarioch! Oh, how I cursed those
damnable Star Lords. For I saw through all the spendid
shimmer of power and gallantry in this young man the inner
core of harsh bitterness. I thought then that his hatred of his
father would make the hatred of Vax as the mewling of a
kitten.

Someone at my back said, not loudly but loudly enough
for us all to hear, "It is the famous Krozair, Pur Zeg. The son
of Pur Dray Prescot!"

"Aye!" shouted Zeg. He whirled past me and the blade
switched from my throat. I did not think there were many
men who would have been allowed to keep a blade at my
throat like that. "Aye! I am the son of) Pur Dray Prescot.
And if any man speaks the name again, I shall—"

With the old venom cutting through my voice so that my
son Zeg swung back, shocked, I said as I had said to Vax,
"And do you hate your father so?"

"If the yetch were here I would strike him down without
another thought than that of justice achieved."

I could see Fazhan, who had gone into the knot of

Krozairs, talking away and nodding his head and pointing at me. He was a good man. Zeg, who had once been three years old and called Segnik, after my comrade Seg Segutorio, swung back to glare at me in a way I fancied I had seen in my mirror.

"You who call yourself Dak! You do not address a Krozair with fitting respect. Do you not know the Krozairs are the only salvation of Zair? Only we can save you. You have been deserting and have been taken up. You will all hang."

My men started yelling at this, and then a Krozair Brother, an experienced fighter, stepped forward and spoke privately to Zeg. I had searched each Krozair face and knew none of them. Had one been present in the Hall of Judgment in Zy then I would have had a pretty dance before I won free. But none had. They had all been out aroving the inner sea, fighting-Krozairs. This Red Brother spoke to Zeg and Zeg turned to me and had the grace to say, "I understand you command in Zandikar, and that King Zinna is dead." And then—and I swear Zeg was a Krozair first, last, and all the time—I saw the abrupt and brutal horror flower in his face.

Before he could agonize too long, I said, "Miam is safe. She is the queen of Zandikar. I am about her business. Cast off your *Golden Chavonth* and pull up to her. Tell you saw me and that all goes well—if I can get free of a pack of chattering Krozairs and go fight Magdaggians."

Some of the Krozairs let rip gasps of outraged horror at this. But time *was* running on. If I didn't do what I intended to do pretty quick it would be too late to save Zandikar. Although even if the city went up in flames I would still do as I intended.

"You speak with a big mouth, Dak."

"Pur Zeg." I said the word and savored it. One day he would tell me how he had achieved the coveted "Z." If we both lived, that was. "I must go. For the sweet sake of Zair, clear your ship from my bows. Do you want the city to fall?"

He glared; but already men were pushing the swifters free. I shouted a few short, harsh commands, for the seamen of *Golden Chavonth* handled out little *Marigold* as though she were a mighty three-banked zhantiller instead of a little chavinter.

"I came straight here as soon as I heard the city was

besieged. The Dikar was open; but I think you will find it
closed by Green swifters by now."

"Thank you for the warning. Now pull into Zandikar and
bid them carry out my instructions faithfully. They are to
concentrate in the strong places and resist. You know your
brother Drak flies here with an aerial armada?"

His face lit up. Well, that might be brotherly love. It
could merely be a warrior's joy that reinforcements were on
the way.

"I will pardon your uncouth manners, fambly, for that
great news. But, the next time we meet, I warn you. Keep
a civil tongue in your head lest you lose it."

I said, "Do you mean the head or the tongue or both? Did
you not receive proper tuition in Kregish?"

Before he could react, for although he was very quick I
think his old father still held an edge there, I bellowed off
forward and my oarsmen settled at their looms. There were
no longer sixty of them, alas, and I turned from the forecastle
and roared back, "are you sailing with us or not? Your
swifter has her oars out. If you do not use them in a moment
or two we'll be on our way."

The Krozairs jumped up onto the bulwarks and ran along
the oars and thence along their own oars to their ship. I
guessed they were fuming. But Zeg might still suspect our
motives and he would wish to be with Miam and where the
fighting was to be expected. What he would say when he saw
Vax intrigued me.

He shouted a last baleful warning as the ships parted company. "Do not forget what I have promised you, Dak, when
you return—if you return." The words spit into the over-
clouded sky. "You have the word of a Krozair."

He had looked resplendent—superb, brilliant—striding
down the blood-soaked deck among the corpses, his weapons
agleam, his helmet flaunting the brave scarlet feathers, his
white surcoat with the coruscating device of the Krzy. He was
my son. And all we could do was shout threats at each other.
So, and to the vast surprise of my men, I bellowed back mild-
ly. "I'll be back. And mind you keep Zandikar safe for
Queen Miam—Krozair."

All the same, as we glided on and at last and thankfully
plunged into the concealment of the rushes, I reflected that
he had been overly mild for a Krozair. I know I have a
daunting way with me; but Zeg was of that stamp of young

men fanatical about their beliefs. That was clear. I had heard it spoken and had joyed in it. He had gone to the sacred Isle of Zy at a very young age, soon after I had disappeared when he'd been three. He had not had the earlier and wider education of Drak. He was obsessed with his Krozair vows, the Disciplines, the mysticism. The Krozairs had molded him completely—or so I had thought. And yet . . . ?

The uproar in that open reach of water might easily bring inquisitive Magdaggian swifters. I fancied Zeg would dispose of them smartly enough, and he had taken the swifter we had captured, manned by her ex-oar-slaves. As for us, we ghosted on and soon were able to turn and so make a landing on the mainland.

Here I had to be extraordinarily nasty to Duhrra and the others.

"No, you pack of fambles! I can get through—I hope. But you would all be taken up. Why, you'd start a-yelling Zair at any moment. This is Green work." And I wrapped about myself the green cloth that I had brought and changed my Red helmet for a captured one sporting green feathers. "See?"

Duhrra said, "I was renegade, also, Gadak."

"Gadak, is it? That proves nothing. I go alone."

"Gadak" was the Grodnim name given to me by Gafard when I'd pretended to become a renegade. Duhrra had never got along with "Guhrra." As for the others— "Take great care on your way back. And tell that fam—tell that Zeg to fight like a Valkan."

Even if they did not fully understand, they would pass the message. Zeg was known to be a prince of Vallia, Zeg of Valka.

I did not wait for them to shove off but sprinted for the nearest cover. I did not even look back. The land here rose from the Dikars, with their ribbons of shining water, and trended upward and then leveled off. I passed through ruined gregarian groves, and through kools of land where the wheat had been cut down and used by damned Grodnims. Soon the camp appeared ahead, rows of tents, with lines of tethered sectrixes, lines of hebras, the artillery park where a few varters were being repaired. One or two fluttrells flew in the sky and so I walked with a brisk military gait, not running and not slouching. If anyone questioned me, I was a scout returning with information.

The park where the vollers had touched down lay over the other side of the camp. This was the main siege camp; there were others on the other flanks of the city walls. It should be mentioned here that I carried an arsenal of weapons, with reason. I had buckled on the Ghittawrer blade, the device removed. I had belted on a Genodder, the Grodnim shortsword, above that, to the right. The great Krozair blade hung down my back, and the green cape hid the hilt. Also I carried the Lohvian longbow and a quiver of arrows. I might not use all of these weapons; I felt it certain I would use some.

When I add that the old seaman's knife snugged over my right hip those of you who have followed my story so far will know that was a habitual fashion with me.

At the center and in a cleared space lofted the ornate green and white tent of the king. I walked through the alleyways between the surrounding tents. Gafard's tent would be nearby. No airboats lifted into the sky, so I was in time. I let out a long breath and stepped past the last tent. Guards ringed the king's abode and tethered hebras waited patiently. The rast was in conference, then. He had slipped up, the cramph.

I put my foot down to stalk arrogantly on and a voice said, "Why, by Grotal the Reducer! Gadak! Gadak, as I live and breathe!"

I turned. Grogor, Gafard's second in command, stood there, hands on hips, his face astounded, gaping at me.

Chapter Nineteen

———◆———

"Then die, Dray Prescot, die!"

"Grogor!" I said, booming it out in hearty good fellowship. "How grand to see a friendly face again, by the Holy Bones of Genodras!"

"Gadak . . ." He goggled at me. "But we all thought you gone to the swifters, dead."

"To the swifters but not dead. I have been remitted. How is our master, Gafard, the King's Striker? He is well, I trust?"

"As well as that prince Glycas will let him be. The king is changed—well, it is not for me to prattle on. So you come to serve my lord Gafard again?"

"My lord Gafard," I said, realizing I'd forgotten the "my lord" bit, thinking so often of him as Gafard. "Aye. If you will take me to him."

"He is closeted with the king and Prince Glycas. They plan this afternoon's strike at that accursed city."

"The siege goes well, I trust?"

"If you trusted less, Gadak, and opened your Grodno-forsaken eyes, you would see how we fare here. Our bellies rumble."

I had eaten well of mergem before I'd quit *Marigold*. This news heartened me. Genod had a large army here, and the way across the Eye of the World from Magdag, and from the nearer Green cities, was long and arduous. With bold sea-rovers like my lad Zeg ranging like sea leem, food would be a problem after they'd eaten the district empty. Logistics play havoc with the calculations of kings.

I handed Grogor a handful of palines. His eyes widened

180

"How came you by these? They fetch golden oars here."

"I remember you shot an arrow at a certain saddle-bird, Grogor. I remember you rode to save my Lady of the Stars." I could not tell him the Lady of the Stars was my daughter Velia. "I think I misjudged you when first we met."

"Aye. Mayhap I did, also. And I give thanks to Grodno for the palines." He put one in his mouth and the paline-look passed hedonistically across his plug-ugly face.

We walked slowly toward Gafard's tent. I had until this afternoon. Rather, I had until the conference ended. I had a plan. It was feeble and must change as events progressed; but as a scheme it ought to be foolproof, given the technology of the inner sea.

The soldiers busy about the unending duties of swods all carried that pinched look of hunger about them. But, also, they held a new and eager look of conquest. I knew why. Their great king had just arrived, with flying boats. Soon, this very afternoon, they would be wafted over the infernal walls of Zandikar, which had withstood every attempt for so long, and then they could run riot within the city in an orgy of rapine. They were soldiers, simple men, and by the reckoning of men of Zair evil until the Last Day and beyond. But to me, a simple sailorman and an equally simple soldier, they were just swods. I would joy to go into action with them against the hated shanks, those devils from over the curve of the world, demons who would give us much trouble in all the lands of the Outer Oceans in the future.

Wo is Kregish for zero. Swods in their rough, jocular way like to dub themselves wo-Deldars, zero-Deldars. It is an irony.

Because this army of swods fought for the Green and King Genod I would have to go into battle against them.

Always I find this unsettling, that one can sing and roister with common soldiers, and find them human beings, and on the next day encounter them in battle and find them transformed into leems. Of course, this holds true for the men of Zairia, and my warriors of Valka and Strombor. As for my Djangs, well, those four-armed demons are fighting-men first and last, and warriors of the hyr Jikai in between.

A number of the men I had known when I served Gafard came up and we talked and I was seemingly free and open in my conversation, telling them I was glad to be remitted from the galleys—a stupidly obvious statement—and hap-

py to be back with Gafard and my comrades. Presently
Grogor said, "The conference is breaking up. The gen-
erals and Chuktars ride off. Soon the three leaders will appear. Then we will know."

As though drawn by a magnet, a crowd of men gathered
in a vast ring around the king's tent. When, at last, he
stepped out, a great cheer went up. "Magdag! Genod! Genod!"

I looked at this yetch, this nulsh, this kleesh whom I had
been instrumental in bringing into this marvelous world of
Kregen. He looked handsome, puffed up with pride, garish
in his green and gold. But he was a fighting-man and
could use the Genodder, the shortsword he had invented and
named, with a skill no other fighting-man of Grodnim could
match.

After him stepped Prince Glycas and Gafard, together,
shoulder to shoulder, and it was clear they struggled for
precedence. As for this Glycas, I remembered him. He might
remember me, for all that it was over fifty years ago I had
stayed in his Emerald Eye Palace and avoided his sister, the
princess Susheeng. He was unpleasant. I would have short
shrift with him.

As for my lord Gafard, Rog of Guamelga, the King's
Striker, Prince of the Central Sea, the Reducer of Zair, Sea
Zhantil, Ghittawrer of Genod, and many another resounding
title, he was the widower of my daughter Velia, my son-in-
law, the hulu, and ripe for mischief.

I remembered what Duhrra had said, and I, too, felt I
would not willingly slay this man Gafard, for all he was a
renegade from Zair, bowing down to Grodno, a hated enemy.
He was a rogue and a rascal, intensely courageous, a Jikaidast, a man.

The noise subsided and the dust clouds settled and the
king spoke. It was all fustian stuff; but it drove heart into the
men and roused them, and gave them enthusiasm. This
cramph Genod, who had murdered my daughter, was ac-
counted a genius at war. He told the men Zimuzz had fallen,
at which I let rip a few shouts, because that was expected.
Now, this very afternoon, he said, we would fly over the
accursed walls of Zandikar. Then it would be every man for
himself. The city would be given over to the sack.

They started in a-yelling, "Zamu! Sanurkazz!" and the
rast promised them those great cities for the sacking,
also.

Amid frantic scenes of wild enthusiasm the king passed among his men. They even began the great shout of "Hai Jikai!" and this I would not shout. Grogor, too, did not shout. He said, sourly, "Wait until the city is ours before we shout the Hai Jikai."

"Let us move nearer to my lord Gafard."

So we forced our way through the throng as the dust rose billowing and the blades flashed in the light of the suns. For the dappled clouds had all passed away and the gloriously mingled, streaming light of the Suns of Scorpio flooded down over that ecstatic scene as a king moved among his army.

The men were halted at last by a line of blank yellow-faced Chuliks. Their long pigtails were dyed green. They wore mail and they would cut down anyone at the order of their Chuktar. Grogor advanced confidently. The king and his advisers had passed beyond the line of Chulik mercenaries, into a cleared space where a small flier rested. They were talking gravely together, with much nodding of heads and gesticulations.

Grogor said to the Hikdar in command of the Chulik detail, "Lahal, Hikdar Gachung. I must speak with my lord Gafard. This man is with me."

"Lahal, Jiktar Grogor. You may pass."

The Chuliks are usually stiff and formal in military matters.

As we passed their impressive line and walked toward the group of high dignitaries by the voller, I said to Grogor, "Nothing was said, then, about your shot at the bird? You escaped?"

"Gafard accepted the loss of his Lady of the Stars. It hurt him. I know that. But the king has the yrium, and the king may do all. My lord Gafard interceded for me, and pleaded I did not know it was the king. There were politics involved." Grogor's face showed what he thought of politics. "My lord Gafard is sorely tried by Prince Glycas."

"The king plays one off against the other? This I do not like, for I believe my lord Gafard to be the better man as mergem is better than dilse."

"Aye."

"And did my lord Gafard truly reconcile himself to the king, afterward? His lady was dead, and it was the king's doing."

"I did not see. No one knows how she died. They say you

were with the body. But you went to the swifters. I think
Glycas had misbehaved himself at the time, and the king in-
clined toward our lord."

The king stood with his back to us, talking and waving
his hands about in graphic gestures. His voice was mellow
and strong and everyone listened intently. Gafard saw Grogor. Then he saw me. His eyes widened. He switched back
at once to listening to the king; but I saw his hand grip
the hilt of his Ghittawrer blade.

A fussy aide bustled up and Grogor cut him to size and
told him we waited for Gafard with news. The king must be
allowed to finish his instructions. We moved off and I heard
Genod saying importantly, "I shall fly over the city now and
inspect the defenses. The rasts of Zairians will never stand
against us, as we descend upon them from the skies. But, by
Goyt, I must conserve my army against the assault on Zamu.
And there is Sanurkazz after." He swung his arms violently.
"You, Gafard, will accompany me."

Glycas, stung, said, "I would fly with you, Majister."

"If you wish, for you may see what has held you up so
long."

Glycas, it was clear, was in King Genod's bad books.

During the time we waited and looked like gawping onkers at the voller, the continual hum and buzz of a great
military camp rose about us. The sense of impending great
deeds filled the air with tension. The suns-light smoked more
brilliantly in every bright trapping and gem and sword-blade.
We all shared the feeling we were gods, treading no mortal
path.

When we heard the sounds indicating that the group was
breaking up, Grogor said, "Let us go and see my lord."

"Yes," I said, and stumbled and sprawled in the dust.

Grogor laughed. "Onker." Then, as I lay there, "You are
all right, Gadak? Nothing broken?"

"My leg," I said. "By Iangle! It stings like the bite of a
lairgodont!"

"Do not move and I will fetch a needleman."

As Grogor ran off I felt again that I would stay my hand
in battle against him, even though he was renegade, hulu.

I heard the men on the other side of the voller. The airboat itself was a roomy craft, with an open central well
with seating around the sides. Her hull was wood over wood-
en formers. She was a simple commercial craft, cheaply

produced in Hamal and sold to Genod. The bloods of the sacred quarter of Ruathytu I had known would never give her room in their vollerdromes. Yet her petal shape conveyed enormous powers here in the Eye of the World.

I stood up when Grogor vanished around her prow, and peeked over the coaming. Gafard was assiduously climbing into the airboat and managing to push Glycas out of the way. The king already stood just aft of the pilot, his back to me.

Glycas—and how I remembered his evil rast-face!—said most petulantly, "Let me up, gernu, you rast."

"Up as high as you like, Prince, cramph," said Gafard.

There was no love lost between these two even in semi-privacy. The king did not move. The pilot sat petrified at his controls. He was a Grodnim. I put both my hands on the coaming.

Men have said I am quick. Well, Djan knows, I have need to be, to stay alive on Kregen.

With a single heave I went up over the coaming. I heard a distant yell, "Onker! Stand aside from the king's flying boat," and I knew no guard in the whole army would risk a shot with the king so near. I jumped across the airboat and knocked the king aside. I hit the control levers, hard and full, to send the boat leaping skyward. I heard an abrupt shriek from the side and rear and guessed Glycas had not made it and had fallen back. If he'd broken his neck it would save the hangman a job. King Genod stumbled back, clearly not understanding what was going on. I caught the pilot around the waist and heaved the poor devil over the side. He fell and did not kill himself.

Then the voller sped up into the bright sky and King Genod, Gafard, the King's Striker, and I faced one another.

No one drew a weapon.

The king hauled himself up. He stared at me with the puzzled look of a man finding a cockroach under his salad.

"You realize you are a dead man?"

I ignored him.

"Gafard," I said. "You know me."

"Aye." He half turned to the king. "This is that wild leem Gadak, who was sent to the swifters." He shook his head. "He must have been remitted, although I did not know."

"What do you here, dead man?" said Genod.

I said, "I was not remitted, Gafard. I escaped. Do you

remember what passed between us the last time I saw you? In the Zhantil's Lair, when you heard this kleesh had stolen away my Lady of the Stars?"

Gafard sucked in his breath. The king's hand hovered over the hilt of his Genodder. That hilt blazed with gems. The blade would be the finest the smithies of Magdag could produce.

"I—I do not fully remember. But the king has the yrium. Surrender yourself to his mercy. We must return to the ground."

"You poor fool! Know you not this genius king of yours is evil? Evil and vile and ready for the justice of Drig's heavy hand?"

The king had had enough. This Genod Gannius had made himself king of Magdag and led the Grodnim confederation. He had humored me. Now he would slay me. He whipped out the Genodder and threw himself into an attacking crouch. The blade gleamed.

"I shall cut you up myself, rast."

"Surrender, Gadak! The king has no equal with the short-sword. Throw yourself on his mercy," Gafard pleaded.

"He knows nothing of mercy." I drew the Genodder at my right side. "Let me show you what he thinks of mercy."

Genod had not come to power merely because he was a genius at war. Anyway, I suspected shrewdly that his genius was a propaganda fiction; he had been successful because of the new army his father had created on the model of my old vosk-skulls from the warrens of Magdag. With a screech our blades met.

He was very good with the shortsword. As always in a fight I go into the combat with the stark knowledge that this could be the last fight, the final conflict, and that I will be shipped out to the Ice Floes of Sicce at the end. This evil king had risen to power as much through his prowess as a fighting-man as through his war genius.

His skin was extraordinarily smooth. Pale and soft like a woman's skin, it covered muscles whipcord tough. He feinted and lunged and I covered and showed the point. He parried and the blades ground resonantly and parted. He jumped back. "Give yourself up, cramph, to the kingly justice!"

I leaped in and twisted the Genodder about in a way that owed nothing to the skills of Green Magdag but rather to the wild outlandish skirlings of my Clansmen. We used the shortsword out there on the wide Plains of Segesthes. In shortsword work a Clansman would have cut up any Genodderman of Magdag, aye, and quaffed his wine as he fought. Hap Loder would have.

Genod's face took on a sudden strained look as he feinted and lunged. Gafard cried out, expecting the blow to be mortal, but the king's blade went nowhere near me and I slashed and his bright green cloak fell away, the golden cords cut through. He stumbled back. But he had courage, the rast, and he came in again. And again I parried and foined with him and so cut away the brilliant gold and green tunic to reveal the mail beneath, and went on and so slashed and cut him about until all his gorgeous apparel had been ripped away and he stood in the mail alone. Then, and only then, I used the old but always cunning lever on him and the Genodder spun from his hand and flew up and out to plunge down to the ground beneath.

He panted. His face had turned lemon-green. His eyes were wild upon me as he shrank back.

"If you are the best Genodderman in Magdag, you cramph," I said, "your Zair-forsaken land is doomed, and praise to Zair for that!"

"Who are you?" he croaked.

Gafard did not draw. I flicked the sword about, between them, and I said to Gafard, "Tell him who I am."

"You—" Gafard's hands trembled. He gripped the hilt of his Ghittawrer longsword and the scabbard shook. "You are Gadak, who was Dak, and yet I think—"

"Yes, Gafard. You think?"

"What you said, there in the Zhantil's Lair. I have tried to think. You would not go after my Lady of the Stars, even though I pleaded as best I could—and you knew I loved her—and—"

"Aye, you loved her, Gafard. She told me that. And she loved you. Never was man more blessed than to receive the love of my Lady of the Stars."

"Yes—you would not go—and then—then you did go. Did I say something, anything—I cannot remember—"

I did not know if he was speaking the truth. Yet the horrific scene in the hunting lodge when I had discovered that the Lady of the Stars was my daughter could have been so painful to him that he had shut it out of his mind. It is known. I glared at him.

"You told me, in all truth, who my Lady of the Stars was."

"Ah! And then you went?"

"Yes."

He trembled uncontrollably now. He had doted on his lady, and he had yearned to emulate the exploits of her father, saying there was a matter between him and Pur Dray. Now I had realized he did not mean he wished to fight me, as I had then thought. He had wished to talk to his father-in-law. As was, in very truth, proper. For I would have a hand in the bokkertu.

The king roused himself. He looked ghastly. "What is all this nonsense, Gafard! Kill the cramph, here and now!"

"I do not think I can do that, Majister."

"Then try, you ungrateful cramph!"

"Tell him who I am, Gafard."

Gafard's face had lost all its color. His bronze tan floated on his skin. He looked frenzied. "I—I think—"

"Why should I not slay you now, Gafard—you who bow down to his kleesh of a king? Oh, yes, Gafard, you know who I am. You have dreamed of this meeting. You save relics. You say there is a matter between us. By Zair! There is a matter between us!"

He gasped and tried to speak and his mouth merely opened and closed.

"There is a matter! I want to know why you fawn on this foul object, and let him steal away my daughter, Velia!"

He did not fall. In truth, the shock of the meeting would have felled a lesser man with all the passionate longings he had put into just such a confrontation. He wet his lips. The cords in his neck strained like ropes in a hurricane. He croaked, and tried again, and, at last, he could say the words.

"Pur Dray! Pur Dray Prescot! The Lord of Strombor! Krozair of Zy!"

The king shrieked at this, and cowered away, his hands fumbling at his throat. Like a fool, I ignored him.

"No, Gafard—*son-in-law!* I am no longer a Krozair of Zy, for I am Apushniad. But—yes, I am Dray Prescot!"

For a moment no one spoke. The moment was too heavy for mere words.

The king levered himself up. His anguished face bore the look of a madman. His hand fumbled at his neck.

"Dray Prescot! The Bane of Grodno!" His hand whipped the cunning little throwing knife from the sheath at his back. "Then die, Dray Prescot, die!"

Chapter Twenty

———◆———

The Siege of Zandikar: IV.

Of partings and of meetings

"Die, Dray Prescot, die!"

The glittering throwing knife hurtled from the fingers of the king straight at my face.

And, in that selfsame instant, as though time shuttered through a macabre repetition, I caught a single flashing glimpse over the side of the voller of a gorgeous scarlet and golden bird of prey in full diving vicious attack upon a shining white dove.

The two scenes merged and melded in my eyes and became one.

The golden and scarlet raptor of the Star Lords, their spy and messenger, striking with black-taloned claws at the white dove of the Savanti, and the glittering terchick, the Kregan throwing knife, hurled full at my face, were one and the same. I saw the Savanti dove hesitate and swerve and the lancing blow of scarlet and gold shriek past. The Genodder in my fist sprang up and twitched in the old cunning Disciplines and the terchick rang like a gong-note of despair, clanging against the blade and springing in a gleaming curve away into the vast reaches of the sky. The king's mouth slobbered wetly and he began to claw out his Ghittawrer longsword.

"He is a Krozair, Majister," said Gafard, staring at me with hunger and despair.

"You call this object 'Majister,' Gafard. Yet he stole my daughter away from you, and now she is dead. You are a man. I know that. You prated on about the Lord of Strombor, and you emulated my deeds and sought my renown. I would surrender all those deeds and give all that renown if my Velia were back with me, alive!"

He pushed himself up. He had stopped shaking. "I, too, Pur Dray, would give everything I own, everything I am—"

"The girl was a fool, a shishi!" shrieked Genod. "I am the king. It is my right to take—"

"Your rights will be allowed you when you are judged. For I take you back to Zandikar. There you will be judged for murder."

"Murder?" Gafard's jaw muscles ridged. He stared at me. His eyes held a look no man should suffer—a look I had borne as I cradled my Velia in my arms and watched her die.

"Aye, Gafard—murder. This kleesh's fluttrell was wounded by Grogor's shot. The bird was falling. Velia was callously thrown off by this kleesh to save himself."

"It is a lie!" Genod staggered up, distraught, panting, whooping great gulps of air. He had drawn his Ghittawrer blade with the tawdry emblem of his Green Brotherhood upon it. "A lie!"

"I never heard the Lord of Strombor was a Krozair who lied."

"I speak the truth, Gafard. This kleesh whom you worship threw my daughter down to her death—threw down your wife!"

Once the first stone is dislodged in a wall or a dam the final pressure mounts swiftly and more swiftly to the point of breaking and utter collapse. This Gafard—the King's Striker, Sea Zhantil, my *son-in-law*—had revered the genius king Genod, the king with the yrium, had worshiped my daughter Velia, and had envied my reputation upon the Eye of the World and had attempted to emulate me. Zair knows, the poor hulu was a tormented man. Struck and buffeted by passions and beliefs, by desires and duties, he had been caught in a mind-shattering trap. Renegade, loyal Grodnim of Magdag, once a loyal Zairian, he now faced the final collapse of everything in his life. He had been tortured in his ib by beliefs and truths beyond the breaking of a mortal man. Even as King Genod, foaming, berserk, launched himself forward with the Ghittawrer blade lifting, so Gafard bellowed and flung himself at the king.

"King Genod!"

"Stand aside, Gafard, you rast, while I cut down this devil."

"Genod—murderer!" Gafard's howl pricked the nape of the neck. "I have served you faithfully. I revered you past reason. You repay me by murdering my Velia, the only woman in the world—"

"Lies! Lies!"

They stood for perhaps a half dozen heartbeats, their chests laboring to draw breath as they shouted, their faces demoniac with convulsive rage and revelation.

Then Genod lunged viciously forward, shrieking he would slay us both, and Gafard, with a snarl like a wild beast dragged heels first from its lair into the hostile world, leaped on the king, one hand to his throat, the other around his waist. So they struggled, bodies locked, animated with hatred and passion.

The rest of their contorted yells were lost as they struggled. The Ghittawrer blade slashed down and Gafard ignored it and forced the king back. I jumped forward to separate them, for I wanted to take Genod for trial—I truly believe I wished this—and the struggle carried them raving to the coaming of the voller.

Without a pause in their struggle one with the other they toppled over the coaming and pitched out over the side of the voller. I put my hand on the coaming and looked down.

Over and over they toppled, falling through the thin air as my Velia had fallen. They still fought as they fell. I did not turn away with a shudder. I watched them as they dwindled and fell away and so I remained, graven, watching as the king and Gafard, the King's Striker, smashed to red jelly in the central square of Zandikar.

The single thought burning in my brain as I brought the voller to land was that Grogor must not be slain in the coming battle, for Grogor would know where Didi, the daughter of Gafard and Velia, was kept hidden. Somewhere in Magdag or on one of Gafard's estates; yes, Grogor would take me to my granddaughter.

The kyro filled with a rushing clamor as the people and the soldiers ran. Life, which had for a moment turned aside, now resumed the reins. Gafard was dead. There would be a proper time to mourn. I did not forget that apocalyptic vi-

"The struggle carried them to the coaming of the voller."

sion of the Gdoinye, the spy of the Star Lords, and its de-
liberate attack on the white dove of the Savanti. I knew,
with that special doom I feel is laid upon me, that the toils
of supernatural manipulations had been only temporarily
evaded.

The consternation and then the bemused wonder and then
the joyful acclamations seized all Zandikar. Everyone understood what the death of this vile king Genod would mean. I
had to quiet the uproar, raising my hands, bellowing to
make them listen.

"Prince Glycas is not dead. That cramph will lead now.
We must still fight!"

"Aye!" they bellowed. And then I heard the name the
people of Zandikar shouted, the name they screeched in their
determination to resist to the end. "Aye, Zadak! We will
fight and never surrender! We fight for Zadak and Zandikar!"

In the hullaballoo I found Queen Miam. Zeg stood at
her side and they were both removed from common cares,
entranced with each other—as was very proper in ordinary times; but of little use to us here in the siege. Others
crowded around.

"Who is this Zadak, Miam? I would care to meet him."

She laughed—Miam's laugh was always a wonder. "I think
I should like that, also." She clung on to Zeg's arm. He
looked down on her with that look—well, we all know
about that. She beckoned to me. "I introduce you with the
full pappattu to Zadak. For the Dak that was is the Zadak of
Zandikar. Do you agree?"

I repeated the formula. "I agree, Queen Miam. I thank
you."

Then they all began cheering. Well, the famous old "Z"
had been added to my name, and that was all very well and
fine; but the battle remained to be won. The feeling was a
strange one. As I seldom had used King Zo's gift of the
title of Sea Zhantil, so I seldom used Zadray. I would always
think of the Sea Zhantil as being Gafard. He had earned the
title. I said to Zeg and Vax, harshly, coldly, "Come with me."

Zeg was too mazed with love to bristle, and Vax knew me
by now. They followed me, these two hulking sons of mine,
and we strode through the people to the cleared area where
the king of Magdag and his favorite lay in the dust.

They had fought bitterly until the end. Genod had landed

first. Gafard was not, therefore, so badly crushed. The fingers of the King's Striker were still tightly wrapped around the throat of the king. He had choked the kleesh. I just hoped Genod had not been dead before he hit.

I turned them over and freed the gripping fingers. Blood ran everywhere. I pulled Gafard over onto his back. He flopped.

"Look on this man's face, Vax. Look well." I spoke with a savage bitterness that chilled Vax. "Look on this man's face, Zeg. Look well. Remember him. Remember him."

Zeg started to say something, a farrago about my calling him Pur Zeg and being respectful to a Krozair Brother.

"Look, Zeg, on this man's face. Make sure you remember every line of it." I bent down and brushed my fingers and thumb over the black moustaches. I forced them away from their silly downturned Magdaggian shape and brushed them up into the old arrogant Zairian fashion. "Look on this man Gafard. There are those to whom you will be asked to speak of Gafard. Do not forget him."

I stalked away and Zeg caught my shoulder and said, harshly, "You may be called Zadak of Zandikar now, Dak the Insolent. But I shall not tolerate your insolence! Either you—"

I swung about and shook his hand free. I glared at him. He did not flinch back—for which I was pleased—but he stopped talking. "Do not say it, Pur Zeg, Krozair of Zy, jernu, Prince. Do not say what you will regret."

What might have happened then, Zair knows; a shrilling shout racketed from the walls and so we all knew the last fight had begun.

There were things to be done. I said to Vax, "Prince Zeg will take care of the queen now. We have one vol—flying boat. Will you take her, with fighting-men, and do what you can?"

Before Vax could answer and so show me up for the onker I was, Duhrra boomed his idiotic bellow. "Duh—Dak! Vax flew the flying boat when we had to leave you on the beach. I'm going with him. It is all arranged."

I did not smile. "So be it." I glared at my son. "And may Zair and this Opaz you speak of go with you."

Everyone ran to take up their appointed stations. Everyone felt convinced this was the last fight. We watched as the vollers rose from the camp of the Grodnims. They

soared up and formed ready to sweep over the walls of
Zandikar. We all let out huge shouts of joy when two fliers
collided. And we all shouted with joy again when two more
suddenly dropped down to crash onto the ground. No one
here—apart from myself and my two sons—could understand why the airboats should fall and crash.

"Glycas is out for all the glory himself. Well, we will give
him a bellyful before the day is done."

We all knew the city was doomed, for we had nothing
with which to counteract the fliers. In that moment as the
vollers, all flying their green swifter pennons and standards,
soared up to destroy us, a fresh series of shouts broke out
from the seaward walls. I looked back—and *up.*

Queen Miam put a hand on Zeg's arm, and swayed. Zeg
held her. Roz Janri and Pallan Zavarin exclaimed in joy.
Up there, sweeping in over the city, flew vollers. And each
flier bore the red flags of Zair.

"It is my brother, Prince Drak!" roared Zeg. "It must be!
By Zair! He cuts his time fine!"

I was busily counting the vollers sweeping in so grandly
with their red banners flying. Fifty! Fifty against over ninety.
The plans must change. I bellowed out the orders. Sniz blew
his guts out. Messengers galloped. We would hold the walls as
we had done for so long. With vollers to fight vollers we had
a chance.

As the main bulk of the Zairian aerial armada sailed on
over the city to engage the oncoming Green fleet, the lead
ship curved through the sky. We waved a multitude of red
flags from our tower atop the Palace of Fragrant Incense,
and Drak brought his flagship down in a courtyard below. We
all met in the High Hall, halfway between up and down, and
the greetings! The roarings! The back-thumpings!

I stood in the shadows, and I looked at my eldest son.

Drak had been fourteen when I'd been ejected from
Kregen and thrust back to Earth. Now he was a big,
tough mature man, grown into Kregan manhood. The marks
of power were on him, and yet I judged—I hoped, by Vox!—
that he had not forgotten the lessons drummed into him by
Delia and me, lessons designed to prevent the disease of un-
controllable power from corrupting him. I had the gloomiest
of forebodings that for Zeg power had already done its not-
so-insidious work. The two brothers embraced each other
with genuine warmth, and Zeg said, swiftly, that Jaidur was

here and aloft, at which Drak said that, by Vox, that was where *he* should be, but he had alighted to learn our plans. So he was not altogether a headlong fool, then.

"And where is Zadak that he may come forward!" said Miam, who was known to Drak and who kissed him with sisterly affection.

It was no use shilly-shallying anymore in the shadows of the High Hall. I stamped a scowl over my ugly old face and stepped forward. If Drak recognized me that would not make any difference to the battle. I planted myself down, and I growled out, "Llahal, Prince Drak, Krozair. If you hold the zigging Grodnim flying boats in check, we will hold the walls."

Drak looked at me, taken aback. Then his eyebrows lifted by a hairbreadth and a shadow passed over his face. I glared at him malignantly.

"The queen has told me of you, Zadak. I give you Lahal. I am outnumbered two to one. But we will hold the Grodnims until not one of us flies."

He spoke up in a grave way, as a man with the cares of high office speaks. I liked the set of his head on his shoulders, the way he held himself. If Vax was still a young tearaway and Zeg a haughty and imperious killer, Drak was a darkly powerful man of affairs, versed in the ways of Kregen, a true prince of Vallia.

What a situation! I stood with my three sons, and could not acknowledge them, could not stride forward and clasp them in my arms. I suppose something more demoniacal than mere malignity showed on my face. I half turned away and shouted, "The prince has spoken! We resist to the end!"

"Hai!" came the answering shouts. "Hai, Jikai!"

"You—" said my son Drak. "We have never met, I know, and yet, something in you—it is odd." On that darkly handsome face of his, in which the beauty of his mother had somehow not been altogether overlaid by my own ugly features, although he was not as handsome as Vax, and not as brilliant in appearance as Zeg, a small, puzzled smile flitted. "It is a long time ago, now, and I grieve for that. But, by Vox, you remind me of my father."

"And do you hate your father, as your brothers do?"

"Of course he does!" Zeg said sharply. "For we have been cruelly treated. Apushniad! Let us get to work."

"Hatred?" said Drak. "Sometimes I think—but, this is a

private affair, of the family and of honor. I give you respect for your defense of Zandikar, Zadak. But this is not a matter to discuss in public."

"I agree. Before you go aloft, I beg a favor. Go down with me to the central square. There is a man I would wish you to see before he is dumped in an unmarked grave."

The last was not strictly true. I'd see that a marker was set up—if I lived. So Drak, too, stared down on the dead face of his brother-in-law. I spoke to him as I had to Zeg and Vax. He understood I wanted to boast of my prowess, and he frowned, and I did not disabuse him. He soared aloft to join his little fleet as the two aerial armadas clashed.

The fight that followed bellowed and clanged away in grisly style. We faced great odds. One enormous advantage we had, for the men of Vallia and Valka flying our vollers were trained men, many of them of the Vallian Air Service and their experience in the air served them well in the fight against twice their number. Even then I saw a couple of Vallian vollers flutter to the ground, victims of the inferior workmanship with which Hamal cursed all the fliers she sold abroad.

The tactics of Glycas were simple. While some fliers attempted to get through and land parties of men inside the city, others settled just inside the walls and made determined onslaughts on the gates to open them to the waiting army. These we attacked with grim and savage ferocity, knowing that the opening of one gate would finish us. We fought desperately. But I saw, as I was staggering back from a charge that had destroyed the men from four fliers but had withered our own men away, that we were losing. More and more fliers settled inside and the green banners waved thickly in clumps, here and there. At any moment now a gate would go down and the damned Grodnims would be in.

"I think," said Zeg as he wiped his dripping blade, "they have us now."

"Do not speak like that, Zeg!"

He glared at me, his eyes overbright, his mouth ugly.

"You and I will settle this, if we live. You deserve to be jikaidered for your foulmouthed insolence. Ha! My brother Drak was right when he compared you with our father! He must be just such a braggart as you."

If that was not fair I had no time to care as once again we went hammer and tongs into a pack of Fristles running screeching, from a newly landed flier. Our varters shot-in our attack and we routed them. The Zandikarese archers proved their worth on this day, and my Lohvian longbow sang sweetly whenever a target looked likely. But, all the same, we could last little longer.

A particularly fierce attack developed against that nodal central gate of the landward wall. Outside, waiting, the Magdaggian army stood at ease, drawn up in formation, ready to burst in. Over our heads the vollers circled and clashed and men and fliers fell from the sky. Many a green flag smashed into the dust and many a red flag followed. Our strength was being whittled away, and yet even as our fliers dwindled in numbers so did the Grodnim vollers shrink. There remained the force ready to launch itself at the central gate, and here we positioned ourselves to withstand the assault that might end all.

"If only our mean old devil of a grandfather had spared Drak good vollers!" said Zeg, with a vicious burst of anger. "He has them, for our cramph of a father took them in the Battle of Jholaix."

"We must fight with what we have, lad." I made up my mind. "If the city does fall, you must take a voller and Miam and escape."

He roared at me then, as a Valkan prince might roar. I bellowed over his furious protests. "Do you want to see what will happen to Miam? Are you that callous and hardhearted —and stupid?"

"And the warriors and the people, you rast! Do I leave them?"

"If they cannot escape, at least you and Miam—"

He turned away from me, unable to answer so base a suggestion as it should be answered, with a blow or the sword, for through all his Zairian fervor he recognized this Zadak was useful to Zandikar in a fight. He did say, bitterly, "But *you* will escape?"

I did not answer. Sniz was there, a bloody bandage around his head. "Blow, Sniz! Blow as you have never blown before."

Everything depended on this gate. Glycas had ceased to throw his fliers haphazardly into the city, where we waited for them and shot his soldiers up as they disembarked. Now he put everything into this last attack. The vollers descended and we could see their brave green banners, the fierce glint of weapons, and hear the ferocious shrilling war chants. "Magdag! Grodno!"

"Zair!" we yelled, and our archers shot. "Zair! Zandikar!"

The Green vollers descended in clouds, like flies onto a carcass. The wall, the gate-towers, the courtyards, filled with battling men. We heard the shrill yelping of men and trumpets from outside. With a crash that tore at our heartstrings we saw the gate burst in with a smother of flying chips of wood. The gate burst and went down and hordes of Green mailed warriors broke through, yelling in triumph.

"Now is the end!" bellowed Zeg and he leaped forward, swirling his Krozair longsword above his head, resplendent, shining in mail and blood, smashing a bloody trail through the Greens. I used the Lohvian longbow and preserved his life, as Seg had done for me in the long-ago. Other red banners pressed in from the side and for a space, a tiny space, we held them. But we could not hold the pressure. We sagged back. We sagged and stumbled back, and wounded men fell and dead men were crushed and it seemed that this final moment was the end.

We saw the ranks of Green draw back a space and knew they summoned up their energies for the last smashing attack. Duhrra stood at my side, splashed with blood, fearsome in his might. Vax was with him. Their flier had been smashed and they had lived so that they might die here, at the gate of Zandikar. Drak was there, calm and powerful, darkly dominant, giving orders that tightened up a flank. Our exhausted men ran to do his bidding. So, for that tiny space, we stood there, Drak, Zeg, and Jaidur—for that was Vax's name. We stood there, three sons who did not know their hated father stood with them in the final hour, and I, that same father who had so failed his sons.

I saw the green-clad ranks forming for the next charge, saw them sorting themselves out after the skirling charge that had driven them through the gate. Now they formed the phalanx, that phalanx I had created in the warrens of Magdag. I saw the pikes all slanting forward, the halberdiers and swordsmen in the front ranks. The sextets of crossbowmen took up their positions in flank. This was a mighty force, this killing instrument of war. It would roll over us, as we smashed with our swords, roll over us and obliterate us. Theory might say otherwise; but I had trained well and I

"Like a clump of thistledown, an enormous skyship landed before the gate."

knew Genod's father had carried on that training, and King Genod, who was now dead, the rast, had profited by it.

So we braced ourselves for the final charge of that superb machine of war. Then I saw men looking up and a shadow pressed down over the gateway. Like a clump of thistledown in lightness and like a floating solid fortress for power, an enormous skyship landed gently before the gate and stoppered the smashed opening with solid lenken walls bristling with varters and longbowmen.

The sleeting discharge of darts and shafts shattered the phalanx. The smashing force of varter-driven rocks carved bloody pathways through rived mail and tattered flesh. The Archers of Valka drove their shafts pitilessly into the gaps. The shields of the phalanx could not withstand the magnitude of the blows: rocks and darts and shafts. The phalanx was shredded to pulp.

"By Opaz!" said Drak. "By Zair!" said Zeg. "By Vox!" said Vax.

I did not say anything. Excited screams burst out all about us. The men of Zandikar knew when succor had arrived. I saw the huge bulk of the skyship, enormous, deck piled on deck, all sustained and driven through the air by the power of the aerial mechanism, the silver boxes, deep in her hull. I looked. She seemed smothered with flags. There was the red of Zairia. But, over all, dominating and fluttering in the brave Kregen sunshine—Old Superb! My own flag, the yellow cross on the scarlet ground. Old Superb, my battle flag, floating in the streaming rays of the Suns of Scorpio.

At the jackstaff flew the yellow saltire on the red ground, the flag of the Empire of Vallia. Many red and white flags of Valka, famous in song, fluttered from the masts. And there were other flags, also, flags I recognized as the flags of friends.

Another shadow sped across the ground and we all looked up, a flower-bed of faces, and another huge skyship circled up there and rained death and destruction down upon the Grodnim army.

As though casually, a varter-sped rock flew and knocked from the sky the last Grodnim voller. It snapped and fell.

My three sons were gabbling away together, and Miam clasped Zeg, and I turned away, for even Duhrra stood by Vax, beaming in his cheerful idiotic way. Roz Janri and

Pallan Zavarin joined them. I heard what was said, Drak dominating all.

"We have been saved by warriors from my own country. See the flags, the Vallian, the Valkan. And yet—Old Superb —our father's flag. That has not been flown for many years."

"It is of no consequence!" shouted Zeg as we waited for the people from the skyship to join us. "See the Blue Mountain Boys! See the flags of Falinur and the Black Mountains! That means Seg and Inch! And the valkavol standards of Valka!"

The skyship was lifting to join her sisters in the sky as they went methodically about exterminating the least sign of Green. Now a fresh wonder was vouchsafed us. The people from the skyship were approaching us. But we looked up. A mass of flying specks leaped from the ship, fanning out, and the wide wings of saddle-birds beat against the sky. Orange streamers identified them, if the flutduins had not— my Djangs! Those ferocious four-armed warrior Djangs! How the fluttrells wearing the green plunged and scattered like breeze-driven smoke!

I swallowed down, hard. By God! I am an old cynical case-hardened warrior. But in that moment—in that glorious moment—I relished as seldom I relished the mingled sunshine of Kregen, the heady intoxicating air, and the deep sure knowledge of friendship I know I do not deserve but which has blessed me in my new life on the planet four hundred light-years from the world of my birth.

They were all there. It seemed to me they were *all* there. Seg and Inch, striding on, beaming. Turko the Shield, Balass the Hawk, Naghan the Gnat, Oby, Melow the Supple. Korf Aighos was there, Tilly, Kytun Kholin Dorn, his four arms windmilling in his excitement, but Ortyg Fellin Coper was not there, as was proper, for he would hold Djanduin when Kytun and I were both away. And—Prince Varden Wanek strode along brave in the powder blue of the Ewards. And, with him, Gloag! And Hap Loder! Incredible! I gaped. What had she been up to? Raising half of Kregen after me?

The Wizard of Loh, Khe-Hi-Bjanching, strode on busily talking to Evold Scavander, two wise Sans absorbed in arcane lore despite their surroundings. And there were others there I knew, men like Wersting Rogahan, and Jiktar Orlon Llordar. I guessed Vangar ti Valkanium and Tom Tomor,

Elten of Avanar, were aloft conducting the aerial operations and finishing the Magdaggians.

Drak and Zeg and Vax took a few paces forward, free of
the rest of us, as the crowd from the skyship approached. It
struck none of us to rush forward. We stood. And, among
the crowd walking toward us all smiling and laughing—I
might have guessed!—staggered two rascals skylarking and
upturning bottles. "Stylor!" they crowed, beaming and drinking by turns. Oh, yes, they were there, my two favorite rascals, my two oar-comrades, Nath and Zolta.

So the crowd around Queen Miam waited, and the three
princes of Vallia stepped forth proudly in this moment of
victory. I stood a little to one side of them, in the random
shadow of a tower, and I, too, savored the moment of victory. But more than that I savored, I luxuriated in, I stared
devouringly at she who walked at the head of all my friends.
Slender, lissome, superb, clad in russet hunting leathers, with
the brave old scarlet sash about her, the rapier and the dagger swinging at her sides, her long brown hair free about
her shoulders with the suns casting gorgeous auburn high-
lights in that lush profusion of beauty, she walked in light,
glorious, glorious. . . .

Drak and Zeg and Vax who was Jaidur took another step
forward. They held out their arms in welcome. I stood to
the side and watched, for I could not see their faces, but I
know they were smiling and happy. Her three sons welcomed her, and they called, "Mother!" Drak and Zeg and
Jaidur, happy, laughing, calling, "Mother!"

She lifted her own arms. She was smiling and I felt myself
trembling, felt the choke, the ache in my throat.

"Mother!" called the three brothers and held out their
arms.

She held out her own arms and began to run because she
could not hold back in regal dignity any longer. The moment
for ritual observances had flown. No longer was she the
Princess Majestrix, imperial granddaughter of the emperor
of Vallia, she was a woman and her heart, like mine, was
bursting. Straight toward her three sons she ran. I stood to
the rear of them and to the side, in the shadows, and I felt
all the crushing weight of twenty-one years pressing down
on me. Directly toward the outstretched arms of those three
stalwart young men ran their mother and they broke and
ran toward her in filial love.

Straight past them she ran. Past their outstretched arms, past the welcoming smiles upon their faces, past the three of them, and so I stood forward. And she threw herself into my arms and I held her close, close, and I could not see anything in the whole world of Kregen but my Delia.

Chapter Twenty-one

Krozair of Zy

"My *father!*" "That insolent rast my *father!*" "The hyr Jikai Zadak my *father!*"

Well, poor lads, it was hard for them.

There is little left to tell.

I, Dray Prescot, Prince Majister of Vallia, Strom of Valka, King of Djanduin, Lord of Strombor—and much else besides —held my Delia and I most certainly would not let her go. We gathered in the High Hall and there was the most sumptuous shindig.

I forced away the dark and terrible news I must tell Delia. Her daughter Velia was dead. But she had news for me that set me back, for she had gone home from the inner sea when Seg and Inch had come for her on the island of Zi after I had seen her in a stinking fish cell. Those two had stolen a skyship from the emperor and gone looking for me. Seg had been in Erthyrdrin and Inch in Ng'groga when my letters at last reached them. But they had taken Delia back, for she had seen me and understood that with the help of Nath and Zolta I must work out my own salvation. At home in Esser Rarioch she had given birth to a daughter. We would call this dearly beloved daughter Velia.

"So now you know why I made you look at the dead face of Gafard. He was not an altogether evil man." The three faces of my sons reflected indescribable emotions. "He was your brother-in-law."

Delia insisted on looking, also, and she turned away and held me close, and said, "Dear Velia. Dear Velia."

She would overcome her sorrow in time.

As to Zeg and Jaidur, they were hot for continuing the war against the Grodnims. The situation of the Eye of the World was now back to where it had been before Genod had set out on his road of conquest. With his genius for war removed, the Red southern shore would be cleansed of the Green centers of infection. From Zimuzz west to Shazmos all would be Red once more. Drak put his chin in his hands and said he had to return to Vallia, for trouble brewed there and the Racters were not the only ones involved.

Just what their attitude to me would be, now that they knew just who I was, remained to be seen. They studiously avoided any mention of the past differences. But I said, "I go to Zy. There is a matter between me and Pur Kazz, the Grand Archbold."

As Krozairs of Zy, Drak and Zeg would attend. Delia said, simply, "I'm not letting you out of my sight again, and you needn't think otherwise."

I gave orders that resulted in a disheveled, bloody, swearing Grogor being brought in and dumped down, all messy and filthy, before me. "Jiktar Grogor!" I said and his head snapped up. "You will do a certain thing for me, or, by Zair, you'll find out where our lord Gafard has gone!"

"Gadak—?"

He shook his head, stunned, when he was told.

So we took our fleet of skyships off to Zy. Seg and Inch had simply stolen the huge vessels. What the emperor would say did not worry them. He had been mean with Drak, saying that what consequence was it to him of a struggle in some distant and forgotten sea around the world? I promised to sort him out when we returned to Vallia. And before I could do that the Apushniad must be removed. I recalled the scarlet and golden Gdoinye, and the white Savanti dove. Vast forces moved behind the scenes here, supernatural powers that sought to control our lives, and I felt a hint of evasiveness, a suggestion of a lack of full control. I wanted to see Zena Iztar again; but she made no occult appearance. And so we flew to Zy.

You may well imagine the carryings-on in the skyships as our old friends rejoiced. It had been a long time. The news! The events that had passed on Kregen—well, all will be told in due time, as they fit inho the jigsaw of motives and events of my life on Kregen under the Suns of Scorpio.

The Krozairs of Zy had been apprised of our coming and

awaited us in the Outer Hall, for so many with me were not Krozairs. Pur Kazz, the Grand Archbold, sat on the Ombor Throne, for that was proper. The Krozairs sat ranked in their stalls along one side and my people sat on the other. If it came to a fight I would not like to predict the outcome. I most certainly felt torn. But a few four-armed Djangs, and Hap's Clansmen, and the Archers of Valka, and the Blue Mountain Boys, and—well, the Krozairs of Zy are renowned warriors, and I feel that had we come to handstrokes a Kregan Götterdämmerung would have ensued. Pride is a fearful thing. I determined to remain cool. It was a good intention.

Pur Zenkiren, vastly recovered and almost back to his old self, greeted me kindly. "Pur Kazz is sick, Dray. He has ordered certain things that I, for one, cannot approve of. I think you may find support—if your cause is just."

"I did not answer the Call because I was unable to do so. I take my vows as a Krzy far too seriously to lie about them. I was not able to answer the Call, and after I have told Delia, you will be the first to hear what, I fear, you may not believe."

Then he said something that rocked me.

"I have talked with Zena Iztar. She is a remarkable woman. She tells me she works for Zair."

I gaped at him like any onker. He went on quickly to tell me that Zena Iztar confirmed my inability to answer the Azhurad. From what he said I understood he did not know the full extent of Zena Iztar's supernatural powers—that I had not been on Kregen at the time of the Call. But he was fully aware that some of the mysticism of the Krozairs—of which I do not speak—had revealed itself.

The adjudicator sat on his throne. Pur Kazz, on the Ombor Throne—the genuine one moved here, for there is only the one—leaned over and spoke to the adjudicator and the proceedings opened.

"This is a preliminary hearing," said the adjudicator. Well, of course. The Krzy would not settle so important a matter with so many non-Krozairs present. If I could win here, then the final hearing in the Hall of Judgment should also be won. But not necessarily. The case was put afresh.

"You, Dray Prescot, Apushniad, stand condemned on two counts. It is known that it is impossible for a living Brother not to hear the Call. If you did hear and did not come, you stand condemned. If you did not hear, you were never fully a Krzy, you were never pure enough of spirit, your ib remained befouled, and you stand very properly condemned Apushniad."

"Ib-befoulment cannot be proved against me. I have worked for Zair. There are witnesses." I detested this crawling and pleading; but I wanted to go home. "I pretended to turn renegade and serve the vile Grodnims and their evil Grodno. Thus in the end perished this Zair-forsaken king Genod."

"All that is very well!" screeched down Pur Kazz. I glared at him. I felt very differently from the dazed wretch who had stood under his enmity in the Hall of Judgment. The terrible scar down his face drew his mouth into a cruel grimace. His eyes gleamed in the lamplight like two feral leem's eyes. I felt sorry for him. But if he stopped me, as he apparently still intended, I must deal with him. Once, he had been a fine Krzy. "You are condemned and no man here will alter that. I will not allow it, not allow such blasphemy." His voice rose still higher, screeching like steel across metal, and he lapsed into an unintelligible screech. I believe at that point I realized I would win this just fight.

I will not go into all the tortuous arguments. Casuistry is a high art among the Krozairs. I based my claim on deeds open to all. I offered the instance of the clearing of the Grodnims from the southern shore, a process still proceeding but all too plainly about to finalize successfully for the Zairians.

"Impious braggart!" shouted Kazz. "You claim this great work is your doing, when the thanks go to Zair?"

"I helped," I said. I heard the growls from my people and I hoped they wouldn't break out. At least, not yet.

Pur Zenkiren said, "I speak for the Apushniad. He has accomplished much. I would give him the High Jikai!"

"Aye!" bellowed my people. "Dray Prescot! Hai Jikai!"

"If they do not behave they will be ejected," snarled Kazz.

Of them all it had to be Korf Aighos who laughed. I wondered how much loot he had stuffed into his sacks, the great reiver.

The arguments went on. It was becoming clear to all that Pur Kazz, while still retaining his mystical authority as Grand Archbold, was in very truth a sick man. The wound across his face had driven deep into his mind as well as his body. And yet he was the Grand Archbold, and he owed the allegiance of the Krozairs for his position, and his near-divine ordinances must be obeyed. No one there would cross him.

I detested, as I say, what I was slowly being forced to do. In good times a maniacal Grand Archbold may be tolerated. But in times of war and stress, a man is needed at the helm who may hold total affection from Krozairs as well as total authority. Krozairs may not be driven by the whip, to shouts of "Grak."

So I began a new tack in the arguments. I reiterated that I had been unable to answer the Call, and then went on subtly to gnaw away at the position of Pur Kazz himself. I cited his rages, his incoherences. I said that Pur Zenkiren through his great knowledge of the Mysteries knew I spoke the truth, that all who knew the truth knew I did not lie. The Krozairs remained very quiet. My people, too, remained reasonably quiet.

I said, harshly, "Pur Kazz has been wounded. The sword that struck his face struck through to his ib. He is no longer one of us. He is Makib! Makib! He is unfit to hold the high office! The supreme man who should have held the high office of Grand Archbold was foisted off, was betrayed. Now he should receive the high due he deserves. It is Pur Zenkiren who should be Grand Archbold!"

My people were not slow to take up the call, and the yells of Pur Zenkiren for Grand Archbold racketed out as though we shouted for our favorite riders in the zorca races.

Pur Zenkiren flung me a startled look. He stood up and somehow silence returned.

"It is not fitting that such grave matters be discussed in the Outer Hall. These are weighty things. You speak aright, Dray Prescot, and yet I will not speak for myself."

At this Pur Kazz foamed and raved and tried to speak and only produced an eerie gargling. The poor devil was mad, right enough; Makib; insane through no fault of his. But he was not the man to hold down the supreme post of Grand Archbold. The other Krozairs saw this, and yet could do nothing.

So Pur Kazz and I fronted each other.

I just hoped none of my men would shaft the onker.

The final stroke seized him as the adjudicator, alarmed, rose to suspend the proceedings. Pur Kazz, foam around his mouth like the foam as a chunkrah runs itself to death, flopped over the side of the Ombor Throne. He was dying as his aides reached him. In a last moment of lucidity, he said, "Krozair! I am a Krozair of Zy!" Then he died, and, despite all, I was sorry for the poor devil.

After that we adjourned to the Hall of Judgment, where only Krozair Brothers might venture.

I will not detail the events there, for, although I was in the right, the means I had used to prove my point did not exactly make me feel pride. In the event, Pur Zenkiren was unanimously elected Grand Archbold, and I was purged of the Apushniad. Once again I was a Krozair of Zy. Then I set forth my son Jaidur, Jaidur of Valka, Prince of Vallia, also known as Vax Neemusbane, for election. He had completed his training. Again, unanimously, Jaidur was elected and ordained. The ceremony would take place later. For now, Jaidur was a Krzy.

When I told Delia she was pleased.

"When you went away, Dray, and I will tell you of that later, Drak was mad to join the Krozairs, as you had instructed. So I sent Segnik there very young. And he—"

"He will stay in the Eye of the World and become the king of Zandikar. Later on he will mature. Now he is obsessed."

"Yes, Dray. And Jaidur, too, wanted to go—and—"

"I would have liked him to be named for Inch."

She looked up at me. We stood on the high outer terrace of the sacred Isle of Zy. Our friends laughed and sang and drank within hail. She said, "But he is. Inch is only Inch's use-name. Jaidur is Jaidur's use-name. Their real name is the same and is known only to them."

I nodded. It was right.

"You have done what you said you would do." She leaned close.

"Yes, my heart. And I will tell you what I should have told you seasons and seasons ago. But only when we are safe in Esser Rarioch."

"And what of Nath and Zolta?"

"They seem to get on well with the other rascals. I think they might relish a visit home." I held her to me. "And Lela and Dayra?"

"They are about their business. The Sister of the Rose make demands very like your famous Krozairs of Zy."

"Hai!" I said, and I laughed. "But although we have won through against great peril, there is a thing we must do yet."

"Yes. You are a Krozair again, and I am happy. This inner sea is a wonderful place; but I yearn for Vallia!"

"Drak is anxious to return to Vallia. He tells me there are forces at work your father would do well to take notice of. And—"

"Hush, dear heart! The stars shine and the breeze is soft and all the problems of Vallia can wait a while."

"Yet will I call Grogor, who is a renegade and should be chopped for it, and yet who tried to help our daughter Velia."

"Yes—you will tell me of this Gafard?"

"I will."

"Did you know that when Seg heard this king Zo in Sanurkazz had you on his list of infamy, Seg said—did you know?"

"No." But I could imagine.

"Seg just stroked one of his terrible steel-tipped arrows and said, 'If this onker, King Zo, does not rub my old dom's name from his damned list we shall have to pay him a visit.' And, dear heart, he meant it!"

"Oh, aye," I said. "That would be like Seg Segutorio."

"And Inch said his great ax was feeling dry again."

"Let us forget everything for tonight," I said, holding my Delia. She lifted her face to me, rosy in the streaming pink moons-light, for the Maiden with the Many Smiles and She of the Veils smiled down on our foolishness.

"Yes, my heart," said my Delia of the Blue Mountains, my Delia of Delphond.

"Although," I told her as, our arms about each other, we went into the chamber prepared for us, "we must take that great rogue Grogor and go to Green Magdag of the Megaliths and there find our granddaughter, Didi, and bring her home with us."

"Yes. Do you think Gafard would have liked that—for I know Velia would have longed for it."

"I think Gafard would," I said, and turned to close the shutters. I thought I caught a hint of lambent blueness beyond the window.

A Glossary to the Krozair Cycle
of the Saga of Dray Prescot

References to the three books of the cycle are given as:

> TIK: Tides of Kregen
> REK: Renegade of Kregen
> KRK: Krozair of Kregen

NB: Previous glossaries will be found in Volume 5: Prince of Scorpio; Volume 7: Arena of Antares; Volume 11: Armada of Antares.

A

Alley of a Thousand Bangles: jewelry alley in Magdag where Prescot received the poison from the king's conspirators. (REK)

Andapon, Captain: master of the Menaham argenter *Chavonth of Mem* in which Prescot and Duhrra attempted to leave the inner sea. (REK)

Appar: place in Proconia. The Battle of Appar halted Grodnim aggression at the eastern end of the inner sea.

Apushniad: ejection in disgrace from the Orders of Krozairs.

Arsenal of the Jikgernus: imposing military warehouse for the swifters in Magdag.

Athgar the Neemu: ferocious Kataki fought by Vax in the Hyr Jikordur. (KRK)

Azhurad: the Call summoning Krozairs in times of emergency.

B

Bane of Grodno: term of vituperation given by Grodnims to the Krozairs of Zair.

Battle of Pynzalo: in which King Genod's new army commanded by Gafard defeated a Zairian host.

black lotus flowers of Hodan-Set: legendary flowers of evil.

Black Spider Caves of Gratz: a Kregan hell.

Blood of Dag: a bright green wine of Magdag.

Blue Cloud: a high-quality sectrix given to Prescot by Gafard. (REK)

Bright Brilliance of Genodras, the Palace of: chief palace of King Genod in Magdag.

broken from the ib: a ghost.

Buzro's Magic Staff: a Zairian oath.

C

chavinter: a small class of swifter.

Chavonth of Mem: a Menaham argenter. (REK)

"Chuktar with the Glass Eye, The": a rollicking Zairian song.

Cottmer's Caverns: a Kregan hell, possibly part of the Ice Floes of Sicce.

Crazmoz: small town on River of Golden Smiles, home of Duhrra.

crickle nut: rich nut with wrinkled brown shell.

crimson faril: beloved of the Red; Zairian term for gentle-man.

Crimson Magodont: new name of *Green Magodont,* a fine swifter.

crooked mur, a: for a few moments.

D

Dak: an old man, over two hundred years old, who fought gallantly and was slain trying to protect his lord; a Red Brother of the Red Brethren of Jikmarz. Prescot took the name Dak in all honor, during his time of Apushniad.

Dag, River: on the delta of the River Dag stands Magdag.

Dayra: daughter of Delia and Prescot; twin to Jaidur.

dernun: savvy? capish? do you understand? Not very polite.

"Destiny of the Fishmonger of Magdag; The": a cheerfull insulting Zairian song.

Didi: daughter of Velia and Gafard; granddaughter of Delia and Prescot. Hidden safely in Guamelga by Gafard.

Drig's Lanterns: will-o'-the-wisp.

Dolan the Bow: an archer of Zandikar who joined force with Prescot.

Duhrra: a massively built wrestler who lost his right hand

Dubbed "Duhrra of the Days" by Prescot. Hails from Crazmos. An oar-comrade to Prescot and to Vax.

dwabur: measurement of length, approximately five miles.

F

Fazhan ti Rozilloi: ship-Hikdar (first lieutenant) in *Crimson Magodont;* an oar-comrade to Prescot.

Felteraz: a harbor, town, fortress, and estate a few dwaburs east of Sanurkazz. A spot of exceptional beauty. Home of Mayfwy.

Fenzerdrin: peninsula of the southern shore of the inner sea northwest of Sanurkazz.

flibre: remarkably light and strong wood used in swifters.

Fragrant Incense, Palace of: royal palace of Zandikar.

G

Gadak: name given to Prescot, as Dak, in Magdag.

Gafard: Rog of Guamelga, the King's Striker, Prince of the Central Sea, the Reducer of Zair, Sea Zhantil, Ghittawrer of Genod, etc. King Genod's favorite. Son-in-law to Prescot; husband of Velia of Vallia. Renegade.

Gashil: Grodnim patron spirit of footpads.

Genod: King Genod Gannius, son of Gahan Gannius and Valima of Malig. Genius at war; made himself king of Magdag. His parents were saved from death by Prescot on his third visit to Kregen, at the command of the Star Lords.

Genodder: shortsword invented by King Genod.

gernu: Grodnim form of jernu—lord.

Ghittawrer: Grodnim approximation to Krozair.

Ghittawrers of Genod: a Green Brotherhood founded by King Genod.

Glycas: a prince of Magdag; vied with Gafard for king's favor.

Golden Chavonth: dekares swifter commanded by Pur Zeg, Krzy.

Golden Smiles, River of: on which stands Sanurkazz.

Goyt: Grodnim spirit much used in oaths.

Green Brotherhood: Orders of Grodnim chivalry in imitation of the Red Brotherhoods of Zair.

Green Magodont: Magdaggian swifter in which Prescot was oar-slave. (KRK)

gray ones: eerie spirits who greet the traveler to the Ice Floes of Sicce.

Grodno: the deity of the green sun Genodras.

Grogor: Jiktar; second in command to Gafard.

Grom: Grodnim form of Zairian Ztrom—Strom, count.

Grotal the Reducer: horrific Grodnim spirit of destruction.

Guamelga: city and province north of Magdag on River Dag. Gafard was its Rog.

H

Hall of Judgment: small chamber in rock of Isle of Zy where trials are held and judgments given.

Hammer of Retribution: used to smash the sword of a Krozair declared Apushniad.

hebra: four-legged saddle-animal of North Turismond.

hlamek: sand scarf and face protector of South Zairia.

Horn of Azhurad: a device deep within the Isle of Zy used to send out the Call to summon the Krozairs.

huliper pie: a sailors' delicacy of Magdag.

Hyr Jikordur: rules and ritual of challenge and combat in duels.

I

Iangle: Grodnim spirit of sword-fighters.

Ilkenesk, Mountains of: mountain range of South Zairia.

Irwin: Irwin W. Emerson, a Savapim who fought in the Siege of Zandikar. (KRK)

Island of Pliks: tiny island of the inner sea where Prescot and his men learned Zandikar lay under siege.

Ivanovna, Madam: name used by Zena Iztar on Earth.

Ivory Pavilion: palace of Roz Janri in Zandikar.

Iztar, Zena: mysterious woman of supernatural power who assisted Prescot without committing herself to either the Star Lords or the Savanti but appears to be in communication with the Krozairs of Zy.

J

Jaidur: third son of Delia and Prescot; twin to Dayra.

Jade Palace: Gafard's palace in Magdag.

jikai: a word of complex meaning; used in different forms means: Kill! or Bravo! warrior; a noble feat of arms, and many related concepts to do with honor and pride and warrior-status. A jikai may be given for a heroic deed; the High Jikai is extraordinarily difficult to win.

Jikaidast: a professional player of Jikaida.

Jikmarz: a Zairian city of the west coast of the Sea of Swords.

jernu: Zairian term for lord.

K

Kalveng: a seafaring folk with havens along the west coast of Northern Turismond.

Kazz, Pur, of Tremso: Grand Archbold of the Krozairs of Zy.

krahnik: very small form of chunkrah used as draft animal.

Krozair: member of a mystic and martial Order of Chivalry dedicated to Zair. Membership is attained only after long and arduous training in the Disciplines. Prescot mentions at this time three Orders of Krozairs, those of Zy, Zamu, and Zimuzz. To be a Krz is to stand apart from ordinary men.

Krzi: abbreviation for Krozair of Zimuzz.

Krzm: abbreviation for Krozair of Zamu.

Krzy: abbreviation for Krozair of Zy.

L

Lady of the Stars: name of concealment used by Velia of Vallia.

Laggig-Laggu: large conurbation of Grodnim up the River Laggu.

Lahal: universal greeting for friend or acquaintance.

lairgodont: a vicious, quick, difficult-to-kill risslaca. Not overlarge, with scaled body, sinuous neck and back, skull-crushing talons, and serrated fangs in gap-jawed mouth, forked tail. Most common in North Turismond.

Llahal: universal greeting for stranger.

longsword, the Krozair: a perfectly balanced two-handed longsword with wide-spaced handgrips; can be used one-handed; subject of rigorous and demanding training and mystical exercises. A terrible weapon of destruction. The Ghittawrer longsword is an attempt to copy the Krozair longsword, but is generally regarded as inferior. The common longsword is usually a one-handed weapon, although hand-and-a-half swords are known.

M

Magdag: chief city of Grodno on north shore of inner sea.

magodont: resembles the lairgodont of the godont family of risslacas.

Makib: insane.

maktikos: white mice. Informers in ship's company.

Malig: Grodnim fortress-city east of the Grand Canal.

Masks, Palace of: small palace of Magdag owned by King Genod.

mergem: leguminous plant, dried and reconstituted, gives protein, vitamins, minerals, and the like. A high yield for small weight and bulk.

Miam: niece of Roza anri; created Queen of Zandikar by Prescot. Betrothed to Pur Zeg.

Mitronoton: the Reducer of Towers, the Destroyer of Cities; a legendary man-god-devil, part of the mythology of Kregen.

mortil: a wild animal almost as large and powerful as a zhantil.

N

Naghan, Pur, ti Perzefn: Krozair of Zamu. Swifter captain commanding *Pearl* in Render squadron. Fought under Prescot's orders as Render and in Siege of Zandikar.

Nath the Slinger: oar-comrade with Prescot. Comes from Mountains of Ilkenesk; has decided views on archers.

Nazhan: Queen Miam bestowed the "Z" on Pur Naghan during the Siege of Zandikar for smart work in the Dikars. (KRK)

needleman: slang term for doctor.

Net and Trident, The: a tavern on the waterfront in Magdag.

nikobi: Pachaks' code of great integrity to which they adhere when hiring out as mercenaries and paktuns.

nikzo: half a golden zo-piece.

Nodgen the Faithful: chief of King Genod's conspirators attempting to abduct the Lady of the Stars from Gafard. (REK)

Nose of Zogo: promontory between Zandikar and Zamu.

O

"Obdwa Song": marching song of the swods of Magdag.

Oblifanters: under instructions from the Todalpheme of the Akhram, they give orders to the workers for the opening or closing of the Dam of Days.

Odifor: deity sworn on by Fristles.

Oidrictzhn: ancient and evil god of horror summoned up by superstitious villagers along the Shadow Coast. His legend is *Of the Abominations of Oidrictzhn*. Known as the Beast out of Time.

Ombor Throne: throne of the Grand Archbold in the Isle of Zy.

Onyx Sea: in the northeast of the Eye of the World, populated mostly by diffs.

Ophig Mountains: mountain range north of Magdag.

P

Pakkad: legendary figure cast down by Mitronoton, now the symbol for the outcast, the downtrodden, the unwanted, the pariah.

pakmort: symbol of the paktun. A silver mortil-head worn in the same fashion as the pakzhan.

pakzhan: small gold zhantil-head worn on cord looped through a top buttonhole. Symbol of the hyr-paktun. The cord is silk and may be worn over a shoulder knot.

Papachak the All-Powerful: Pachak deity.

Pa-We, Logu: a Pachak hyr-paktun who assisted Prescot and Duhrra to enter Shazmoz. (TIK)

Phangursh: Grodnim city sited at junction of River Daphig with River Dag, west of Mountains of Ophig, north of Magdag.

prijiker: stem-fighter. A warrior who fights from the forecastle and beakhead of a swifter. The post of most danger in ramming.

prychan: very much like a neemu, save that its fur is tawny gold.

pungent ibroi: a disinfectant.

Pur: not a rank or a title (although apparently used as such); a badge of chivalry and honor, a pledge that the holder is a true Krozair. Prefixed to the holder's name, as: Pur Dray.

Pynzalo: fortress-city of Zairia.

Q

quidang!: at once. Equates with, "Aye aye, sir!"

Quinney, Doctor: charlatan who found so-called mediums for Prescot when banished to Earth. He introduced Zena Iztar and so served a purpose and earned his fee. (TIK)

R

Red Brethren: fighting Orders devoted to Zair. Prescot mentions three Red Brotherhoods at this time: those of Lizz and Jikmarz, based on the cities of those names; and the Red Brethren of Zul, based on the city of Zulfiria. The Red Brotherhoods do not possess the same high mysticisms or Disciplines as the Krozairs, and are easier to enter.

Rog: Grodnim term equating with Zairian Roz—Kov, duke.

Roo Throne: throne in the Palace of Fragrant Incense in Zandikar. Roo is Kregish for eleven, and the throne is regarded as the eleventh guardian after the Ten Dikars.

Roz: Zairian term for Kov—duke.

Rukker: a Kataki lord from Urntakkar. Slaved with Prescot on same oar loom. Is haughty and ferocious like all Katakis; but Prescot says he has a touch of humanity. Does not like to discuss things that embarrass him.

S

Sanurkazz: chief city of Zairia.

Scarf of Our Lady Monafeyom, the: when all the seven moons shine at the full together for that brief period.

Sea Werstings: name given by Grodnims to the Kalveng.

Sea Zhantil: title of honor given by King Zo to Prescot when he was the foremost Krozair upon the inner sea. Gafard given the title by King Genod. Prescot thinks of Gafard as the Sea Zhantil, in remembrance.

sectrix: six-legged saddle-animal; blunt-headed, wicked-eyed, pricked of ear, slate-blue hide covered with scanty coarse hair. One of the trix family of animals.

Seeds of Zantristar: clusters of many small islands off Shazmoz.

Seeds of Ganfowang: Grodnim name for Seeds of Zantristar.

Shadow Coast: short stretch of coast between Zimuzz and Zandikar with an evil reputation.

Shagash: Grodnim patron spirit of banquets.

Shazash: Zairian patron spirit of banquets.

Shazmoz: fortress-city of Zairia of the west.

Shorush-Tish: blue-maned sea-god whose temples are found in all the seaports of the Eye of the World.

Sisters of the Rose: seminary of virtue at which Delia and her daughters received much of their education.

Sniz the Horn: Prescot's trumpeter at the Siege of Zandikar. (KRK)

solaik: three-quarter.

Soothe: planet of Antares appearing in the sky of Kregen as a large blue star at approach of orbits. Is a famous Goddess of Love, represented all over Kregen. Prescot says he wonders if the coincidence of Soothe and Venus is a coincidence.

Souk of Silks: in Magdag, where a man was killed in mistake for Prescot. (REK)

Souk of Trophies: in Magdag, where the loot of Zairia is sold.

Stones of Repudiation: twin basaltic blocks across which the sword of a Krozair declared Apushniad is broken.

"Swifter with the Kink, The": a rollicking song of Zairia in which the swifter with the kink appears to ram herself up her own stern.

T

Takroti: minor deity of the Katakis.

Three Mirrors of the Ib: positioned so that a Krozair in the Hall of Judgment may see himself and understand his own dishonor.

Todalpheme: astronomers and mathematicians dedicated to serving all in forecasting the Tides. Immune from slavery.

Tower of True Contentment: tower of the Jade Palace. Here Velia lived when in Magdag with Gafard.

turiloth: a large animal of Turismond, similar to the boloth of Chem, with six tusks, sixteen legs, a tendrilous mass of whiplash tails. The hide is hard and gray along the back, bottle-green along the sides and gray beneath. Normally slow, but fast in a short dash. Has an enormous underslung fanged mouth; is keen scented and has three hearts.

Tyvold ti Vruerdensmot: a Kalveng helped by Prescot to escape from slavery under the Grodnims. (REK)

U

Ugas: diffs of many tribes and nations of Northern Turismond; nomads and city dwellers, not barbarians.

ulm: unit of measurement, approximately 1,500 yards.

Uncle Zobab: patron spirit of Fenzerdrin.

Urntakkar: area north of the Onyx Sea. Home of Rukker the Kataki.

V

Vax: name assumed by Jaidur of Vallia in the Eye of the World. (KRK)

Velia: second daughter of Delia and Prescot; twin to Zeg. Married to Gafard; mother of Didi. Murdered by King Genod. (REK)

Velia: fourth daughter of Delia and Prescot. No twin.

Veng: deity of the Kalveng.

volgodont: flying form of godont. A powerful aerial killer.

Volgodont's Fang: swifter commanded by Gafard. (REK)

Volgodonts' Aerie: hunting lodge near Guamelga.

W

Wabinosk: island of western inner sea used as base by Renders.

warvol: vulturelike carrion-eating bird.

"Weng da!": "Who goes there!"

wo-Deldar: wo is Kregish for zero. Ironical appellation to themselves by swods of most Kregan armies.

Y

Yoggur: area to the northeast of inner sea.

"Your orders, my commands!": Grodnim equivalent to "Quidang!"—"Aye aye, sir."

Z

Zadak: name won by Prescot, as Dak, from Queen Miam. (KRK)

Zagri: a powerful demon spirit of the inner sea.

Zandikar: fortress-city of Zairia, scene of the famous siege.

Zavarin, Nath: Pallan of Zandikar. Very fat; but loyal to his city.

Zenno, King: name assumed by Starkey the Wersting in Zandikar. (KRK)

Zeg: Pur Zeg Prescot, Krzy, Prince of Vallia. Second son of Delia and Prescot; twin to Velia. Grew out of name Segnik.

zhantiller: type of the large swifter of inner sea.

Zhantil's Lair: hunting lodge near Guamelga.

Zhuannar of the Storm: spirit of the sea who raises rashoons.

Zimuzz: fortress-city of Zairia, home of the Krozairs of Zimuzz.

Zinkara, River: runs north from the Mountains of Ilkenesk.

Zinna: deposed king of Zandikar; grandfather of Miam.

zinzer: sixty silver Zairian zinzers make one gold zo-piece.

Zogo the Hrywhip: name used in a Zairian oath.

zo-piece: gold coin of Sanurkazz.

Ztrom: Zairian form of Strom—count.

Zunderhan, Janri, Roz of Thoth Zeresh: noble of Zandikar; uncle of Queen Miam.

DAW BOOKS

ALAN BURT AKERS

Six terrific novels compose the second great series
of adventure of Dray Prescot: The Havilfar Cycle.

☐ **MANHOUNDS OF ANTARES.** Dray Prescot on the unknown continent of Havilfar seeks the secret of the airboats. Book VI. (#UY1124—$1.25)

☐ **ARENA OF ANTARES.** Prescot confronts strange beasts and fiercer men on that enemy continent. Book VII. (#UY1145—$1.25)

☐ **FLIERS OF ANTARES.** In the very heart of his enemies, Prescot roots out the secrets of flying. Book VIII. (#UY1165—$1.25)

☐ **BLADESMAN OF ANTARES.** King or slave? Savior or betrayer? Prescot confronts his choices. Book IX. (#UY1188—$1.25)

☐ **AVENGER OF ANTARES.** Prescot must fight for his enemies in order to save his friends! Book X. (#UY1208—$1.25)

☐ **ARMADA OF ANTARES.** All the forces of two continents mass for the final showdown with Havilfar's ambitious queen. Book XI. (#UY1227—$1.25)

DAW BOOKS are represented by the publishers of Signet
and Mentor Books, **THE NEW AMERICAN LIBRARY, INC.**
